WINTER SEEKS OUT THE LONELY

A SONNY BURTON NOVEL

WINTER SEEKS OUT THE LONELY

LARRY D. SWEAZY

FIVE STAR
A part of Gale, a Cengage Company

GALE
A Cengage Company

LIBRARY OF CONGRESS CATALOGING-IN-PUBLICATION DATA

Names: Sweazy, Larry D., author.
Title: Winter seeks out the lonely / Larry D. Sweazy.
Description: First Edition. | Farmington Hills, Mich. : Five Star, a part of Gale, a Cengage Company, 2021. | Series: A Sonny Burton novel |
Identifiers: LCCN 2020049030 | ISBN 9781432868963 (hardcover)
Subjects: GSAFD: Adventure fiction.
Classification: LCC PS3619.W438 W56 2021 | DDC 813/.6—dc23
LC record available at https://lccn.loc.gov/2020049030

First Edition. First Printing: August 2021
Find us on Facebook—https://www.facebook.com/FiveStarCengage
Visit our website—http://www.gale.cengage.com/fivestar
Contact Five Star Publishing at FiveStar@cengage.com

Printed in Mexico
Print Number: 01   Print Year: 2021

To Rose

"As the flowers are all made sweeter by the sunshine and the dew, so this old world is made brighter by the lives of folks like you."

—Bonnie Parker

CHAPTER ONE

January 13, 1935

Sonny Burton stood on the front porch and watched an open-topped jalopy sputtering down the hardpan road, rolling slow enough to kick into the air any dust worthy of noting. Hollow gray puffs of tired Texas dirt followed the tires, lacking any abracadabra enthusiasm. Anything substantial had already blown away; opportunities, dreams, farmers' hopes, all lost to the sandstorms of the early 1930s. The way Sonny saw it, all of the good topsoil and everything else that went with it would never be found again. The Depression had hung on like a ravenous gray leech sucking the life out of everything it had touched—including him. There was no such thing as a promised land or redemption around the next corner.

The sight of a circus parade on the road in front of his house was a surprise to Sonny. He wasn't aware that the circus was close by. He hadn't been to town in days. The thump of an elephant's foot had roused him from an afternoon nap that was somewhere south of a nightmare. For a split second, he wasn't sure that what he saw in front of him was real. He'd had to wipe his eyes clear of sleep more than once to see that the jalopy was an old Model T Ford converted into a stake truck, black when it was new, but even darker now, coated with the grime of age and miles. Rust had eaten a hole above the wheel well and metal flapped as the Ford rolled along. The truck carried a load of canvas stuffed into the bed as neat as possible. It was the big

7

top; maybe the only tent of the circus—there were no other canvases to be seen. Skinny poles were mounted on both sides of the vehicle, at the doors, with banners coughing in weary flaps, faded red, green, and blue. A longer pole was attached to the back of the truck, extending fifty feet, narrow like the trunk of a tall walnut tree. It rested on a pair of wheels that rolled as slow as the jalopy. A loose string of folks walked on both sides of the tent pole, heads hung low, their clothes ragged and lifeless as the banners, vests and thin shirts pulled close to their ribs to ward off the January chill. Any joy on their faces was saved for greasepaint and Saturday nights—if anybody could afford the dime to get inside the big top. Behind the pole came the great disturber; a beast that looked like it had been carved out of a granite mountain. The elephant was gray as the sky, with loose wrinkled skin, and was in no hurry to go anywhere but forward. A cord-like tail swished through the air; a habit to ward off any insects that might be attracted to it, though it was unneeded in winter. Each step shook the earth. Distant thunder created by four giant feet that stirred old men from their afternoon naps.

Neither Sonny nor Blue, the dog at his side, had ever seen an elephant before. Blue growled under his breath. The fur above his lip was curled, the only part of his coat that was gray. The rest of him was shiny black. When the sun hit him right, the dog looked like it had been dipped in deep blue ink, which was how he came about his name.

Sonny held Blue by the scruff of the neck so he wouldn't set off on an attack protecting his territory. There was no way a gimpy old dog with a bad leg could win a fight with an elephant no matter the spirit and enthusiasm he carried.

A team of four men surrounded the giant gray beast, one at each corner of a lopsided square, leading the animal with a rope that looked thin enough for Blue to chew through. All of the men looked tired and had worn holes in the soles of their boots. Their eyes were vacant and unconcerned about any surrounding threat. The dog's bark meant nothing to them. A rusted chain that wasn't attached to anything rattled around the elephant's neck, and a purple satin bib, shredded by wind and time, swayed with each step. The chain was like a giant piece of jewelry, but not hung there for beauty or glamor. On closer inspection, the chain could be pulled tight to inflict pain or restraint if necessary. The jingle-jangle of the metal constraint was a sad song of coerced behavior. Sonny figured such a thing was needed. There were days when he had his problems convincing Blue who was in charge of things around the house. A chained collar might have come in handy if it could have been made to be humane.

Sundays were made for moving for most circuses. There wasn't a town in Texas that would allow a circus to perform on a church day. Performances of any kind were against state law. One of the chores of the Texas Rangers was to shut them down if anyone opened a ticket booth on the Lord's day of rest. Sonny had closed down more than one circus when he'd been a Ranger, when he was younger, whole, and like Blue, motivated to protect his territory and prove his worth to the world.

It was odd watching the parade, still a surprise, even though Sonny didn't show it. He stood rigid as a fence post, eyeing each animal and person with suspicion. He didn't have any idea where the circus was heading. South, by the way they were going. They would be out of Collingsworth County into Childress County before long. That's all he could tell, all he cared to know. He wasn't a circus-going kind of man. Never had been. Clowns didn't make him laugh and women flying through the air on the trapeze made him nervous. The big top wasn't a serious place as far as he was concerned. It was for fools and thrill seekers, and he didn't consider himself either of those things.

Another jalopy followed the elephant. It was the same as the stake truck, only it carried an assortment of cages instead of a tent. From where Sonny stood, he could see a lion and a tiger lazing among the slow-going commotion. The exotic cats didn't roar or looked bothered by the ride. Both were settled in their places in a cage. Like everything else in the ragtag parade, the cats looked skinny and hungry. Nothing shined, nothing looked appealing enough to lure in a crowd. Maybe that would change when they found their next spot and pitched camp. Maybe there was some kind of sparkle to this circus that he wasn't seeing.

Sonny wondered what it took to feed such an outfit, where they found food when food was hard enough to find for those who had the means to pay for it. Blue growled louder at the sight of the cats. Like the elephants, lions and tigers were a new sight to them both.

"You best get inside," Sonny said, leading the dog to the door with his left hand—the only hand he had. He wore a wood prosthesis on his right arm. That hand was a hook. A cold, silver metal hook fashioned by fire instead of born of flesh. Sometimes he felt like a circus freak himself. Took the stares in town personal even though he knew he shouldn't. People, kids mostly, weren't used to seeing a one-armed man acting like there wasn't anything missing from his life. He'd been an amputee for two years, ever since Bonnie and Clyde had passed through Wellington and decided to shoot their way out of town, wounding him, leaving his arm a victim of gangrene, lying on the operating floor all by itself. He came out better in the end than Bonnie and Clyde did, though he still regretted he wasn't the one to kill them and put a stop to their madness. That trophy had gone to his good friends, Frank Hamer and Maney Gault.

Sonny pushed the door open with his shoulder and ushered Blue inside. "You stay in there till they're gone." Then he closed the door, leaving the hound inside. Blue barked, but Sonny paid him no mind.

He didn't venture off the porch. He stood sentinel, watching as more folks walked behind the second jalopy. None of them bothered to wave. Most of them didn't notice Sonny watching them. He figured they must have been accustomed to being stared at, though he did wonder if it bothered them like it did him.

A team of white horses walked alongside a pair of humped camels. Ribs showed on the horses, their coats vacant of any shine. It had been a long time since they'd had a brush taken to them; their hair looked like a dingy dining-hall rug. Of all the animals, the camels looked the most comfortable, the least depressed or overworked.

Another truck brought up the rear of the circus line, full of people that looked unable to walk. One man was so huge he looked like he must have eaten a piano. He had to weigh five hundred pounds. The fat man sat in the middle of the truck bed as content and bored as the cats in the cages. Sonny was certain the person who sat on the back of the truck, with her shapely legs dangling over the open gate, was a woman even though she wore a thick black beard. She waved and smiled at Sonny. Her blouse was made of red sequins and her ample chest glittered in the late afternoon sun. She was the first shiny thing he'd seen in all of the parade. All he could do was lift his left hand and offer a sideways hello, cut through the air with a half-hearted salutation. The bearded woman cocked her head and let her smile fade away, puzzled by Sonny's response. Or maybe she noticed his hook for the first time, glinting in the sun itself, sending back the sight of an unexpected shiny thing, too. Either way, she broke Sonny's gaze and said something to the fat man behind her. He looked at Sonny but didn't raise a finger. A sad expression stayed on the huge man's face until the circus rolled out of sight.

Sonny stood on the porch long after they were gone, doing his best to conjure what he had seen in his mind so it would stay in his memory. Nothing like that had ever passed by his house before. True to his word, once the excitement was past, he let Blue out of the house.

The dog hurried down the road as quick as it could on his three good legs, dragging the bad one, sniffing about, barking its fool head off, angling away from the pile of steaming elephant dung the humongous animal had left behind. Blue's back leg had been broken, fractured under the tire of a truck—Sonny's truck—which was how he came to live in the house. Guilt and the county veterinarian, Pete Jorgenson, had convinced Sonny that the dog needed a home instead of being put down.

Satisfied that the intruders were gone, Blue stood in the middle of the road with his hackles sharp as pikes, unaware or uncaring that he wasn't whole, and barked one last time after the parade, then ran back to Sonny's side. Guilt had worn off long ago about the accident. Without it, Sonny wouldn't have brought the dog home, wouldn't have had the company of another living creature under his roof. He would have been all alone. His closest neighbor was half a mile away. At night he could see one lone light glowing in the kitchen window of the Harmeson place; it was a constant, comforting star that never disappointed him. In the day, he couldn't see anything but the open barren fields that hadn't produced a crop of cotton in more years than Sonny cared to count. Everyone else around him had gone to California, along with the Okies, or other places that offered a dose of hope and a sad reality once they found their way there. They had only found the sand that had blown on their tail as they went, and nothing more. Okies weren't welcome in California, or much of anywhere else from what Sonny had read in the newspaper or heard on the radio. He wondered if the circus was lost, had turned the wrong way.

Everybody else had gone west instead of south.

"That's all the doin's for today," Sonny said to Blue, wistful, sad in a way. He looked to see if anything else was coming and found the road empty, the way he knew it to be most of the time. The solitude of the land was why he had bought his house in the first place. Now he didn't know if that had been a good decision or not.

There was nothing else to see, only an endless horizon soaked gray, lifeless as a twig, clean as a butcher's blade first thing in the morning. Sonny was sure he could die right then and there, and nobody would notice.

CHAPTER TWO

The next morning Sonny stuck his head out the door to see if there was any sign of the circus or any other scurrilous creatures who might have camped out on his property overnight. All he saw was a lone crow sitting on a fence post like he owned it. It was no surprise that there was nothing else to be seen in the barren view, but the distant whirl and grind of a malnourished engine caught his attention, made him stop before pulling his head back inside. He had been set on putting the dripolator on the stove to start the day, but he abandoned the plan.

He stepped out of the house, stared across the empty field, and saw a familiar truck heading his way. The crow flew off, cawing as it went; annoyed, not angry. Sonny was used to seeing crows, so this was no bother to him. The black scavenger birds seemed to be the only ones making a living, eating carrion and cavorting in contented flocks, these days. It was rare to see one alone. Sonny wasn't a man prone to superstition. He had met a wise Comanche once who had believed the crows carried the souls of the dead to heaven or hell, whichever they deserved. The man feared owls, too; messengers for the dead and not to be meddled with. There were no birds that Sonny feared, but he wondered if he should have.

The truck was driven by Clifford Jones, second cousin to Jonesy, the Collingsworth County sheriff, coming to deliver the day's mail. All of the Joneses seemed to work county or government jobs of one form or another. At least they had a roof over

14

their heads and a chicken in the pot. Even if they were on the dole, nobody'd ever know it because the Joneses didn't share their personal business with anyone outside of the family. They were a proud bunch, and like Sonny, the thought of heading west hadn't crossed their minds. At least as far as he knew.

"Might as well go see Clifford," Sonny said to Blue, who had followed him out the door. The dog bore no ill will against the postman, or most anybody else as far as that went. The dog didn't care for Jesse, Sonny's son, but that was more of an amusement than a concern.

Sonny had to reconsider his previous assumption that his death would have gone unnoticed. The crows would have found him first, then Clifford Jones would have come along to find him stiff, already missing an eye or two, his face pecked unrecognizable. He shuddered at the thought and tried to focus on what was before him, not his imaginary demise, his imaginary trip to hell on the wings of a crow.

A quick push of cold air reminded Sonny that it was still January. He wore a long-sleeved shirt to cover the prosthesis and a pair of heavy work trousers. His coat hung inside the door on a rack made for such a thing, but caught other doodads, too, like Blue's leash and collar for trips into town. His hook was as cold as a midnight icicle.

It had spit snow the night before, but nothing had stuck. The ground was so parched there was no sign of any moisture at all. According to the weatherman on the radio, the high temperature for the day was predicted to reach into the mid-forties, then drop down to the twenties at night. January in the Panhandle could be tricky. Cold one day, then warm the next. Snow wasn't unusual, except in the last few years. There had been no real precipitation to speak of, only spits and drops, not enough to wet a man's throat. Only bits of hard-squeezed water fell from the sky, in one form or another, to offer the good earth an inadequate drink, leaving it, and everyone else, wanting for more.

By the time Clifford Jones pulled the dusty black Ford cargo truck next to the mailbox, Sonny and Blue were already there waiting for him. The heat from the engine wafted from under the hood and washed over Sonny, warding off the winter chill. The hood of the truck shimmered and smelled of raw gasoline and pungent exhaust. Sonny's eyes watered, making him remember how the air in France smelled and tasted when he had fought against the Germans. It didn't take much to remind him of his time as a soldier in the Great War—even though he would have given anything to forget it. He rolled his tongue across the roof of his mouth to rid his memory of the taste of mustard gas and blood.

"Boy, howdy, was that a sight to see," Clifford said, sticking his head out the open truck window. He was typical Jones. Short, stocky, hair thinned to a frazzle—if you could see it. Sonny could never recall seeing Clifford without a hat on his head, at least outside of a building. "That circus must have passed right by here. You see it?"

The postman avoided looking at the hook where Sonny's right hand should have been. Clifford had talked to Sonny enough over the last two years to get used to the idea of him being a one-armed man—but it was obvious he was still uncomfortable with the sight. Sonny understood, to a degree. An amputation was as unnatural as a three-legged dog, or a circus traveling down a deserted farm-to-market road. You could try not to look, but good luck with that.

"We saw it," Sonny said. Blue sat at Sonny's ankle, eyeing the road for any oversized beasts.

"A sad circus, if I say so myself," Clifford went on, "the only one I've seen since the Crash. Looks like they were passin' through, which is a good thing, if you ask me." Clifford looked down to Blue, then back to Sonny. "I wouldn't let him out to wander for a day or two if I was you, and I'd keep a lock on the front door. They stopped past the Harmeson place off that ravine that drops down into the crick."

"I know the place. That creek's been dry for so long I wouldn't call it that now. Odd place to stop if you ask me."

"They had to stop somewheres."

"I guess so. I've got a varmint rifle if need be."

"Of course, you do. But you can't trust them circus folks. Hell, you can't trust no one these days as far as that goes, but I figure you know that more than most about the meanness people do to one another, don't you, Ranger Burton?"

Folks would call him Ranger till the day he died. There was no use fighting it, even though Sonny wanted to. Bonnie Parker took his Ranger days away from him but not from everyone else. Once a Ranger, always a Ranger. But Clifford's words weren't about that. Sonny let Clifford's words trail off into a cold silence. He wasn't in the mood to start a conversation about his recent troubles. Not now, or anytime soon. The act of killing a man was still fresh in his mind, still weighed heavy in the matter of sleeplessness, as he replayed using his hook to kill Billy Bunson over and over again in his mind. *Did he have to kill him?* He knew the answer was yes. Billy would have killed Sonny without a thought. He would have killed everyone in that room, including Edith Grantley. Being there was a favor to the Rangers. Sonny's last act of duty. He was done with all that lawman business.

Clifford continued with his line of thought once he figured out that Sonny wasn't going to bite on the bait he'd dropped. "I heard tell of some trouble with some of those boys gettin' ready to leave out for the Civilian Conservation Corps trainin' in Amarillo."

If there was any man in Collingsworth County who knew

more about every resident than he should have, it was Clifford Jones. He saw the laundry on the line, the good times and the tragedies, as he drove by and deposited letters and frequent duns in the mailboxes of the scattered population. Sonny didn't trust Clifford not to tell his business to the next neighbor who had a few minutes extra to chat—which was why he censored his words in any conversation with the postman. But Sonny liked Clifford, found him a useful source of news that never found its way onto the radio or in the newspaper, the *Wellington Leader.* Just because you didn't trust a man didn't mean you couldn't listen to him.

"One of them boys took offense to somethin' a Mexican said," Clifford continued, "and that boy got the livin' daylights beat out of him. Sheriff's still got the Mexican in jail. At least that fella is gettin' his eggs scrambled for him instead of havin' to scramble them for himself." Clifford chuckled, but Sonny didn't join in. "But that boy, Leo Dozier, lost his CCC spot. It went to an alternate, our cousin, Clyde Jones. How lucky is that for Clyde?"

There must have been more to the story for Jonesy to keep the Mexican in the county jail for a simple assault and battery. Wasn't any of his business what went on in the jail, or behind a badge as far as that went—even if a Jones found some benefit from taking a spot in the CCC line. "That happens," Sonny said. "That Dozier boy gonna be all right?"

"He could still count to three, last I heard, but his vision is fuzzy."

"Could have been worse, I 'spect."

"I fear this is our lot for the rest of our days," Clifford said. "People on edge, fightin' over silly things. I don't know what it's gonna take to break this weary streak we've been mired in."

"A good rain, I'd say."

"One that lasts a month and washes all of the Roosevelts out of Washington."

"No wood to build an ark."

Clifford started to dig in the blue canvas mailbag that sat beside him. "Got a letter for you today is all. Nothin' official the way I see it. That's good news, is it?" He was still fishing, and Sonny still wasn't biting.

Most days Clifford drove by and left the mailbox empty. The box was becoming a place for ants to shelter in and nothing else. Sonny extended his left hand and took the letter. Clifford let a wry smile hang on his face a little longer than he should have after the exchange had been made.

"Every time you stop it's good news, Clifford," Sonny said, stuffing the letter into his breast pocket. He didn't have to read it to know who it was from. The letter had come from Huntsville and the sender was Edith Grantley. Her name and address were written in perfect scrolling letters, unmistakable penmanship across the front, with a sweet woman's smell emitting from it even though it had been shipped from a couple hundred miles away. Each letter looked the same, and no matter how she put it, the content was the same, too: When are you coming back to me?

CHAPTER THREE

Edith Grantley
111 19th Street
Huntsville, Texas
January 7, 1935

My Dearest Sonny,

There are days when it seems like it has been years since
you left this house. And, then other days, it seems like it
was yesterday that you were here, and we stood in the
parlor slow dancing like we were the only two people on
earth. I understand that you had to leave, that you had to
go home to Wellington, but I wanted you to stay. It was
selfish of me. Even now, I worry that I am being too
forward with you, that you will read this letter and toss it
in the trash bin. If only I could see your face. If only you
would answer my letters so that I would know that you are
well.

We have shared a nightmare, you and me. A horrible
trauma that haunts me in the day and the night. It does
you, too. Your life has been a struggle beyond our brief
time together. All of those years as a Ranger, a man who
went to fight the Great War and came back home. Men
who have been changed, scarred by battle. They have
boarded with me. I have seen the thousand-yard stare in
their eyes. I have seen it in your eyes, too. I do not want to

imagine the things you've seen, the things you've had to do in the name of honor, on the right side of the law, with our government's permission to kill. What I have seen in my own home is enough to realize that you will do anything to save yourself and those around you. If I had dreamed of a hero, he would look like you. I am sure that makes your cheeks blush a deep red, but it is true. You saved my life and for that I am grateful.

I have said all of these things before, but I feel I must keep saying them. At least until I see you again, until I hear from you again. Sometimes, I fear that will never happen. If that is how it is to be, can you please tell me soon? I stare down the street daily hoping for a sight of you, for your return to my home. Only then do I think I will be able to sleep through the night. Is there a phone at a nearby farmhouse that I could call? To hear your voice would be enough.

That is that. There is news to share.

I have a new boarder. A woman this time. Ella Lynn Burns. She is the new secretary to the new warden, Haliford Wilson, at the prison. Everything is changing there from what I understand from the men who still take their rooms here. I feared I would lose tenants after the melee that occurred, but not a one has left me. They have rallied around me, and for that I am glad.

With the new governor coming into office, it's time for a clean sweep at the prison. I've heard happy whispers that folks are glad to be free of those Fergusons, especially the governor, Ma. It's all a bit much considering the loss we suffered here in Huntsville. I worry about poor Miss Ziskin. She had been Jeb Rickart's secretary for years. My boarder, Ella, told me that Miss Ziskin has been transferred to the operator panel in the basement. That's better than being put out on the street these days. Anyway, Ella Lynn is in your old room. She's almost thirty and speaks little of her past. She wears a set of wispy hazel eyes, heartbroken and fragile, and there's a white strip on her wedding finger where a ring used to be. I like her. She's neat, tidy, and respectful to the other boarders. I worried at first about having another woman under the roof, but she does not seem interested in anything but her work. I dare not inquire of her past. I think the outcome of such a query is obvious, and I do not want to be rude and pry. She will tell me her story when she is ready, if ever. Like all of my other boarders, she could be gone tomorrow, replaced with a new stranger—or not. That is my lot in this life, in this house.

I think the town is getting back to normal after all the ruckus. The Del Reys are taking the loss of their daughter, Donna, the hardest. Business was hard enough for them—who has the money to pay for an embalming these days? But now they bear the brunt of a damaged reputation. Donna running with that Billy Bunson, even if she was manipulated into his scheme, won't be forgotten anytime soon. I feel sorry for them and send over some food when I have extra. The sidewalk is still marked, and the hobos knock on the back door with frequency. I don't think those elected men in Washington, or Austin for that matter, understand the difficulties and trials most normal folks face in these prolonged hard times. I've never met a man who enjoyed begging for a meal. They want to work is what they want. Hunger is a fierce motivator. We both should count ourselves lucky that we have the means to get through the day. When will it ever end?

As much as I miss you, I have to tell you that I miss Blue even more. I never took to many dogs in my life, but I've told you that. Us townfolk never had much use for dogs like farm folks do. There is little for them to do, and they are another mouth to worry about feeding if you keep them close. But Blue is different. He is a comfort that I have never known. He barked at the backdoor beggars, and as much as I hate to think of such a thing, I imagine he ran more than one of them off. The fact that the dog is devoted to you is another reason for my admiration. He laid in wait every second while you were away and wore a sad look that wasn't there any other time. The joy Blue showed on your return would warm even the iciest heart. Even on three good legs, I swear that dog danced at the sight of you. Please give him a good pat on the head and tell him that I miss him, too.

I did manage to leave the house this last week and go to the picture show. I heard snickers behind my back about a woman attending a show on her own, but I paid those who passed judgment no mind. I was in need of some entertainment. *Bright Eyes* has been playing for a week and I had heard so much chatter about it that I figured I best go see what all of the fuss was about. That little Shirley Temple is something else. She plays an orphan girl taken in by an uppity family against the wishes of her godfather. He wants custody of her for himself. I laughed and cried. But the best part of the show was forgetting for a minute about the state of the world we live in and the emptiness I would face when I returned home. I got my money's worth is what I did. And I'm glad of it. I wonder if they will play this movie at your theater in Wellington. If they do, you should go see it. I think you'll like it. That little girl might make you smile for a minute or two.

Well, I've rambled on for long enough. I'm sure you have better things to do than read a letter from a sappy woman like myself. I meant what I said. Please tell me if you don't plan on coming back. There's a place here for you, Sonny. Maybe I haven't said that in so many words, but I mean it. If times were different, I'd sell this old house and start fresh, but no one has the money to buy and sell such a thing these days. Besides, how could you trust the banks? I won't. Not anymore than folks around here will trust the Del Reys to bury their dead. Once trust is broke, there's no repairing it the way I see it. Give my regards to Jesse, and I hope to hear from you soon. I'll continue to write until you tell me not to.

Cordially,
Edith

Edith Grantley stood over the stove stirring a pan of thin milk. The clock in the entryway ticked, echoing through the sleeping house. She was so accustomed to the regularity of the clock's presence that she took no notice of it at all. The mice had quieted in the walls, too. Their overnight travels put to an end, their quest to survive given a respite like the rest of the folks and creatures in Huntsville. No moon shone in the sky. It was a dark night full of rolling clouds and a steady wind out of the west. The screen door rattled against the latch like someone was trying to get inside, but Edith knew better. She'd checked the door three times and looked out into the backyard to see nothing moving; no new renters at the wrong door, or hungry hobos chancing the late hour for a bit of bread or leftover cheese. The yard was as vacant and lonely as the boardinghouse kitchen.

She wore a quilted housecoat over a thin flannel nightdress. Her feet were covered by a pair of old black socks stolen out of her husband's drawer before he'd died. The socks needed darning, but that chore was the least of her worries. Being presentable, or fashionable in any sense, was not a concern. It was the middle of the night. Sleep was elusive for Edith. It had been since Walter P. Flynn, a boarder and lightning rod salesman, had been murdered in her parlor. It was only by the grace of God and the luck of having Sonny Burton in residence that she had survived the ordeal. If it could be called that: *An ordeal.* Nightmares haunted her all hours of the day. She saw blood everywhere even though it had been cleaned and washed from the floor and walls. To the eye that wasn't anointed with the truth and recent history of the house, there was no sign of the struggle. But paint and bleach could not erase the sight of death from Edith's mind. She was certain that she could still smell blood in the parlor; invisible particles of death trapped in the fabric of the woven wool rug. The upright piano sat with the lid closed, as needy for a touch as she was. Not one note of music had been played since Billy Bunson had invaded the house and stole away her sense of security, comfort, and the presence of her Sonny.

The bitter smell of the warm milk didn't entice her to drink it, only told her that if she didn't remove it from the flame it would be scalded and wasted. Even with three boarders in the house, there was little left over to waste. She was far from wealthy, but she had a sock full of bills tucked under her mattress for a rainy day.

Edith poured the milk in a waiting coffee cup and let it sit to cool before she would even consider drinking it. Intent on washing the pan and putting it away first—but something stopped her. Footsteps approached behind her.

She turned, startled, then calmed at the sight of Marcel Pryor, her longest boarder. Edith had gotten past normal formalities with Marcel, unlike Mr. Day and Miss Burns. Marcel was a thin, normal-sized man with a Roman nose, soft chin, and a tussle of unmanageable black hair on top of his head. His job as a prison guard required a haircut of military precision, which Marcel abided by on the sides and the back, but he kept a length of the hair on top, usually plastered down with pomade to suit the attitudes of his superiors. He had a girl he was sweet on in New Orleans and would disappear for a string of days when he could accumulate time off from the prison. There was never any talk of marriage or of the girl moving to Huntsville. Edith didn't know her name and had never seen a picture of her. She took Marcel's word that the girl of his dreams really existed. If not, and Marcel was doing something else on his journeys, well, that was none of her business. She liked Marcel, trusted him, and if he wasn't twenty-five years younger than her, she might have tried to tempt him into her bed a long time ago. They shared a loneliness that was obvious.

"I thought I heard you moving about," Marcel said. He wore a nightshirt covered by a thin olive-green robe. There was a hint of French on the tip of his tongue even though he had been born in Louisiana. His mother had been a cancan dancer from France and his father had been a ship's captain from Liverpool, England. They'd met in New Orleans and Marcel's mother spoke French and little English. His voice had a natural softness to it that was pleasant to Edith's ear; his accent and intense eyes were unusual, worth paying attention to.

"Sleep eludes me," Edith answered. She showed him her cup of warmed milk. "There's a little left. Would you like some?"

"Yes, that would be nice." Marcel sat down at the small dinette table next to the dry sink. A longer, more formal table sat in the dining room. It was there that the boarders took their daily meals. The kitchen was Edith's domain, reserved for her and the occasional guest. She didn't eat with the boarders, fighting familiarity as much as she could. Favors needed to be avoided on the days the rent was due.

Edith walked over and set her cup down in front of Marcel. "You usually don't have trouble sleeping. Are you all right?"

A look of protest crossed his dark blue eyes but disappeared when he saw that Edith was in no mood to argue about good manners. They knew each other well enough to have some unspoken vocabulary between them.

"A tiring day at work is all," Marcel said. "Some days it feels as if I am a prisoner, too, jailed for a crime that I didn't commit." He took a sip of the steaming milk and eyed her over the rim of the cup.

Edith was tempted to remind Marcel that he was a lucky man. Having a steady job these days was a gift most men could only dream about. But she restrained herself and poured what milk remained into another cup for herself.

"You think I am ungrateful," he said. Both of their voices were low, aware of the time of night, that the other boarders slept in their beds above them on the second floor. Voices carried through the furnace grates, turning them into whispers of betrayal if one wasn't careful.

"I thought it, but I was wrong to think such a thing. I have never set foot on the grounds of the prison. Who am I to condemn you for feeling caged in when . . ." Edith stopped, looked away from Marcel, then took a deep drink of the warm milk.

Silence filled the room between them. Tick, tock. A creak of lumber high in the trusses of the house. Edith's heart matched the beat of the clock. The middle of the night shared their insomnia.

"When you feel caged, too?" Marcel said.

"Yes, how did you know?"

"I have watched you wither since Sonny Burton left for his home."

"It's more than that."

"Walter's death was traumatic."

"I can't get it out of my mind." Her words were more of a gasp for air than an admittance.

Marcel dug into the right pocket of his robe and pulled out a pack of Camels. "Do you mind?" He raised the cigarettes for permission, even though the next action he took belied his request. He was already tapping out a cigarette before Edith spoke.

"No, not at all." Edith set her coffee cup down, opened a drawer next to the stove, pulled out an orange ceramic ashtray, and took it to Marcel. He had lit a Camel and put the matches and pack back in his pocket by the time she got to the table. Her deceased husband, Henry, smoked Camels. She liked the smell of them. The Turkish blend of the tobacco comforted her.

"I do not have a cure to remove your nightmare, Edith," Marcel said, blowing out a lungful of blue smoke.

Edith retook her position next to the stove and cradled the cup of milk in her hand.

"But it has been my experience that time will cause the shock of the trauma to fade," he continued. "That is little help, but I think you suffer from a malady worse than the repercussions of witnessing a murder in your own home."

"And what is that?"

"A broken heart, *mademoiselle*. You lost your luster the day that Sonny Burton and his dog climbed into that truck and drove away. You have not been the same since. And you were more than smitten with him. I could tell when he first arrived. He stirred something in you that had been sleeping for a long time." Marcel paused and took another drag off the cigarette, then resumed from where he'd left off. "I beg your pardon for being so direct. I know a little about love and broken hearts. I know them when I see them, when I hear them."

Edith lowered her head and sighed. *Had it been so obvious?* she wondered. But Marcel's assumption was not a revelation or an offense. His words were as comforting as the cigarette smoke. She was glad he cared enough to speak so direct to her. "He's not answering my letters," she said. "I fear I have lost him or made a fool of myself. One I can live with, the other, I am not so sure. I had become resigned to the fact that love was a thing of the past. Its arrival surprised me more than I can say. I never thought I'd feel so deep for another man after losing Henry. My world revolved around him, his hopes and dreams, then his every breath, begging him not to leave me here alone. I thought we were going to live happily ever after. And we did for a time. But that time was not long enough. I'd resolved myself to being alone for the rest of my days, and then Sonny Burton walked through that door, wounded, confident, his weary eyes searching every inch of me in a way that I think surprised us both."

"Sonny Burton is a complicated man." The cigarette burned between Marcel's long, yellowed fingertips at a slow pace. He made no offer to comfort Edith with anything but his words.

"I wait for him every day, staring out the back door, doing my best to will him into existence."

"Like a caged animal."

Smoke swirled in front of Marcel's face, obscuring his blue eyes, but Edith didn't break his gaze. "What would you suggest I do?"

"The thing we all want to do but are afraid of. Break free."

"Go to him?"

"What is stopping you?"

"I hadn't thought about leaving. How could I walk away from this house?"

"He can never come back here." Marcel took another drag off the Camel and bored a hole into her soul with his stare. "It would be like returning to the battlefields in France. None of us can do that. Our hearts would collapse, and our veins would explode. We left so much there, like he left so much here, in the parlor. He knew that man who stole the lock off your door and the lightness from your dreams. He had a history with him. He only killed him to save you. Otherwise, I think Sonny Burton

29

would have let Billy Bunson kill him and put him out of his misery."

"You talked to him?"

"Enough to understand him a little."

"I have to go to him?"

"Yes," Marcel said, grinding out the cigarette. "I think you do, or I fear you will never see him again."

CHAPTER FOUR

Sonny stared at Edith's letter long after he finished reading it. His hand trembled for a long second, and he had the itch to grab a pen and start writing a letter to her right away. He could hear her voice in his head reading the letter to him, like she was standing in the same room—instead of writing from hundreds of miles away. It was impossible to write with his left hand and expect anyone to be able to read the scratches he left on the paper. He missed the ease of writing, of shifting his truck, of reaching for a cup of coffee, and taking the use of his right hand for granted. The doctor had told him it would take several years to adjust to losing the arm, but that had not happened yet. Some nights when he lay sleepless in bed, he could feel the tips of his missing fingers, pain throbbing in the bicep of his right arm. Of course, neither were real. They were called phantom pains, like the arm was a ghost of itself. He could almost believe in that kind of unreal thing. The pain was as real as sticking a pin in his eye.

Instead of attempting to write, Sonny took the letter over to the desk that sat in the front room and put it down on a pile next to the typewriter. The desk sat next to a tall Atwater Kent radio, a gift for Martha on the last wedding anniversary they had celebrated together. The electric set had a veneer cabinet that looked new, untouched, because it was on most days. There were few programs that interested Sonny other than the weather and news. The top of the radio was covered with dust along with an empty doily in the center. There used to be a sepia-toned picture of him and Martha taken in Austin sitting there, but Sonny had put the portrait away after her funeral and never replaced it with anything.

He stared at the typewriter, at three of Edith's letters that he had left unanswered, and he understood the panic in the words on the page of her recent letter. Edith didn't deserve to feel like he had abandoned her. She didn't deserve that at all. She had been kind to him. She had shown him love when he'd been lost on the desert island of old age, surrounded by a sea of blood and bullets.

Sonny sat down and stared at the Olivetti like it was a piano, like he had no idea what key was what. Treble, bass, who knew? But the typewriter was marked with the alphabet, but in an order that started with Q instead of A. How hard could pounding out a letter to Edith be? It didn't matter. He could feel the heartbreak in Edith's letter. He couldn't ignore the fact that she was waiting on him any longer. He wasn't the kind of man to hurt someone with intention. Never had been, but he *was* hurting her. How could he tell her that he never wanted to set foot in Huntsville again? That all he wanted to do was hole up in his house and die? He couldn't. But, yet, he had to.

Sonny Burton
RR #1, Box 78
Wellington, Texas
January 14, 1935

Dear Edith,
Your letter came today, and I wanted to answer it right away. Please forgive the previous letters that I have not answered. I want you to know that I think of you often, and of my time in Huntsville. I view our time together

32

fondly. You were a bright flower in an empty field. A surprise and a beauty that I was not ever expecting to find.

The truth is, I had to scour the confines of Wellington to find a typewriter, of which there were none to be found, so I ordered one from the Sears & Roebuck catalog and have only now come to attain possession of the thing. I think I will find writing easier using this contraption than trying to scribble a legible note with my left hand. Still, I must type with one hand and that presents a challenge. If I can dress myself, I can darn well find the decency to answer your letters. It has taken me hours to write this much.

I'm sorry to tell you that returning to Huntsville before Dolly Rickart's trial is not going to happen. My distance has nothing to do with you, and more about the nightmare that occurred there. Billy Bunson cannot harm anyone ever again, I see his death, and the death of the others that he caused as my burden to carry. I couldn't look those Del Reys in the eyes if I met them on the street. Miss Ziskin, either. Her life has been altered by my inability to intervene in a meanness that I have known for a long time. And then there is Billy himself. I failed him the most. I had plenty of chances over the years to rescue him from his sorry plight, but each time that opportunity came my way, it slipped through my hands. If I had changed him a bunch of people would still be alive right now—including Billy himself. I mourn for his loss, as odd as that seems, as much as the others.

My darkest hours of the night are filled with images of Billy that I cannot pry from my mind. I'm sorry I had to kill him in your house, in front of you, but I had no choice. We share in the shock of that. Midnight is a cavalcade of relentless horror stories. I toss and turn in the bed worse than I did after I lost my arm or came home from France.

I'm not sure that I will come to terms with what happened in Huntsville anytime soon. Do not fret, though, I will see you again. I will return to Huntsville because I must, but for now, I feel like the comfort of my own home, as isolated as it is, is the best place for me to recuperate from that tragedy. I fear I would be poor company for you in the state I find myself in everyday when I wake.

Jesse comes by every so often to check on me, to talk about our days in Huntsville. That time together has brought us closer than we've ever been, given us a memory to share that we did not have before. He was a good partner, and that came as a surprise to us both. He shares your relief at the change in governorship. Being a Ranger under Ma Ferguson presented challenges for Jesse. A nickel and a phone call from Ma could make any man a Ranger. The organization is chock-full of tyrants and renegades who have no business claiming to be lawmen, much less a Ranger. Jesse is a by-the-book man, of which I am proud, and takes no favor for anyone who commits a crime. He is not a man to look the other way. I am glad to be free of the politics of the current-day Rangers, and I am sure, like the prison system, the Texas Rangers are going to go through some welcome changes under this new governor, Allred and his men. There needs to be a good housecleaning if you ask me, but I am last on the list of opinions most of those folks care to ask. I am glad of that, too. My days as a Ranger are over with, and I am surprised that I am happy about that. I am anxious to spend the remainder of my days without the charge of peeling right from wrong.

I wish I shared your enthusiasm for the picture show. I have not been in a long time. I don't think I would enjoy the antics of that Shirley Temple. I am sure she is a talented girl, but the world seems too dark for her smile, or eyes, to brighten it for any length of time for me. One of our movie theaters, the Ritz, has suffered from a serious fire. The projectors were saved, but there was extensive damage. Lucky for folks who enjoy the picture show that there is more than one theater in town.

Blue is fine, sitting at my feet as I struggle to type this letter to you. Since when does W follow Q? The English on this contraption seems like a foreign language to me. Blue doesn't like the noise this Olivetti makes. Me, either. I was never much of a letter writer when I had both of my hands. I wrote to Martha from France, but not near as much as she would have liked me to. There was little to talk about, or that I wanted to relay about the war, other than I was safe and still alive. That seemed enough then, but not so much now. Times are different and you deserve more than that from me, all things considered. I am sorry for any discomfort my silence has caused you.

I didn't know what to say or how I would say what needed said in response to your letters. Thank you for them. Your voice fills an emptiness in this house, even on paper. Sears & Roebuck has rescued me, us, with this metal heap that sings with taps and rings. I will try to be more prompt in my replies.

The most exciting thing around here to happen was a circus passed by the house yesterday. It is the first time in my life that I have ever seen a live elephant. It was bigger than I ever imagined it would be and the windows shook in their frames when it walked by. Old Blue about had a fit. I had to hold him back with all of the might of my good hand. I worried the beast would have stomped him to death if the dog escaped me and got tangled among those giant feet. I'm surprised such things as circuses still exist in these days of struggle and strain.

I wish I could tell you when this Depression was going to end, but like you, I have my fears that it never will. These grim days might well out last us all. Those fellas in Washington can't turn around a ship that's sinking if you ask me.

We need rain is what we need. Rain and hope. Neither of which is on the horizon as I look out my window.

Regardless of what you might think, I look forward to your letters. Please continue to be well.

Sincerely,
Sonny

A knock at the door startled Sonny out of a shallow sleep. Blue scampered out of the small bedroom to investigate, barking as he set off a vicious alarm that hurt Sonny's ears. By the judge of the light, the sun hadn't been awake for long. A thin stream of soft yellow sunlight pushed into the room below the shade. Dust particles floated like tiny diamonds in the air lit by the hungry sunshine. The clock ticked toward eight, a much later time than Sonny stirred awake. He'd had no reason to rise with the chickens since he didn't have any. Blue's deep protective voice echoed throughout the small house, forcing Sonny to consider there might be a threat beyond the door.

Another knock came, more anxious this time. Sonny dropped his feet to the floor and walked over to the chair where he'd left his clothes from the night before. "I'll be right there," he hollered as he struggled to pull on his pants with his left hand. He'd fallen asleep in his undershirt and boxers. There wasn't time to strap on the prosthesis. He grabbed his shirt and slid it on his good arm, leaving the empty sleeve to dangle limp like the circus banners had. On other days he would have made sure to holster his handgun, his father's 1873 Colt Army Revolver. But he didn't stop and pull the gun out of the bureau. There didn't seem to be time. Besides, there was a varmint gun loaded and ready to fire sitting next to the kitchen door if he needed it.

By the time he got to the kitchen, Blue had stopped barking and was sniffing at the base of the door, wagging his tail. Sonny saw a familiar silhouette through the curtains that covered the window in the door. "What's the matter, Aldo?" he said as he opened the door with heft, calming himself with a deep breath. Blue bolted out of the house as fast as he could, happy to see the Mexican.

Aldo Hernandez pulled his hand back, retracting from another knock. He wore a worried look on his weathered brown face. He had shiny black hair, dense as a bird's nest, with gray streaks sprouting on his sideburns. His skin was leathery, looked wrinkled and pruned from working in the sun most of his early life. His family had been migrant workers and had traveled all over the country following vegetable and fruit seasons, picking tomatoes, cabbage, apples, and more, until he settled in Wellington and took to being the janitor at the one and only hospital in the county. He was in his late thirties, early forties at the most, but looked much older. Aldo and Sonny had become friends when Sonny was in the hospital after getting shot by Bonnie Parker.

"Ah, my favorite *perro*," Aldo said to Blue, rubbing the dog's head. "He looks good, *Señor* Sonny. He like it here with you. I knew he would."

Sonny wore a puzzled look on his face. Somewhere in the distance a robin sang, welcoming the day. It was an odd bit of noise since there were no trees in Sonny's yard. The trees had either died or had been cut down for fuel long ago. The air was cold, but that didn't seem to bother Aldo. He was dressed for work, wore a long-sleeved shirt with a fresh pack of Chesterfields sticking out of the pocket and a pair of dark blue Dickies to match the shirt. It was as close to a uniform as Sonny had ever seen the man in.

"It's awful early, Aldo. Come on in and have some coffee." Sonny stood back and opened the door to let the man into his house.

"If you are sure," Aldo said, stepping inside the kitchen. Blue followed him, staying at his side.

"I haven't seen you for a month of Sundays, so I figure there is a reason you are here so early in the morning banging on my door. It's not an emergency, is it?"

Sonny headed to the two-burner stove—the gas manifold was hidden behind painted white sheet metal—grabbed a match and lit a burner with the flame after striking it. A brief smell of gas flittered upward, then disappeared, eaten by the fire and sudden warmth.

"I am in need of a favor." Aldo sat down at the dinette that was pushed tight against the wall. A calendar was tacked over the table. One side of the dinette was stacked with newspapers. "But I suspect you are already aware of that."

Sonny was in mid-reach for the can of Arbuckle's coffee, but Aldo's words froze his arm level with the open shelf above the stove. He knew the tone, the implication of the need. "I have no money if that is what you're after."

"No one has any money."

"That's true."

"You have time on your hands," Aldo said, looking away from Sonny.

"I wish that were true." Sonny finished the reach for the coffee, then prepared the dripolator, a small two-part aluminum container that held water and a basket for the coffee to drain through.

"I am sorry, I didn't mean anything by what I said."

"It's a figure of speech. I have time on my one hand."

Aldo drew in a deep breath. "You are the only one I could come to."

"I've heard that before." Sonny's spine stiffened without any prompting from him. It was a quick physical response that resulted from the pain of familiar tension and another man's unease. No one seemed to accept that he wasn't a Ranger anymore, that he couldn't help them with their troubles, legal or otherwise.

"My cousin, Rafael, is in the county jail."

Sonny turned on the flame to warm the coffee, then faced Aldo. "For assault and battery?"

"*Sí*. I knew you would know."

"People tell me things without having to be asked. It's always been that way."

"That is why I come to you with matters such as this, *Señor* Sonny."

"This doesn't have anything to do with Carmen, does it?"

Aldo shook his head, then looked past Sonny, out the window, avoiding eye contact, like he was ashamed. "Carmen is fine. Home with the *bebé.*"

"I was hoping you would say that."

"She would be dead if it were not for you."

"Jesse had a hand in that, too. He would have saved her if I wasn't around." The dripolator started to drop coffee into the container below the basket and the rich familiar smell of Arbuckle's filled the room. It was a warm and comfortable aroma, but there was a matter of coldness situated between Sonny and Aldo. The trouble with Carmen had forced Sonny out of the house after he had lost his arm. He'd almost lost his life in the process of acting on another favor for Aldo. "No matter the trouble, my days of helping out are over, Aldo. I've done my time. Sheriff Jones is a decent man. He's fair to everyone, even to them coloreds on the south side of town. You need to go to him if this matter concerns the law."

Aldo's shoulders sagged, and the puffy bulbs under his eyes

seemed to grow darker. "Not everyone in this state is equal under the law. If Rafael was white, he wouldn't be—" Aldo stopped, didn't say anything else.

The tension in Sonny's body was obvious. Even Sonny had his boundaries when it came to be discussing a Mexican's place in the world. He stared at the dripolator, waiting for it to complete its task. He remained silent until the coffee was ready, then poured Aldo a cup and handed it to him.

"*Gracias.*" Aldo took the cup and wrapped both of his hands around it to warm his palms. It was cold in the kitchen even with the stove burner flickering.

Aldo stared at the dark brown liquid like he was trying to read tea leaves, trying to figure out what to say next to encourage Sonny to listen to his plea. Sonny knew the look. He turned his back and filled his own cup of coffee.

"Rafael," Aldo went on, "he was there because of Sheriff Jones. But they cannot tell anyone. His left eye is still swollen shut and his face looks like a grape."

"What do you mean Rafael was there because of the sheriff?" Sonny turned around, unable to stop himself from asking the question.

"He is a, how you say it, a snitch?"

"Some people call it that," Sonny said. "What was he doing with those CCC boys? Seems like he was asking for trouble by going there, especially on a Saturday night. Coloreds have a hard enough time getting into the corp. Jonesy must have known there'd be trouble. You get a bunch of anxious men drunk on sour liquor and a Mexican comes walking in like he belongs there, somebody's bound to throw a punch. No offense, mind you, Aldo."

"It wasn't like that. Rafael was going to be on the crew. He is a good boy. Graduated from high school, got a ribbon for running track. Rafael, he was never in no trouble."

"He must have done something to be a snitch for Jonesy."

Aldo shrugged. "He was there to keep an ear out for the sheriff. I thought the sheriff, he would tell you why or what he was after. Rafael took some tequila and shared it around. He says he drank too much and passed out. He came to when someone was beating him in the face. Another man, Leo Dozier, he lay not far from Rafael."

"The Doziers are well-known," Sonny said. "The boy's father oversees the junkyard and runs a wrecker service on the north side of Wellington."

"*Sí*, Wilmer. He's a good man."

"Why is the sheriff still holding Rafael for assault and battery?"

"Everybody says Rafael started the fight, but Rafael, he don't remember no fight. He didn't have anything against this man, Dozier. They were all just drinking, that is all. My guess is he thought the tequila would make someone talk, say something he was listening for."

"Something doesn't sound right."

"Rafael, he is in serious trouble, and Sheriff Jones can't help him, even if he is a snitch for him. It would come out that Rafael has been helping the sheriff, and that it was the sheriff that suggested he join the CCC. That might not look good next time the election comes around. That's why I came to you for help. The law, it cannot help Rafael. Only you can."

Sonny took a sip of coffee, and said, "Whatever Rafael has got himself into, then he will have to get himself out of it. If there's witnesses and the stories are consistent, a judge and jury will go the way of the crowd. You can't argue with that. Maybe Rafael doesn't remember. Jonesy can advocate for Rafael, tell the judge why he sent him to be with those boys."

"No, I don't think he will do that."

"You need to find out why Rafael was a snitch."

"He is an innocent man. My cousin, he has *niños*, two little ones that still hang on their *mamacita's* skirt. What will happen to them? I have trouble feeding the mouths in my own house. I cannot take them in."

"Were you there?"

"No, but . . ."

"Then you can't assume what happened. Tequila is a powerful drink. I've seen sane fellas jump off of roofs for the fun of it, drunk on that stuff."

Aldo still held the cup of coffee but hadn't taken a sip of it for himself. Blue sat next to the Mexican's ankle, offering what comfort he could. It was easy to tell by Aldo's tone that he was upset. "I do not wish to beg, *Señor* Sonny."

"Won't do you any good."

"Would it hurt you to talk to the sheriff? To make sure there's nothing more that can be done. He trusts you, will listen to you like no one else. Maybe he will tell you why he had Rafael walk into the middle of those white boys. He won't tell me. Even Rafael is silent."

Sonny knew that Aldo was right, that Jonesy might talk to him. He didn't like it, but he had to admit that it was so. He sighed, doing his best not to sound too resolute. Sometimes he came across more determined to stay out of things than he meant to. "Okay. I have a letter to mail at the post office. I'll stop by and talk to Jonesy, but that's all, you understand? It's only a talk, that's all. I wouldn't do this for anyone else but you, Aldo."

"*Gracias, Señor* Sonny, *gracias*," Aldo said, with a smile replacing his doom-filled face.

"Don't get your hopes high and unbound, Aldo, it's only a talk and nothing more. You hear?"

"I hear, but I am happy is all," Aldo said. "If anybody can help Rafael, it is you, *Señor* Sonny. It is you."

CHAPTER FIVE

Edith held the Smith & Wesson .38 in her hands with the barrel pointed at a bale of straw. A thin wisp of blue smoke spiraled upward, and the smell of gunpowder invaded her nose. Her ears rang from the shot, and her fingers could still feel the vibration of the controlled explosion that had blasted inside the gun's steel casing.

"I still don't see the reason for this, Marcel," she said as disdain clung to her thin cheeks. Her face was chilled by the January wind pushing down from the north. Freezing temperatures in Huntsville were rare, but the mercury had touched ice overnight.

Marcel stood next to Edith dressed in his prison guard uniform, fresh off a shift, stiff as a sergeant getting ready to send a soldier off to battle. "You will be a woman on the road alone. It is a five-hundred-mile trip to Wellington on unknown roads and through Fort Worth, too. You must be prepared to defend yourself if the need arises."

Edith dropped the .38 to her side. She had never had a desire to be anything like Bonnie Parker. "You are a sweet man, Marcel, but I can't take your gun."

"I have another. You must take it."

"This is a bad idea."

"Cold feet will not warm the regret you feel if you are still here and Sonny Burton is still there."

"I should talk to him first before I leave out. What if he does not want me there? What if my arrival angers him?"

"Then you will have your answer, and your house will be waiting here for you on your return."

"It is too much to ask of you to look after things for me while I am away."

"I have spoken to Mr. Day. Our shifts are on a different rotation. We will look after your concerns for a time. It is the least we can do for you. Now, try again. Be more confident of your aim."

Edith stood rigid, determined to rebel against Marcel's command, but her feet didn't agree with her mind. She knew he was right. Anything could happen in five hundred miles. She should be prepared to take care of herself. She had never traveled alone for such a great distance. If she were being honest, she was as afraid of that as she was of being rejected by Sonny when she arrived in Wellington unannounced. At least she would know where she stood. Marcel was right about that.

She steadied herself, drew the pistol so the target was sighted, breathed deep, exhaled, then pulled the trigger before taking another breath. She was ready for the jolt from the firing, ready for the pungent smell of gunpowder.

"Much better," Marcel said with a clap of his hands. "Much better. A few more rounds and I think you'll have it."

"Are you sure?"

"Yes, of course. You're a natural."

The yellow 1928 Pierce Arrow Model 81 Runabout sat outside the house, packed and ready to go. The rumble seat was stowed, and the canvas top pulled tight to protect the interior from the weather. Henry had bought the Pierce for Edith before he had got sick. The mill had been running at full bore, two shifts a day, six days a week, everything was good for almost everyone in Huntsville. There was no sign of the trouble to come on the horizon, to Henry or the stock market. The automobile sat stored in the carriage house except for the rare time Edith needed to drive a distance. She kept it in operating shape out of respect for Henry. He had loved the car, bright like a sun rolling down the road, with smart black fenders, and the convertible top, perfect for the long, hot Texas summer days. Whether the Pierce could make the distance of the trip was another question. It hadn't been tested. The miles on it were low, and Edith's confidence behind the wheel was in league with her gun-handling skills.

The morning was bright, the sky clear, with no immediate threats visible. All that was holding Edith back was Edith. She stood with her hand on the door handle, one foot on the running board, one foot on the graveled alleyway. Marcel stood with his arms crossed, full of assurance that Edith was doing the right thing.

"I am not the kind of woman to walk in somewhere uninvited, Marcel. Perhaps I should send a telegram to ask Sonny's permission."

"You could do that. It would be an easy out for him as well as you."

"You are a difficult man, Marcel Pryor."

A smile crossed his lips. "It is not me forcing you on this journey. It is your heart. You felt Sonny's heart, too. But he is not the kind of man to invite you into his home, either. There are wounds bearing tough scars on the surface of his skin. We both could see that. Time is short for you both. If you stay here that love will melt away. His presence in your life will be nothing more than a memory. What are you waiting for?"

Edith stepped off the running board, walked over to Marcel, and gave him a peck on the cheek, leaving a set of prints from her fresh lipstick. "Thank you," she said. "How did you get to be so wise?"

"I have let things slip from my grasp. Not acted when my heart demanded that I do. I quit the chase too soon. And now look at me? I work in a prison with men like me who gave up on themselves too soon and took the easy way out. I don't want to see you spend your life like me is all."

"But you have your girl in New Orleans."

"Alas, another loss on my part. She is to be married to a lawyer in Monroe. How could I ever compete with that?"

"I'm sorry." Edith kissed him on the cheek again, only she let her lips linger a little longer. "You're a good man. There'll be another girl to steal your heart."

"Maybe. Until then, I will live my life looking forward to the day when I can do what you are doing, fleeing the bars that hold me. Be safe, Edith. Your house will be here waiting for you on your return."

Edith agreed, then went to the Pierce, settled herself in the driver's seat, and started the engine. She sat, letting the automobile idle, warming to a purr. The Smith & Wesson was under her seat with six chambers loaded with fresh cartridges. A map sat in the seat next to her with her journey plotted out to the stop. The trip was going to take two days, only because she was in no hurry, with a visit in Fort Worth. It had been a long time since she had been to the city, and her only living aunt still lived there. She planned on paying the woman a visit if the weather and time cooperated.

With the engine warmed and no more reason to stall, Edith put the engine in gear and drove away, offering Marcel a quick wave. She tried not to look at the house. Any gaze would have tethered her to it, pulled her back like she was attached by an invisible rubber band. But that didn't happen. Edith was as certain of her adventure as she could be. She couldn't wait for Sonny to answer her any longer. She had to go find out for herself where she stood with him. One way or another, she was going to set her heart right. Marcel had been spot-on. Time was growing short for them both. Neither of them was youthful nor spry. It was now or never.

The mechanics of going into town took twice as long for Sonny as it used to. Life had been a lot easier when he'd had two hands. Not only was writing a letter next to impossible, shaving had turned into an art form. Each swipe of the razor was a risk—his face bore a new crop of minuscule nicks and scars to remind him of his lack of skills with a sharp blade. The remaining left hand lacked coordination, strength, and confidence, and on top of everything else, he had developed an unpredictable tremor in it since returning from Huntsville. Sometimes the shake was there and sometimes it wasn't. Sharp objects and tremors don't mix. It was a good thing he'd retired from wearing a gun on his hip for a living. Aiming an uncertain barrel would be difficult. Unfortunately, he had a new weapon, a hook that had taken a man's life. He didn't need a gun to kill someone if the need arose.

Aldo waited in the kitchen as Sonny got ready. Out of habit, Sonny had turned on the radio as he'd passed by it. The weather report came first, then news from Washington. Nothing new. The broadcaster's voice was cold, dreary, and gray no matter the subject. The radio was nothing more than comfort, contact from the outside world to remind Sonny that there was something going on beyond his four walls. Without it the only noise would come from the wind, or Blue, who so far hadn't developed the ability to hold much of a conversation.

Sonny washed the remaining shaving cream from his face, put everything where it belonged, buttoned his shirt the rest of the way, then headed to the kitchen. Aldo and Blue were right where he'd left them, sitting at the dinette still as a rabbit wary of a circling hawk.

Aldo stood when Sonny walked into the room. "I am sorry to bother you. I know you don't want to do this thing I have asked of you."

Sonny stopped inside the doorframe that separated the front room and the kitchen. "I need to get some sugar and staples, anyway. It's all right, Aldo. Come on, I'll drop you off at the hospital on my way, unless you want to go to the sheriff's office with me?"

"No, I have to get to work." Aldo looked at his watch with a worried look.

"You're going to be late."

"They will not mind. I will not be late by much. I will have more worry when the new hospital on Fifteenth Street is completed."

"It looked almost ready the last time I went past."

"The new hospital will be open later this year. Many more beds, and many more things to keep clean. I hope I can do it all. At least there will be room for more sick people in Wellington. That is a hopeful thing."

"You should have told me that you were in a hurry."

"I have asked too much of you the way it is. It is difficult for you to do the daily things."

Sonny sighed, then made his way into the front room to turn off the radio. He grabbed the letter to Edith that sat next to the Olivetti, stamped and ready to go, and made sure he didn't need anything else. "Come on, let's go then," he said, as he walked back into the kitchen and made his way to the door.

Aldo and Blue followed him outside. Sonny hesitated for a second as he considered leaving Blue behind, but he changed his mind, heeding Clifford's warning. The circus people were still close by as far as he knew.

Sonny dropped the gate of his '29 Ford pickup, and Blue jumped into the bed without any trouble. The dog had figured out how to compensate for his bad leg by taking a running jump. There seemed to be nothing that Blue couldn't do, after being hit, that he couldn't do before, except run after elephants a little faster than he wanted to.

Aldo joined Sonny in the cab, and it wasn't long before they were on the road, heading toward town. Silence settled between the two men. The Model A's engine didn't purr, it growled and shook with the change of gears. Sonny's one-handed timing was never going to be great. The road was hard and bumpy, and there was a constant vibration that sounded like a squadron of angry wasps had invaded the truck's interior. Besides, the way Sonny saw it, everything that had needed to be said between the two of them already had been. Conversation had never been one of his strong points.

They passed the Harmesons' place, a farm battered by the wind and the Depression. The clapboards were sandblasted of any color, and the windows were smudged with a decade of dirt. A thin milk cow stood next to the barn staring off into the distance. Beyond the cow, a set of ragged clothes flapped in the wind on a clothesline, offering the only color in the landscape; faded blue pants, brown shirts, and white sheets that had seen too much bleach and wear. The bedclothes looked like giant surrender flags waving for the enemy to stop their attack. A black Model T sat next to the house, but no one was outside. Chickens pecked at gravel, filling their gizzards, unaware of anything but themselves. It looked like the morning chores were done and over with.

A little way down the road, still cutting through Harmeson land, beyond a rise, Sonny wasn't surprised to see the circus where Clifford Jones had said they had stopped for camp. He slowed as he went by, not paying too much attention to where he was heading. A wood bridge with no rails stretched across a dry creek, adding to the vibration in the truck as he drove over it.

Aldo looked out the window in wonder. "I had heard they'd passed through."

"I thought they were moving on." Sonny glanced over his shoulder to check on Blue. The dog was standing on the wheel well, hackles raised, his nose pointed straight at the camp. There was no sign of the elephant or the African cats. The big top had been erected on flat ground overlooking a barren ravine. Sonny figured the animals were either inside the tent or behind it. The trucks and jalopies he'd seen in the parade were scattered about, and a few men wandered around, but there didn't look to be much going on. The banners weren't set to fly, announcing a performance. It might as well have been Sunday all over again.

"It is strange for them to be heading south so late," Aldo said.

Sonny wondered what made Aldo think of such a thing. "Maybe they're like birds, need the warmth in the winter."

"Elephants would need a *grande* coat in the north country," Aldo said, still looking out the window. They were past the circus now, and he had to crane his neck to keep it in sight. Sonny focused his attention back to the road ahead of him, then checked on Blue again, who had settled down once the circus had faded from view.

"You ever travel with anything like that?"

"Me?" Aldo said. "Oh, no, *Señor* Sonny. But traveling all over like I did, going from picking apples in Washington state to tomatoes in California, and beyond, you see lots of things on the road. The circus, it has seasons like everything else. North in the summer, south in the winter, from one town to the next. The thing I liked about picking was we would stay in one place for months on end. There was time to get familiar with a place, *comprendes*? A circus, they are here one day and gone the next.

You never get to appreciate anyplace. All you do is empty pockets of coins if you can and move on. I think it would be a lonely life."

"I understand. I had my seasons as a Ranger, too. I was traveling, going from one feud to the next, one camp to the next. Martha, my late wife, she didn't like that life much. I was gone a lot of the time. She held a grudge against me for leaving her so much, leaving her to raise Jesse on her own. I guess, she had a right to her grudge. I was out doing what I wanted, while she stayed back in one rented place or another, never able to do much but take care of what needed taking care of. That's why I settled down and bought this place in Wellington, to atone for my roaming. Then Martha went and died on me. I guess I should have bought a place sooner, but I couldn't."

"There is no way to relive the past, *Señor* Sonny. My guess is those circus people have no place else to go, or they would have left for their home by now."

"I imagine you're right, Aldo," Sonny said, as he looked into the rearview mirror. He didn't see anything but the trail of dust he was leaving behind, and an emptiness beyond the cloud that would never be filled.

CHAPTER SIX

The current hospital was a clean, freshly painted white two-story Victorian-style house that sat a block from downtown. It had served Wellington for a lot of years, but even in its decent shape the hospital couldn't compare to the new one being built on Fifteenth Street. Surgery was conducted in the basement, and the top floor held the sickrooms where Sonny had healed after his amputation. There were four beds to a room, and more in the attic if the need arose. Aldo was a janitor, handyman, or errand boy if that was what Doc Meyers needed him to be. The hospital was a small operation and there was one full-time nurse, Betty Maxwell, that everybody called Nurse Betty. Betty'd had some of her own problems in the past, got all twisted around in the mess with Aldo's daughter, but after a few months off, she'd gone right back to work at the hospital, helping people heal like she had Sonny. It was Betty who had convinced him that his life would be better if he wore a prosthesis. The hospital glowed like an oasis in a dead forest in the early morning light.

Sonny pulled to the curb to let Aldo out of the truck and left the motor idling. "I'll see what I can do to help Rafael. You remember what I said about keeping your hopes in check, don't you?"

Aldo's fingers were wrapped around the door handle, and his head was hung so low his chin almost touched his chest. "I am sorry I asked you to do this."

Sonny stared forward, toward town, doing his best not to

look at the hospital or Aldo. "It's the least I can do for you, Aldo. I don't mind." It was a white lie and he hoped he was convincing.

Aldo shook his head, opened the door, and pushed his way out of the truck. "*Gracias, Señor* Sonny, *gracias.*"

Sonny watched the man go to work, looked in the rearview mirror to check on Blue, then put the truck in gear and shimmied away from the hospital as fast as he could.

There was no heater in Sonny's truck. Some of the new Model A's had a vent that came in through the dash that pushed hot air off the engine into the interior. It sounded fancy and smelly to Sonny. He still missed the days of riding a horse everywhere he went. There was no protection from the weather in any way on the back of a decent mount. You had to deal with whatever came your way, which was the problem with the world today. Everybody drove dry in their automobiles while it was raining. It made people soft. Too much luxury was a bad thing. He didn't mind the chill in the air. His window was halfway down, ensuring that he was fully awake before he started asking Jonesy questions he didn't want to.

The county sheriff's office was located in the new courthouse. Built in 1931 to replace the original courthouse after Pearl City lost out as the county seat. The courthouse was made of light-colored brick, a three-story building with square corners and a flat roof. It looked more like a school than a government building. Carved limestone figures of justice and Roman fasces stood over the arched entrance on the south side of the building. More decorative panels were adorned over the first-floor windows, depicting scenes that featured the county's pioneers. In the early days, there were a lot of cattle farmers in Collingsworth County, but the agricultural mainstay had switched over to cotton when it became more profitable. Cotton was easy to grow in the climate and the soil before the sandstorms took all of the good topsoil west. There were still farmers struggling against the weather, the government, and the energy it took to be optimistic about their latest crop. As long as there were humans, the world would need cotton. There was no denying that.

Sonny parked the truck, told Blue to stay, and headed inside. His pace was even, not brisk. Beyond talking to Jonesy, he had the letter to Edith to mail, and some food to shop for at the grocers before he headed back home. The letter rode high in his breast pocket and his grocery list hung on the corner of his memory along with the pangs of persistent hunger. He hadn't taken the time to eat breakfast.

The inside of the courthouse still held a pervasive new smell to it; wood that hadn't seasoned and paint that gleamed and hadn't begun to crack and peel. The ceilings were inset, edged to look like copper but were hand-painted in hard-edged squares. Hanging bronze lights, centered in insets, offered simple white globes of radiant light. The floors were tiled, and one footstep echoed all of the way down the long hall and back. When there were a lot of people coming and going—before and after a trial—the hall sounded like it was filled with thunder tossed down from the heavens by angry and impatient gods.

Sonny knew his way to the sheriff's office. Out of habit, he had taken off his hat, a worn, brown-felt Stetson, as soon as he had stepped inside the courthouse. He carried the hat with his left hand, which gave him no ability to straighten his hair. If he tried to smooch it down, he might poke his eye out with the hook.

A receptionist guarded the entrance to the sheriff's office. Vandetta Glade was a thin, gray-haired woman, and was related to Jonesy in one way or another. A cousin, in-law, or a combination of both, Sonny wasn't sure which. He had got to know Vandetta when he had kept a small office in the basement in his

Ranger days. She was a spinster who had fluttered her eyes at him after Martha had died. He ignored the invitation then and had no desire to face such a thing again but knew he would. Vandetta Glade was as persistent as a honeybee in the spring.

"Well, looka here," Vandetta said as Sonny walked into the office. "Aren't you a sight for sore eyes, Lester Burton. I haven't seen you since that ruckus with Hugh Beaverwood. Such a shame, that man. Who would have ever thought?" She didn't take a breath, and kept on talking, staring straight at Sonny, tapping a pencil in her hand, looking him over head to toe, judging him like he was a bull for sale at an auction. The top of her desk was as organized as the alphabet, everything in its place. "Well, I guess we all would have suspected something was off with Hugh if we'd have let our minds wander, now wouldn't we? But we mustn't allow that, should we? Think ill of our neighbors even when it's hard not to. How have you been, Lester? Would you like a cup of coffee? I put on a fresh pot. Sheriff likes his coffee hot and fresh. I have to keep it that way. Yes, I sure do."

Sonny smiled and wondered how many cups of coffee the woman drank every day. Vandetta Glade was about the only person in Wellington who called him by his given name, Lester. Sonny was a nickname that had stuck so early in his life that almost no one knew the difference now. "It's good to see you, too, Vandetta. I don't get out much these days."

"Winter's that way. All folks want to stay inside. Or at least, they should. Sure would save the sheriff some time and trouble, wouldn't it?" With that Vandetta leaned forward and offered Sonny the flutter and gaze that he knew was coming. He ignored it, like usual.

"It would. Jonesy wouldn't happen to be in his office, would he?"

Offering no sign of rejection, Vandetta glanced over her

shoulder to a closed door that said Hiram P. Jones, Sheriff, Collingswood County, Texas, in temporary letters pasted onto frosted glass. The sheriff's position was elected not appointed.

"He is, but I gotta tell you, Lester, he's in a foul mood."

"Could you tell him I'm here?"

"If that's what you want."

"It is." He watched Vandetta get out of her chair and remembered that she had a hard time walking. She was hunched over with a bulge on her back that you couldn't see when she was sitting down. It took a reasonable amount of effort to hold her head high, her chin even with the floor, to see where she was going. If she was five-foot-tall, it was only by a cat's whisker.

The woman knocked on, then cracked open, the door. "Lester Burton's here to see you."

Jonesy didn't say anything right away. There was a shuffle of paper, a resetting of something heavy on his desk. Sonny didn't look into the office. He looked at the toes of his boots and tucked his hook behind his back. His hat felt like a thin life raft incapable of holding him afloat.

Silence followed Vandetta's interruption. The clip-clop of someone walking by the office on the tile floors with the perfect timing of a hurried heartbeat broke the discomfort. A groan joined in from somewhere deep in the bowels of the courthouse as the coal furnace fought to heat the gargantuan building. Then, Jonesy added to the institutional song, and said in a tired voice, "Send him in."

Vandetta pushed the office door open the rest of the way, then motioned for Sonny to go inside. He hesitated, fought off the desire to turn around and walk straight out of the courthouse and go home. The last thing he wanted to do was step into something he might not be able to get out of.

Sheriff Jones stood from behind the desk and offered Sonny his stubby hand. Jonesy was short and wide, had the face of a bulldog, a soft heart, and a solid spine, determined to uphold the law. Today, he slouched a bit and his brown long-sleeved shirt was frayed at the cuff. Most days he was as put together as an Army drill sergeant. They'd worked well together when the times had demanded it. The sheriff was no different than Aldo Hernandez. He'd made his way to Sonny's doorstep asking for help more than once or campaigned for Sonny's intervention when it came to solving one legal problem or another—even after he gave up being a Ranger *and* lost his arm.

Sonny shook the sheriff's right hand with his left with as much strength as he could. It was a limp shake, which bothered Sonny to no end, but there was nothing he could do about it. He knew how Texan men judged handshakes. He'd done it himself. A weak handshake meant he was less a man, inept, something to be weary of.

"What brings you this way, Sonny?" Jonesy said, sitting back down in his worn leather high-back chair.

Sonny looked at the stacks of papers on the sheriff's desk, not regretting his loss of employment and the demands of the documentation side of the law. "I've got some staples I need from the grocers. I thought I'd stop by and say hello."

Jonesy settled into his chair and clasped his hands together like he was about to twiddle his thumbs. "Is that so? I can't recall a time in my entire life that Sonny Burton ever stopped by my office to chew the fat. We ain't never been runnin' buddies, you and me, now, have we? Seems to me you got business on your mind, even though you claim to have resigned from such things."

Sonny looked at his toes again, wished there was a window to take his attention away, but there wasn't. "I 'spect any business of sorts is hard for any man to quit. Even an old fool like me."

"You started keepin' chickens yet? I hear tell in the *Leader* that Tom Young's gonna sell fifty hens along with his span horses, and everything else that ain't nailed down on his place."

"I steer clear of them farm sales if I can. Don't want to profit off another man's troubles if I can avoid it. Besides, I don't want to consider the mess a chicken makes. I don't eat that many eggs the way it is. The Harmesons see to it I get an egg or two every now and then even if I don't need one. Chickens and other stock tie a man down. I'm no farmer, Jonesy."

The sheriff examined every twitch Sonny made. A ray of overhead electric light glinted off his badge as he took a deep breath. Jonesy looked half-amused, half-pissed-off, by the interruption. "You plannin' on takin' off sometime soon for parts unknown? California, maybe?"

Sonny shrugged his shoulders. "I've got a trial to attend to in Huntsville before long, so there's that. You gonna stop by and feed my chickens while I'm away?"

"I don't think I would."

"There you have it."

"It was a difficult time for you down in Huntsville. But I have to tell you that I'm relieved you kept that Billy Bunson trouble away from here. We've had our fair share of tussles with hard criminals, includin' too much of Bonnie and Clyde between you and me. I still see that bullet-riddled car of Barrow's that Carl Halstaad pulled out of the river and put back together. He's got some nerve, that old man, takin' peoples' nickels for a ride around the courthouse square. Sorry I mentioned it."

"I'm used to it."

"You are. Maybe too used to it." Jonesy pulled himself to the desk and propped his elbows on the surface. "You want to tell me what this visit's all about, Sonny? Or do I have to guess?"

"I think you might, beings I've been associated with Aldo Hernandez every now and then."

"You could do worse for yourself than chumin' with Mexicans

like Aldo Hernandez. I had a talk with him myself recently."

"I heard."

"There isn't a damned thing I can do to help Rafael out of the mess he's got himself into."

Both men stiffened, staking their footing in a standoff or a showdown, Sonny wasn't sure which. Jonesy was more defensive and antagonistic than he'd expected him to be. "That's not the way I heard it. I heard you sent Rafael into the lion's den with a bottle of tequila. Seems a little out of character for you to do something like that 'less you had a good reason. I've never known you to sacrifice any man without a good cause, Jonesy, Mexican or otherwise."

"You don't want to stick your nose into this, Sonny." The sheriff stood, then leaned forward on the desk with his hands flat down and glared at Sonny like he was a hobo rolled in off the street. "I suggest you take yourself on the errands you got to run and tell Aldo Hernandez that the fate of his cousin will be handled in the court like every other ordinary man in this county. If he'd like to come and watch the proceedings, he's more than welcome. It's still a free country, unlike those places in Europe I hear tell about on the radio and see on the newsreels at the picture show. Shame about that fire at the Ritz, ain't it?"

"I guess it is." Sonny stared at the sheriff, a man he'd been comfortable with, but didn't recognize an inch of. He started to take his leave, aware that the ice under his feet was starting to crack, but he stopped before opening the door. "You're not in any trouble are you, Jonesy?"

The suggestion lit a flame atop of the sheriff's ears and turned them red hot as a kitchen burner. "Now why in the hell would you ask me something like that?"

"A feeling is all," Sonny said. "Sorry, I didn't mean to insult you. I'll be around if you need me, Jonesy." He didn't give the sheriff a chance to say anything he might regret. Sonny fled the office like the floor under his feet had turned from ice to fire. He hurried past Vandetta without saying goodbye, without offering even a nod. Stale air threatened to choke him, to cut him off from the living world. And he found himself unprepared to quit breathing, to walk away from the fight when something seemed wrong and needed fixing.

CHAPTER SEVEN

The road stretched out before Edith Grantley like a long, dark brown ribbon. She was well past Madisonville, the first town of any size outside of Huntsville, before any sense of calmness settled over her. The roar of the Pierce's engine was constant, and the ride was soft and comfortable, making it easy to let her mind wander. There was little traffic on the two-lane road, and the land was flat as the sole of a shoe with farmhouses dotted here and about. Smaller clusters of houses were strung out between the ranches and stretches of thick woodlands. Most of the houses were vacant, curtains dangling in shattered windows, screen doors half open, ready for a gust of wind to slam them shut. Edith kept a steady eye on the fuel gauge, which didn't look like it had moved at all since she'd started her journey. Any day-to-day worries she held remained behind her, in her house, under the care of Marcel and the reliable Mr. Day. Dread, however, lived under her skin, fearing the reception she would get when Sonny Burton saw her coming his way. Edith wasn't sure that she could take Sonny's rejection if that was what was to come, but she was certain she couldn't live without knowing once and for all how he felt about her. Marcel had been right. Time was running out for both of them. A glance at the rearview reflected a fifty-eight-year-old woman's thin face with graying hair that she didn't recognize. She looked away and turned her focus back to the road.

A tree line skirted the left side of the hard dirt road, full of naked hardwoods, live oak, elm, and hickory, all taking their January rest; limbs bare and skeletal reaching to the sky, hanging over the road in a tangle of sleeping desire. The right side of the road was open pastureland with a thick pecan grove sitting high on a rise. There were no cattle or other livestock to be seen. They had either been sold off, eaten, or shipped to the slaughterhouse to see the rancher through the winter—if the ranch was still viable, not shattered by withering hope, financial markets a thousand miles away, or Washington blowhards who had no idea how to fix what they'd broken.

The vast blue Texas sky reached out in front of Edith, forcing her to look past the Pierce's hood ornament, a silver archer, bow pulled back ready to release, a helmet on his head to protect him in the battle he was leaning into. There were no storm clouds on the horizon, no winds to worry her, only feathery cirrus clouds, thin, transparent white strokes that looked more like images born from an artist's imagination than a collection of vapors. All things north looked inviting, the road clear and empty, the kind of good driving weather Edith had wished for.

It had been a long time since she had taken the Pierce out for a spin. The car drew attention no matter where she went, which was why she stored it away in the carriage house, a hidden gem, a set of wheels that promised freedom and adventure, all the reasons Henry had bought the automobile for her in the first place. Except he didn't predict the Depression or count on dying, making the automobile a grim reminder of better days with no promise that they would ever return. She had no choice but to drive the Pierce Arrow to Wellington; it was that or take the bus, which she was loath to do. The shiny yellow automobile was the only set of wheels she owned. There was no need for another one, living where she lived. Everything she needed was within walking distance from her boardinghouse. And like the house, a structure that was way too big for her needs, the Pierce was extravagant, a luxury, a reach beyond the grasp. Henry's, not hers. He'd liked the finer things in life—as well he should have. Her deceased husband had worked hard all of his life, from the time he was a boy, sweeping the floors at the mill after school to the day he died, making decisions about the future when he should have been more concerned about the present. The mill was his mistress, a lover who had kept him awake at night, took all of his energy, the better part of him. The convertible was a gift to console Edith for his absence, for his dedication to something other than her, and she had accepted it with a smile and a silent sigh, let down that she would have to drive the Pierce alone—when she drove it at all.

There was no way she could drive the road she was on, for the reason she was on it, in the automobile she was sitting in, without thinking of Henry. Sweet Henry. The image of him in her mind was still clear, anchored in the port of her grief, like a waiting ship set to sail to points unknown. She had met Henry on the boardwalk in Houston, the place of her birth, the year the Texas Constitution was ratified, and where she thought she would live for the rest of her life. Her own family's fortune had been gained in wars and lost in hurricanes, then rebuilt again with an inherited grit and determination required of all of her siblings—six sisters born to a man who owned an iron foundry. There had been no son to pass the business on to, and so, accepting his fate, her father demanded more of his girls than most other men did of women. He treated their sex as equal because he had no choice, and because he was a smart, calculating man. Her father saw the talents of his daughters before anyone else did and knew he could exploit them in a parental way that would guarantee his life's work would survive long after he had died. He had been right about that, but not in the way he had wanted. Edith, being the oldest, was his most trusted, the obvious successor to head the foundry. She loved the business, loved working by her father's side, loved being the favorite. Until that changed. Edith was never the same after Henry Grantley walked into her life. A half head taller than she was, thin and fit, well-dressed, well-mannered, and himself an heir to a three-generation family business. She would have followed Henry to Saturn and back—and that's where Huntsville might as well have been to her father. When she left on her marriage day, Edith broke her father's heart, and gave her sister Erma the best present she thought she'd ever get. Erma was wrong about that, too. Her father died three years later, standing in the foundry office, of a heart attack. There had been no signs, no warning. He fell over dead. Then the Panic of '07 came along with banks and trust companies filing bankruptcy, catching Erma over-leveraged and unaware that the business was crumbling under her feet. Their finances soon collapsed, and all of the foundry was sold for parts, and the rest of the sisters and her mother were cast out into the world without skills or the desire to have them. Henry did his best to take them all in. The mill had survived the panic, was successful and growing every day. The prison was the mill's lifeblood, like it was for a lot of other businesses in Huntsville, but Henry was ambitious, knew that he couldn't rest all of his hope and fortune on one revenue vein. In a matter of years, the prison was a small fraction of the mill's business. Erma was jealous and resentful, especially after their mother died. A ruckus exploded after their mother's funeral, severing the family, sending Erma and the remaining sisters to other parts of the country. Henry and Edith were left in the oversized house by themselves, hoping to grow their own family. A family, son or daughter, that never came. The loneliness broke their hearts, and Edith blamed herself, felt it was her fault that she couldn't give Henry the one thing he wanted most—a son. Henry never let on like he felt cheated by not having children. Instead, he doted on Edith, tried to give her everything she wanted. And then he died, leaving her in the house alone, certain that she would never love again.

Driving down the road in the Pierce Arrow, the rumble of the engine and vibration kept her awake, but Edith realized that she was crying. Tears streamed down her face with as much force as they had the day she had buried Henry. She slammed the steering wheel with her hand, enraged at herself and Henry. The world had fallen from under her feet almost from the day Henry had died. The stock market had crashed, the mill went under—even though she tried to save it, but she couldn't—and she was left penniless, dependent on strangers to knock on the door to let a room to keep food in the larder. Then Sonny Burton walked into her life, bringing a cold-blooded killer with him. She pulled her foot off the accelerator at the thought, was tempted to stop, turnaround, and go home. But she knew this one thing: If it hadn't been for Billy Bunson, she would have never met Sonny Burton, would have never danced with him in the parlor and fallen in love with him. A storm had brought her the promise of hope and renewal, a glimpse of spring during a long winter. Life was so unpredictable that she could hardly stand it sometimes. Instead of stopping, she put her foot back on the pedal and brought the Pierce to a steady speed. There was no way she was going to turn back. Not now. Because the truth was, she had nothing to go back to. Nothing but solitary nights and the memory of blood dripping off the keys of her piano.

Edith pulled the Pierce Arrow into the first gas station she could find in Corsicana. Two red gas pumps, round and six feet tall, with a white pump in the middle, stood in front of a small wood-frame building with a sign, Magnolia, written across the front in green block letters. A red Pegasus was situated on both ends of the sign, taking flight into the air. An air tube lay across the pavement, and a distant bell rang when Edith drove across it and came to a stop next to the pumps.

A gas jockey, dressed in a bright bleached white uniform, ran out the front door of the Magnolia station with a happy look on his face. He looked to be sixteen or seventeen and had hair the color of motor oil. "Can I help you, ma'am?" he said, before Edith could get the window rolled all of the way down.

"Fill her up, please," Edith said.

"With ethyl?"

"Yes, that would be fine."

"This sure is a beauty," the jockey said, admiring the yellow Pierce Arrow like he had never seen anything like it before.

"Thank you."

The boy smiled, showing a gap between his front teeth, then hurried away, ready to attack his task with more enthusiasm than Edith had expected. She smiled to herself, happy for the stop and human contact.

"Do you have a Dr. Pepper box inside?" Edith called out.

The jockey was already to the rear of the Pierce. He skidded to a stop. "Yes, ma'am, we sure do. Would you like for me to get a cold one for you while I'm at it?"

"No, that's all right. I'll get it myself. I need a stretch." It was true. Edith wasn't accustomed to sitting down for so long and thinking about Henry had left her feeling wrung out. She needed a breath of fresh air.

"Chet'll be happy to help you out," the jockey said, then went about gassing up the Pierce.

Edith exited the automobile, rolled her shoulders, and flexed the toes in her traveling shoes, black leather pumps with low heels. She reached back inside the automobile, grabbed her purse, then made her way to the front of the Magnolia station, checking out the area around her.

The Magnolia station sat on the outskirts of Corsicana. A grain elevator sat next to a set of railroad tracks across the street. A rusted boxcar, with the doors slid wide open, stood alone, either ready to be pulled by the next train or abandoned from the last. There were no hobos hanging around, and Edith was thankful of that. She'd had enough of the beggars at her back door. The air smelled of gasoline, oil, and coal smoke. A rising round smokestack stood above a red brick building next to the Magnolia. It looked like a miniature foundry outfitted into a welding shop of some kind. Bits and parts of oil derricks were stacked alongside the building, waiting to be assembled or carted off. The area reminded Edith of the place she'd lived in Houston as a girl; industrial, gritty, full of thick-skinned working men. She was comfortable and relaxed her shoulders as she opened the door and walked inside the station.

"Why, hello, there," a man said from behind the counter. He was twice as old as the gas jockey, wore a similar uniform, only his was stained with grease marks on the elbows and had a name patch sewed to his chest that said: Chet.

"Hello," Edith said, heading straight for the Dr. Pepper box. She opened the cold lid and pulled out a bottle, focused on the dark, sweet drink. She popped off the cap on the opener and took a long drink on the way to the counter. She hadn't realized how thirsty she was.

"That'll be five cents," Chet said, staring at Edith. "Ain't never seen the likes of you around here." He squinted at Edith in a way that made her uncomfortable.

"I'm on a trip north." Edith sat the glass bottle on the counter and dug into her purse for a nickel.

"Where to?"

Edith stared at the man, at this Chet, and wondered if he was being friendlier than normal or if he was only making small talk. "North," she said.

"Oh." Chet hit a key on the green NCR cash register and a bell sounded as the drawer pushed out in front of him. He snuffed his nose like he'd been hit, then held out his grimy hand in expectation of payment.

Edith dropped the coin into Chet's hand. "I'm sorry, I didn't mean to be rude."

"You're traveling alone. I understand." He put the nickel in its proper slot and forced a smile. "Anything else I can get you?"

"Yes, is there a ladies' room I can use?"

"Around back. It should be unlocked."

"Thank you." Edith settled her purse, gripped the Dr. Pepper, and headed outside.

The gas jockey was coming her way. "Your gas tank's full, and I washed your windshield for you."

"My, you work fast."

"Thank you. I'm happy to have a job. We all are around here."

"It looks a little quiet."

"There's still some businesses that have needs. The oil fields keep Otis Halloway's factory goin' and there's a truck depot around the bend that ferries goods around the state. We're here for them. One or two of them go out of business, I'll be on the bread line."

"I'm sorry to hear that."

"Oh, it's all right," the gas jockey said. "Better days are right around the corner." He smiled wide, then said, "The gas'll be three dollars and two cents. You took fifteen point five gallons. Good thing you stopped. There ain't another station like this for a good fifty miles. You might not have made it to wherever it is you're a goin'. I'd be a little uneasy if'n I was you out on the road all by myself."

"No one likes to travel alone. Excuse me a second." Edith

hurried to the passenger side of the Pierce and put her Dr. Pepper on the floorboard, then dug into her purse again to pay her bill. "Here you go," she said, handing the jockey his money, and a little more, a tip for his top-flight attitude. The jockey's smile was infectious.

He looked at the bills and no coins and turned to go inside. "I'll get your change. Hold on."

"No need. Keep it." It was Edith's turn to smile.

"Golly, ma'am, nobody tips these days. Thank you. Wait till I tell Chet." He almost hopped and skipped inside, leaving Edith alone to make her visit to the ladies' room.

She hurried to the back of the Magnolia station, startling a stray tabby cat as she went. Once she was finished with her business, she walked back outside, readying herself to get back on the road. She stopped short of the corner of the building as she took in a man walking around her automobile. He was tall and thin, wearing a waistcoat made of denim, a pair of Levi's, cowboy boots that looked worn and mud-soaked, and a dim, white straw cowboy hat that was frayed at the rim. It was a summer hat but looked like it might have been the only one the man owned. A lit cigarette dangled out of the corner of his mouth as he walked around the Pierce, trailing his fingers over the top of the right front fender. He stopped when he saw Edith staring at him.

"Boy, howdy, ain't it somethin'." He didn't smile or nod but held Edith's gaze like he was trying to bore inside her skull. Then he dropped his eyes down her body, making Edith feel uncomfortable as a push of wind tapped her back and wound around her. "I ain't seen an automobile this fancy in a long, long time," the man said, taking the cigarette out of his mouth.

Edith stood ridged, unwilling to move, silent and on edge. The man walked around the front of the Pierce still trailing his fingers across it, until he got to the hood ornament. He grabbed the archer by the head and tried to shake it to see if it moved. It didn't.

"Don't," Edith said from instinct, without censoring herself.

The man smiled, raised his hand off the archer, took a drag off his cigarette, exhaled, then tossed the butt onto the ground and stabbed it out with the pointed toe of his boot. "I ain't gonna hurt it." There was no water, but there was an audible sizzle, dying fire gasping into dust.

Edith sucked in a deep breath of dry air, hoped that Chet and the gas jockey would notice her predicament, but she couldn't wait. She walked to the rear of the Pierce, opposite the man. Her plan was to avoid him, get inside and drive away as quick as she could. Her heart was beating like she'd run a hundred-yard dash. Her face was flushed, and she could feel sweat forming on the back of her neck.

The man met her at the door. "You ain't gonna run off before you talk to me now, are you, lady? You are a lady, aren't you? All nice and purty in a bright yellow chariot?" He sniffed loud with animated effort, then looked up and down the front of her again. "Where's your prince?"

His actions and tone made Edith cringe. She wished she could vomit on command. *Where are you, Chet? Can't you see that I need help?* "Excuse me. I'm late and I must leave," she said, grabbing the door handle. There was no way she could force the man out of the way. She didn't have the strength, but she wasn't going to show him that. Edith yanked the door open anyway, and it surprised the man. He stumbled backward.

"Oh, you got spunk. I like that." He regained his balance and went to take a step for Edith.

"Hey, there, you bum," a voice called out. "What are you doing?" It was the gas jockey, not Chet, his face painted with a look of horror. He ran out of the Magnolia station, acting as the rescuer she'd expected.

Edith took advantage of the distraction, slid into the front seat of the Pierce, and slammed the door. It was all she could do to fumble through the steps of ignition to start the automobile, but she did. The engine revved to life, and without thinking about anything other than fleeing, she put the Pierce in gear and pushed down on the accelerator as hard as she could. The gas jockey had to jump out of the way to avoid getting hit. The rear wheels shot a rooster tail of dirt and gravel behind the Pierce as she sped away.

Edith looked in the rearview mirror to see the man in the cowboy hat standing his ground, ignoring the gas jockey's attempt to shoo him away, staring after her as she fled. She shivered and sighed, glad for the escape. For peace of mind and to calm her nerves, she reached under the seat and touched the Smith & Wesson to make sure it was still there. It was. She was grateful that Marcel had insisted she take the gun on the trip.

When Edith looked into the rearview mirror, the man had vanished. She had gone far enough for him to be out of sight. Relieved, now all she had to do was decide if she was going to keep heading north or turn around and hightail it home.

CHAPTER EIGHT

Sonny stopped outside the courthouse to take stock of the conversation he'd had with the sheriff. He was unsettled by Jonesy's attitude and tone. There was more going on with this Rafael Hernandez business than he had first thought. Even though he didn't say so, Jonesy had told him to mind his own damn business. If Sonny was a smart man, that was what he'd do. But he'd never considered himself smart. His curiosity got him into trouble in one way or another. But maybe now was time for a change. Maybe he really did need to retire and keep chickens. Accepting his fate as a one-armed useless old man would save him a lot of grief. If it were only that easy. Something was wrong. A familiar flare had lit inside Sonny's brain. Call it instinct, intuition, a hunch, or aged experience, it didn't matter. Jonesy wasn't acting like himself, and that unsettled Sonny—for Jonesy's sake, and Rafael's.

There was nothing he could do about any of it other than keep his ears and eyes open a little wider. He headed away from the courthouse at a slow pace. Blue wagged his tail and jumped onto the wheel well as Sonny approached the truck. It would only take a pat on top of the head to urge the dog back in the bed. After doing that, Sonny stopped and looked across the red-brick-paved street to the line of businesses that faced the courthouse square. His stomach growled from the lack of breakfast. Bacon and eggs from the café sounded good. There was more than one café situated around the courthouse square to serve the comings and goings of the county seat. It was the one place within fifty miles where lawyers and farmers could sit shoulder to shoulder. If there was gossip to be heard about the sheriff, he might hear it there.

A loud, angry voice captured his attention, took his mind away from hunger and the nagging feeling about Jonesy.

A familiar black stake truck poked out into the street, the bed empty, with the driver's side door standing wide open. Sonny spied three people standing next to the jalopy. Well, he thought they were three people. He almost rubbed his eyes to make sure he wasn't seeing things or caught sideways in some kind of daytime nightmare. The truck was one of the circus jalopies he'd seen pass by his house. Further inspection told him that he was wide awake when he realized he knew one of the men, Heck Kilbride. Sonny and Heck, and a few other of the Kilbrides, had had a few run-ins when Sonny had worn the Ranger badge. It didn't surprise him that Heck was doing the yelling—telling two people to get the hell out of his town.

One of the people from the circus parade was the focus of Heck's attention. The bearded lady stood hunkered behind the tallest man Sonny had ever seen. The man must have been eight-foot-tall, skinny as a rail, ladders for legs, ears the size of saucers, and a nose a skier could do a long jump off of. Heck continued to give the two a hard time without any regard to onlookers like Sonny and a few other folks who had been called out of the drugstore and the Percy Wells Department Store by the ruckus.

"You stay here," Sonny said to Blue, who had also been drawn to the confrontation. The dog let out a low growl as Sonny walked across the street, but he did what he was told.

The phantom pain in Sonny's invisible right hand twitched as habit forced Sonny to touch his sidearm for comfort and security. The Colt wasn't there any more than the fingers were.

He was unarmed. But that didn't slow Sonny's stride. He marched right into the confrontation without any hesitation or regard to Heck's pugilistic reputation.

"What seems to be the trouble here, Heck?" Sonny said, coming to a stop next to the tall man. The bearded lady studied Sonny from head to toe as if she were trying to determine whether he was a friend of Heck's or not.

Heck Kilbride's dim blue eyes had dilated with so much anger that his black pupils had flooded the entirety of his eyes; they looked bottomless, filled with steaming tar. All he needed was a bucket of feathers and the strength and will to capture the two interlopers and he would have had everything he needed to play the executioner he'd wanted to be.

The tall man stared down at Heck, and Sonny, too, with a serene look on his face. He looked unfazed by the outburst. Maybe he was used to it.

"What the hell do you want, Sonny Burton?" Heck said. He was short as a cement block and about as dense. The tall man made Heck look like a miniature bull. "This ain't got nothin' to do with you."

"What's it got to do with then, Heck?" Sonny said, as calm as he could, avoiding eye contact with the bearded lady. The tall man's eyes were in the clouds.

"Ain't no need for these freaks to be here, is all. They ain't welcome. Now go on and mind your own goddamned business," Heck answered.

"So, you're working with the Chamber of Commerce now, are you?"

"Huh?"

Sonny stepped forward, angling himself in between the tall man and Heck. "I think you're the one that best be moving on, Heck. We need to let these folks get done what they need to get done." He turned back, and for the first time engaged the bearded woman. "You won't be here long, will you, ma'am?"

Before the woman could answer, Heck bellowed, "That ain't no woman. I ain't never seen no woman with hair on her face like that."

Sonny snapped his head around, took sight of Heck's smooth face that hadn't seen a razor in days, and said, "You're jealous, Heck Kilbride. Now, why don't you do what I told you to and move on. The show's over. You've had your fun drawing attention to yourself, having your say, and throwing your two cents in where it don't belong. Doesn't matter what you've seen or not seen. This here woman deserves the same amount of respect as your momma. Now, go on and get before me and you have a bigger problem." Sonny words echoed across the sidewalk and filtered through the growing crowd. They seethed with anger and authority, and didn't diminish until they were a block away, past the Ritz Theater.

Heck Kilbride jerked his head to the side like he'd been punched in the jaw. He stepped forward with his elbow jutting forward while he balled his right hand into a fist. "Don't go talkin' about my ma like that."

Sonny didn't back down. He stiffened, stepped forward, and did the same thing, putting himself within an arm's reach of Heck. Only he didn't have a fist to form. No matter how hard he tried, he couldn't produce one. All he had was the hook, and it stood in between him and Heck like a sword drawn, not a punch to be thrown. His body reacted before his mind could stop it. Sixty-some-odd years of being right-handed had left him unskilled as a south paw. The thought of such a thing had never crossed his mind. Learning to shoot left-handed, how to shift the truck and drive it, had been his focus, not throwing a left-handed punch. Not protecting himself in a fight. He had thought those days were over with.

The hook glinted in the midmorning sun as Sonny stopped

the metal appendage's trajectory upward. He realized the implied threat by the look in Heck Kilbride's enraged eyes. The anger turned to fear, to recognition that Sonny's hook was more of a weapon than his hand was. It was like Sonny had pulled out a knife in surprise, prepared to defend himself to the death.

Heck rocked back, making sure he was out of reach. "Put that damn thing down, Sonny Burton."

Horror overtook Sonny. Everywhere he looked people were staring at him with fear and disgust in their eyes. Or maybe that's what he thought he saw, what he would see if he was one of them, staring at a man who used a hook instead of a hand to fight his battles with. He dropped his arm to his side and let it dangle.

"I'm sorry, Heck, I didn't mean anything by it. Just habit is all," Sonny said. His mouth went dry as a fallow cotton field in August.

The apology didn't sate Heck's fearful appetite. He kept retreating with a look on his face that Sonny couldn't read. It was half, "I got you," and half realization of something that had not occurred to Heck until that moment: Sonny Burton was more dangerous than he had ever been.

"You're a freak, Sonny Burton. You ain't no different than them. You don't belong here, either. You get. You just get out of here now," Heck said.

Before Sonny could respond, the bearded lady reached out and touched his shoulder. "We're gonna leave, mister. We don't need no trouble. You should, too." And with that, she pulled back and nodded to the tall man. He seemed to understand what she meant but said nothing. The man looked serene, like he was unable to talk—like Blue. Sonny wondered if the tall man was dense, no smarter than a dog.

The tall man climbed into the back of the stake truck and sat down with his back propped up by the cab. His head shot over the roof by a good foot. Everyone ignored Heck, who fumed in front of the crowd.

The woman opened the jalopy's door and slid behind the steering wheel with ease. She said "Thank you" to Sonny before closing the door and starting the truck's engine. It sputtered and hacked to life like an old man throwing a coughing fit until all of the pistons sang together in harmony. A black cloud of exhaust pushed out of the rear of the truck and floated upward, dimming the sun for a brief second.

Sonny stood out of the way as the truck backed out, then headed out of the square toward the Harmeson place. He had no choice but to do the same thing. He wasn't going to feel welcome for one more second on the Wellington, Texas, town square if he stayed there. Heck Kilbride stood his ground, and the crowd watched and waited for what was next, not saying a word.

Sonny headed south on West Avenue until he reached the post office. He walked in and deposited the letter without saying a word to anyone he passed by. The post office was a busy place. The hook was stuffed in his pants pocket, a precarious deception, but he didn't care if the sharp point gouged his skin. He was in no mood for stares or whispers. All he wanted to do was mail Edith's letter and be on his way. That was all. And the plan had almost worked. Almost. He was about to reach for the door, about to make his exit, when he heard someone call out his name.

"Hey, Sonny, what are you doin' here?" It was Clifford Jones. The last person Sonny expected or hoped to see. He figured the man would be out running his route.

Sonny stopped and turned around. "Oh, hey, Clifford, I didn't see you."

"It's okay." Clifford stood at the postmaster's door, wearing a curious look on his face, and his regular work attire.

"I had a letter to mail," Sonny said.

"I could have picked it up."

"I was going to be in town. Seemed like the speedy thing to do instead of waiting until tomorrow. Why aren't you out delivering the mail?"

"My truck broke down. I'm headin' out now."

"You're going to have a late day." Sonny still had his hook jammed in his pants pocket. He started to push the door open, to say goodbye to Clifford.

"That's my life. Did you hear someone stole Tom Young's milk cow?"

Sonny stopped. "I thought he was selling everything."

Clifford added emphasis with a quick twitch to his neck. "He is, 'cept now he's short a cow. I bet it was those circus people who done it. I mean, what else are you gonna feed a lion? A hundred cans of corned beef hash?"

"Because they have a lion doesn't mean they're thieves."

"Makes sense to me is all. I figure Jonesy or one of his deputies will have to have a talk with 'em to see."

"Be hard to prove if you're right," Sonny said.

"How do you figure?"

"Probably nothing left between the lion, tiger, and whatever else they've got to feed."

"I would think so."

"I'll keep an ear out if I hear anything."

"They're not far from you."

"No. No, they're not." Sonny looked out the door to Blue. He was standing in the truck bed, waiting for Sonny to return. The dog was starting to shiver. "I need to go, Clifford. It was good seeing you."

"You, too, Sonny. Be careful out there."

"I will. No need to worry about that," Sonny said.

CHAPTER NINE

Sonny hurried to the truck, more concerned about the gloomy sky and coming weather than he had been all day. The morning had been clear with the temperatures above freezing, but the afternoon sky was changing, going gray, thick and roiling with wind. The air was cooler with a forceful gust. It bit through his thin jacket, unwelcome and not planned for. "Come on, Blue, get in the cab with me," he said, dropping the tailgate. Blue hurried off the bed and lit onto the ground. The dog let out a slight whimper. His enthusiasm had caused him to land on his bad leg and put more weight on it than it could take. The whimper forced Blue to stop. He normally would have run straight to the cab, happy to be inside.

"You all right, boy?" Sonny said, taking his attention away from the sky. The last thing he wanted to do was get caught in a sandstorm, but his guilt was heavier than that fear.

Blue spun around, barked, and ran to the driver's side of the truck. Sonny relaxed and followed, opening the door as soon as he got to it. Blue jumped right in and settled down in the passenger seat like he rode there all of the time, which was not the case. Riding inside the truck was a treat, or when bad weather threatened. He didn't want to make the dog too soft.

Sonny followed suit and hurried inside, settling behind the steering wheel as quick as he could. There was no sign of a sandstorm yet, but that didn't mean one couldn't come along. Gray clouds that promised rain were like those blowhards who

79

had caused all the current problems in the first place, all show and no go.

The thought of a storm pushed Sonny to get going. He had a few more stops to make. No sense in wasting a trip into town. He needed sugar and a few other staples. The closest place to stop was the Vallance Grocery. The only problem with that was they didn't carry Arbuckle's coffee. He'd have to settle for a glass jar of Twin BB coffee. Last time he was there he'd paid twenty-nine cents for a pound. Highway robbery is what that was. Nothing less. But he didn't say anything. He grumbled when he'd counted out the pennies, then complained about the taste of the coffee to Blue every time he drank a cup. The dog was a good listener.

Before he went too far, he was going to have to stop and get gasoline at Cal Sugg's service station across the street from the high school. Sonny clicked the starter button on the floor, pulled down the throttle, and went through the rest of the physical operation to start the truck. The engine barked and groaned like Blue did when he was being stubborn and tired. It caught hold after a couple of grinds and cycles. Sonny eased off the brake and rolled out of the post office parking lot, then headed down to Fifteenth Street. If he turned left, he'd go by the new hospital. But he turned right, with the high school right in front of him, and pulled into the service station. An attendant, a young boy that Sonny didn't recognize, was at the driver's window as soon as he brought the truck to a stop.

"What can I get you, Mister Burton?" the kid said.

Sonny looked at him twice, and realized it was Cal Sugg's youngest son, Bob. "Oh, sorry I didn't see that it was you, Bob. Last time I saw you, you were a little squirt tailing after your momma, hanging onto her apron strings. How is she these days?"

"Good as far as I can tell. What can I get for you?" Bob

rubbed his bare hands together.

"Better top off the tank with that winter grade you've been advertising in the *Leader*. Truck's getting a little cranky with this January weather upon us."

Bob was of average height, his head was level to the top of the truck, and his face was as smooth as that bully's on the square. He seemed like a congenial boy, which made sense, with his family being in the service business. Cal Suggs had a reputation as a decent man.

"I heard it's gonna snow a bit tonight. I wonder how you keep an elephant warm?" Bob said.

"You heard about that circus out by the Harmesons', huh?"

"Everybody's talkin' about it. That and Tom Young's missing cows."

"I heard it was a cow."

"Ted Neilson said it was a herd of cows. It puzzles me how those folks got away with such a thing in broad daylight, but it sure seems like they did. Probably got a system, if you ask me. Go into a town, distract folks with a parade, while another crew is behind the scenes scoping out food for those lions. They get what they need, then off they go in the middle of the night."

"That's some plan, Bob."

"It's what I'd do if I had all them mouths to feed."

Before Sonny could say another word, a clattering truck pulled in on the other side of the pumps. It was a jalopy Sonny recognized. It was the black stake truck with the bearded lady driving and the tall man sitting in the back. "Well, Bob, it looks like you're in luck. Those are the circus folks right there. Maybe you can tell them about your plan and see if they admit to it."

Bob Sugg's face turned red as a ripe plum. He gasped a bit in search of something to say. "Well, I best get your gas, Mr. Burton. Nice talkin' to you."

"Nice talking to you, too, Bob," Sonny said. He was talking

to the wind. Bob was already gone, hurrying to his tasks of pumping gasoline, checking the oil, and washing the windshield.

Sonny felt bad for giving the boy a hard time, but that only lasted a second or so. He looked over to the truck, took in the lady, then scanned backwards through the stakes of the truck. There was a massive heap covered up with a tarp lying in front of the tall man. A heap that could have been a cow. No body parts were showing, so it was hard to tell for sure.

Sonny got out of the truck and headed over to the driver's side, buffeted by the wind as he went. The wind was strong enough to blow the toupee off a bald man's head. "Hey, there," he said to the bearded lady.

She looked at him with suspicion, then seemed to relax as she took in his face. "You're that fella from downtown." She was a little on the plump side with hair as black as coal and skin as white as the horses in the circus parade. Her blue eyes narrowed, and she still wore the red sparkly long-sleeved blouse. Sonny wondered if she was cold, or if her thick hair and well-manicured beard helped to keep her warm.

"I am," he said. "I'd apologize for Heck Kilbride, but that's not my place."

"Oh, don't you worry none about that, mister. If I had a nickel every time a man called me a freak, I'd be richer than them Rockefellers." Her voice was tinged with a Southern drawl, but it wasn't Texan. Maybe she was from Alabama or Mississippi, Sonny wasn't sure.

"Still, that's no way to treat a lady," he said.

She laughed, letting her eyes go wide. "So, you think I'm a lady?"

Sonny blushed a bit, then said, "I imagine I do."

"Well, that's mighty kind of you."

Sonny saw that the tall man was looking down at him with the same odd look on his face he'd wore during Heck's tirade.

"Your friend here doesn't seem to be much company."

"Paul? He's no company at all. He's a deaf mute. Grew out of his ears and tongue is what he did." The woman leaned her head out of the truck and whispered. "We're not even sure that Paul is his real name. Paul was stitched in his one and only shirt when he came to us. We call him Paul Bunyan is what we do. My husband sends him along for protection, not that I need it. But Paul's a good deterrent even though I've never seen him kill a fly. I can take care of myself, but my husband insists. Who am I to argue?"

Bob Suggs appeared next to Sonny. "You're set and ready to go, Mister Burton."

Sonny dug his wallet out of his trousers. "How much do I owe you?"

"Fifty-nine cents."

"Boy, that winter grade's expensive."

"You was about empty."

Sonny opened the change compartment of the wallet with his left hand while pressing it against his side with the hook. Another balancing act that he had practiced and was getting better at. He counted out the coins he needed. "I'll tell your pa you did a fine job the next time I see him," he said as he dropped the money in Bob's open hand, put his wallet away, and slid the hook back in his pocket, out of sight.

"That'd be swell of you, Mr. Burton. It sure would be." Bob turned to the woman, trying his best to ignore the tall man, and said, "Can I help you, ma'am?" He stuttered on the *ma'am* with uncertainty.

"Fill it up, please," the bearded lady said.

Bob hesitated, like he wanted to ask something else, then thought better of it, and disappeared behind the truck, looking for the gas tank.

"He wanted to ask me if I had the money to pay," the woman

said. "I'm used to that, too."

"There's a rumor going around town that some of the circus people stole a cow from Tom Young," Sonny said.

"There's always a rumor going around town when we roll in." There was disgust in the woman's voice. "Why do you care, anyway? Who are you?"

"Telling you what I heard, is all. That way you won't be surprised when the sheriff comes around." Sonny looked to the bed of the truck again. The woman was focused on him like he was the only man in the world.

"We're never surprised when the law comes calling."

"I doubt you are. My name's Sonny Burton. I live outside of town. You all went by my house yesterday. Woke me from a nap and set my dog off barking."

"I'd apologize for that if we'd have done it on purpose. But since we didn't, I won't. I'm Avalon Blackbeard in the ring, but my friends call me Frances. Frances Avalon." Her drawl got thicker when she said her real name; there was an echo of regret bound to her words that wasn't there before. She stuck her chubby right hand out and offered Sonny a shake. He hesitated, had the hook stuffed in his pocket. "Come on, I've shook worse things than a hook before," she said. "I saw you in town, remember. You're not one of us, but folks around here treat you like you are."

Sonny looked over his shoulder. He'd lost track of Bob Suggs. He found the boy at the front of the one-and-a-half-ton vehicle with his head stuffed under the hood. No one else had pulled into the lot, and the automobiles on the road were too far away to see what was going on. The wind continued to push at him, urging him forward. He looked Frances in the eye, trying to determine if he should trust her or not. There was no way to tell. He was still distracted by the beard on her face and the soft lilt of the sweet voice that came out of her mouth. There didn't seem to be anything to lose, so he did what the bearded lady suggested. He pulled his hook out of his pocket and offered the steel appendage to Frances like it was a real hand. She took the hook in her clasp, and gave it a firm shake, which was not what Sonny had been expecting.

"You need to toughen up, Sonny Burton," Frances said. "We all got our stories, and there's lots of things about us that ain't perfect. Every one of us. The sooner you figure that out, the stronger that arm and that shake will be."

"There's no arm there." He didn't like being lectured. He didn't like it at all.

"Says you. That's why." Frances let go of the hook, and Sonny allowed it to drop next to his side. His mouth turned dry, not sure what had happened. A shiver ran down his spine and he had the desire to flee and find the warmest fireplace he could find and sit in front of it for the rest of the day.

Frances leaned over inside the cab, snatched a piece of paper off the seat, then pushed it out the window, offering it to Sonny. "That's the bill of sale for that cow in the back there. That's Tom Young's signature on it. Now you could say it was forged, but I'll be happy to walk you and that sheriff of yours down to Tom's place and have him prove it was him that sold us the beef." She flapped the paper at him. "Go on, look."

"That's not necessary. If you say Tom sold it to you, then I believe you."

Frances retracted the bill of sale. "You hold yourself like a lawman, Sonny Burton. Like a man who's used to askin' all the questions."

"I was a Texas Ranger for a long time."

"What are you now?"

"Nothing but a man having a conversation with a stranger."

"There are worse things."

Bob pulled his head out from under the hood, hurried back

to the pump, and pulled the nozzle out of the gas tank. A look of relief crossed his face as a couple of drops of petrol fell to the ground. "That was close," he muttered, then made his way to the other side of Sonny. "That'll be a dollar and three cents, ma'am."

Frances looked down, did some rearranging of things out of sight, and handed Bob his money. He took it and said, "Thank you." Then stepped back, huddling his arms across his chest like it was fifty degrees below zero.

"You're welcome," Frances said, as she started the truck. "It was nice to meet you, Sonny Burton. Stop by and see us. We'll be camped out for a few days, taking a rest from the road. Or until someone figures out a reason to run us off."

"Thanks for the offer. It was nice to meet you, too, Frances."

She put the jalopy in gear and pulled away slowly. Paul waved as he went past, and Sonny offered him the same in return.

Sonny and Bob Suggs stood there and watched until the truck was on the road, almost out of sight before either of them spoke a word.

"Well," Bob said, "you don't see that every day."

"No, sir," Sonny answered, "you sure don't."

CHAPTER TEN

Edith kept the archer, the hood ornament, of the Pierce Arrow headed north. Turning around would have forced her to pass by the Magnolia station and cross paths with that dirty cowboy. She could have taken a different route, but one hadn't offered itself yet. Besides, the last thing she needed to do was get lost. She couldn't count on another gas jockey to come along and give her the opportunity to flee. Her heart was still racing a bit from the uncomfortable encounter. The possibility of such a thing hadn't seemed possible when Marcel was training her how to handle the Smith & Wesson, but it was now. Edith knew she would have to be vigilant, aware that she was alone, that the automobile she was driving reflected an image of money and success, and so did she. Which was a surprise to her. Her struggle had been confined to inside her own house, and the small world she traversed in to keep it going. She owned the deed to her house, had a mattress full of money—in comparison to most people—and had reliable boarders who more than paid for her living expenses. But yet, a personal depression had befallen her after the murder in the parlor and Sonny's departure. All she could see were her own problems, until now. Until she had ventured out into the world and saw more suffering than her own. It was that realization that kept her on the road, driving toward Wellington, instead of returning home.

It took Edith another twenty miles to relax. The engine's rumble soothed the jitters under her skin. She pushed forward, hoping to get to Fort Worth before she stopped for the night. The day was still long, stretched out before her like the road she was on; sparse, vacant farmhouses and little traffic. Blue sky continued to offer her pleasant driving weather as the sun ticked like a lazy clock hand overhead. Evening was hours away. But the best thing of all was that she wouldn't have to stop for gas anytime soon. A bite to eat, however, would be necessary. The Dr. Pepper was no meal, and Edith had only brought some snacks with her, hoping to eat in cafés along the road, or stop in a grocery store to buy something to get her through the drive. She saw now that this part of her plan wasn't thought through at all. None of it was, really. The trip to see Sonny was one of the most impulsive actions Edith had ever taken. At least since Henry had died. She had done little more than pack a bag and shoot a few bullets into a hay bale before fleeing Huntsville like it was on fire.

The one-story, detached building constructed with a long and wide overhang sat next to the road, under a huge lighted sign that said: Breakfast, Lunch, and Dinner. The café looked a little like a former train depot, but that didn't seem right. There were no railroad tracks to be seen anywhere near the little restaurant. A spotlight on the ground was angled at the sign several yards off the road to attract nighttime drivers, but there was no need for the light to burn. The sun blazed like a white plate dangling in the fading January sky as it dipped toward the horizon on a slow rope. Color had been squeezed out of the sky like a sheet run through a wringer and left crumpled on the floor. The thin streaks of clouds had metastasized into tumbles and rolls of gray that promised an uptick in the wind, and maybe some much needed rain. The sky had been full of false promises for too many years to count. No one trusted their eyes anymore. Clouds were con men dressed in white uniforms.

Edith was relieved to find Thompson's Café when she did. It looked like an oasis in a deserted land, though it wasn't any more optimistic than any of the other forlorn buildings she'd seen as she drove into Ennis.

It had been a long time since she'd been to Ennis. Henry had mill customers there, a few small bakeries that served the once-thriving town, but the cotton and the railroads were its major money makers. The last time Edith had been in Ennis was with Henry in the spring before he died. The roads had been lined with blooming bluebonnets, every fedora on the heads of men, business and common workers alike, looked new, without any fade or wear to be seen. Store windows gleamed in the sunlight with pride, and smiles were easy, not painful like pulled teeth without any elixirs to make them more tolerable. The good old days were really that, and there was nothing in view that suggested they would return anytime soon. There were no flowers in January, nothing but a growing gloom that did little to heighten Edith's mood. She had spent too much time alone in the automobile thinking about things that made her sad.

Edith felt like a fool, or maybe a lovesick teenager, which was never her style, for making the drive in the first place.

She pulled in the parking lot, drawn to the café like a moth to the blinking open sign in the window. There were no other automobiles in front of the café. An older Model A sedan sat at the back of the building, along with a dusty pickup truck that reminded Edith of Sonny's vehicle. If only he were in Ennis and her travels were over, but she knew that would be like wishing on a star and expecting that wish to come true. Life didn't work like that.

Regardless, she parked the Pierce as close to the entrance as she could and hurried inside like she was expecting to see someone she knew. A bell twinkled, announcing her presence as she made her way inside.

The interior looked like she thought it would. Rows of booths with the tables covered in thin white tablecloths, with a long bar with round seats protruding out of the floor, pedestals with flat orange vinyl blooms on top. Beyond the counter an open pass-through window gave a view of the kitchen; a clean flat-top stove, two ovens, and an organized table with a resting meat slicer.

A tired waitress stood at the farthest end, next to the cash register, smoking a cigarette, staring off in the distance, unmoved by the opportunity of a new customer. There was no one else in the café, and the cook, wherever he might be, was not in sight, either. The place smelled of bacon grease and tobacco smoke.

Edith stopped on the worn mat, wondering if the café was open for business. She was about to ask the waitress when her question was answered.

"Have a seat any place you like, honey." The waitress ground out her cigarette in an ashtray next to the cash register, then grabbed a menu off the counter. She was younger than Edith, in her late twenties or early thirties, it was hard to tell for sure, and had a curvy figure stuffed in a white uniform that came to a stop above the knee. A cap was adorned to the waitress's piled-up hair that matched the color of the pedestal seats. She wore an apron strapped to her waist, also orange, that was soiled from the day's business. The stains didn't look permanent. Her face was lined, void of makeup or lipstick, and her brown eyes looked tired and bored, like the rest of the interior of the café.

By the time the waitress, whose name tag said she was called Stella, reached the table Edith had chosen, she had pulled a pencil from behind her ear and a small order pad out of a pocket hand-sewn into the apron. "What can I get you?"

"Do you have any coffee?" Edith said. The boost she had got from the Dr. Pepper had worn off miles ago.

"I'll have to make a fresh pot." Stella made it sound like that would take a lot of effort.

Edith wasn't deterred. "That's fine. I can wait. But could I have a glass of water in the meantime?"

"Sure, whatever you want. The lunch specials are over and the dinner specials ain't ready yet. You'll have to order off the menu."

"I'm sure I can find something."

Stella didn't say anything else. She spun on her heels and cut through an opening in the counter, and yelled into the pass-through, "Fire up the grill, Glenn. We got a customer in the seat."

Edith situated herself in the booth seat and tried to get comfortable. The air was a little cool, and she felt a chill wrapping around her ankles. She was out of her element, almost like she was outside her own skin, not herself. The feeling had more to do with the trip than the café. There was nothing wrong with the place. It was what she needed. A quiet place to eat and regain some strength. And confidence, she thought to herself. The cowboy had left her unsettled and aware of every sound and movement around her.

Stella the waitress returned with the glass of water and Edith ordered a club sandwich and a bowl of coleslaw. "Save some room for some pecan pie, honey. Glenn bakes the best pecan pies in Ellis County. Folks used to drive down from Dallas to have a slice. Can you imagine such a thing now? Most days, we're lucky this place is still standin'."

Edith smiled, and said, "I'll save some room for that pie. It's been a long time since I've had pecan pie." It was a lie. Edith had baked four pecan pies a month ago, right before Christmas. She cooked an extravagant holiday dinner for her boarders and this past year had been no exception, even though she had not been in a festive mood. Two of her pies had been served then.

The other two, along with as much food and money as she could part with, went to the breadline at the First Methodist Church.

Stella spun around on her heels again and disappeared into the kitchen. Edith could hear voices, the exchange of the order between the waitress and the cook. She took a sip of the water and relaxed again in the booth. Her mind wandered, but instead of to the past, or behind her, she looked forward to Wellington, to Sonny. There was no question she knew little of him, that they had not spent a lot of time together. Not enough time, in some minds, for her to take a journey such as the one she had embarked on. But Edith was certain that she could read a man's intention by his tender touch, the longing in his eyes, and the gentle words he spoke in private and in public. Gentleness did not come easy to men broken like Sonny Burton. He had no hidden agendas when it came to women. If Edith could have guessed, Sonny avoided women instead of pursuing them—even as a young man, after finding himself in a loveless marriage. He didn't stray. He stayed true to his vows. Sonny had felt the electricity between the two of them—there was no denying that—and they had come together in one beautiful moment, one moment that neither of them had planned on, sought after, or ever thought would happen to them. That in itself was reason enough to get into the Pierce and drive the distance north the meeting demanded. It would be better if Sonny knew she was coming, that he had invited her. How would she really feel if he rejected her, sent her packing? Edith knew she would be crushed, heartbroken, a fool with a long drive home.

"Here you go, honey," Stella said as she set a steaming cup of coffee down in front of her.

"Thank you."

"Cream or sugar?"

"Black's fine."

"That's the way I like it, too." Stella lingered like she wanted to talk or say something else.

Edith took a slow sip of the coffee. "Strong, too. This will help keep me going."

"I thought maybe you was waitin' on somebody."

"No, only passing through."

"You're travelin' on your own?" Stella craned her neck sideways, so she could see out the window. "In that?"

"It's the only automobile I have."

"It must be nice."

"Yes, I guess it is." Edith still held the cup of coffee and was in the process of setting it down when she realized by the look on Stella's face that she had misunderstood what the waitress had meant. "Oh, it's not like that. My deceased husband bought the Pierce for me when times were good, not like they are now."

A frown had settled on Stella's face and without knowing it or not, she had crossed her arms, resting them across her ample chest. "I ain't never been ken to times as good as that."

Edith smiled from discomfort and looked Stella in the eye. "I'm sorry, I didn't mean to offend you. Because folks had some nice things left from another life doesn't make things easy for them. I'll admit, I'm lucky, but if I was living in a perfect place, I wouldn't be on the road, or sitting here talking to you."

"Where you headed?"

Edith hesitated like she had with Chet in the Magnolia station, but Stella was a woman, not an unknown man. She felt more comfortable with the waitress, even though she was uncomfortable with the conversation and the attitude she had faced. "Wellington. In the panhandle."

"You've got a ways to go." It was obvious that Stella had nothing to do. There were no other customers. All of the tables had been bussed, and there were no orders to serve. She was waiting on Glenn the cook to set Edith's club sandwich on the

shelf in the pass-through. She looked over her shoulder every
ten seconds or so, like it was a tic.

"I have an aunt in Fort Worth. I'm planning on staying with
her overnight."

"That's probably a good plan." Something outside got Stella's
attention, and she focused on it, looking away from Edith. "You
sure you're not waitin' on somebody?"

"No, why?"

"There's a man leanin' on the front fender of your automobile, smokin' a cigarette like he's waitin' on *you*."

CHAPTER ELEVEN

Grit and small pebbles peppered the truck's windshield with so much force that Sonny feared the glass was going to shatter. He had seen the storm coming from Sugg's service station and thought he'd have time to stop and get the groceries he needed before it hit, but that had been a poor miscalculation. After a quick trip to the Vallance Grocery, he headed for home, driving straight into the storm, confronted by an angry, unrelenting wind. By the time the steady gusts started to sing he was too far out of town to turn around to go back, and too far from home to make it there safely. There was little shelter outside of Wellington. There was nothing but wide-open cotton fields, dormant or abandoned for the winter, and no bridges or tunnels to hunker down in.

The sky had weaved all of the clouds together into a sullen gray blanket, hung vertical from the ground to the heavens, sweeping toward him, threatening to collapse and smother everything in its path. By Sonny's watch, it was midmorning even though the world around him said something different. It seemed like dusk was racing toward nighttime, in a hurry to relent to the darkness. He had his headlights on so he could see the road ahead of him. Twenty yards at best. Visibility was only going to get worse the farther away from town he drove.

What if I die here? he thought. *No one would find me for a week. No one but the crows or coyotes. I'd rather die at home. Or in Huntsville with Edith at my bedside.*

Sonny took it as a surprise that he would think of Edith Grantley in the time of need. Or maybe it wasn't. Maybe his longing meant something more than he cared to admit. Either way, he wasn't ready to die yet. Not today. If ever. The letter from Huntsville had fertilized his regret and his loneliness. *Maybe it had been a mistake leaving there after all.*

Sonny gripped the steering wheel as tight as he could with his left hand and anchored the hook opposite it to keep the truck on the road. Blue looked worried, and pushed himself into the corner of the seat, against the door, as if he was trying to mold his body into the Detroit steel and become part of the truck so he wouldn't blow away. A box of groceries sat on the floor. Two cans of beans rattled against another can of salmon. They pushed against a box of saltines, which was convulsing like something was trying to escape it. A five-pound bag of sugar sat next to the box, wedged against the firewall. The engine ran strong, with the pistons pumping as hard as they could. Sonny worried that the mechanical orchestra under the hood wouldn't last. There was no way the Model A could keep running if all it breathed was dirty air, full of sand and dirt. Something was bound to clog.

He leaned forward to see the road as clear as he could. It would have been impossible to keep going forward if the berm wasn't a little higher than the road. That guide wouldn't last. The road planed out the closer to home he got. To make things worse, a load of sand and dirt had started to collect on the windshield. Small grains tapped at the glass like bird shot, then slid downward. It sounded like a hundred men were shooting at him. Some of the newer, fancier automobiles had electric wipers, but the Model A truck wasn't equipped with modern doodads. He could pull over and wipe off the dirt himself or keep driving and hope the obstruction would blow off. Or he could reach out with his left hand and clear his view the best he could, steadying the steering wheel with his weak hook. There were no good options. He chose to keep driving. He didn't have the balance, coordination, or the right hand to hold the truck straight enough in the violent wind to keep himself on the road. Hoping to encourage the sand and dirt off the glass, Sonny pulled the throttle down, and forced the truck to go faster than it had in a long time. Blue whined and tried to bury his head in the seat.

"It'll be all right, boy. Don't worry, I'll get us home." Sonny didn't believe the words that came out of his mouth any more than the dog did. There was a crack of fear in each syllable that usually wasn't there.

Sonny's breath started to fog the windshield, frustrating him even more. He could only hope that there was no one else on the road this far out of town. If they were, he'd plow into them before he had a chance to put on the brakes. He was driving on faith and stubbornness more than plain sight.

Another mile down the road, he was about to stop the truck. Visibility had diminished to almost nothing. Sand exploded into the interior through every crack that it could find. The whoosh of the wind was so strong it sounded like a locomotive was sitting on top of the truck, promising not to lose steam anytime soon. It wouldn't matter if he was driving or sitting on the side of the road, he was going to be buried alive no matter what he did.

To Sonny's surprise, the wind cooperated, blew sideways, cleaned the windshield off, then paused for a brief second. Long enough for him to see down the road a stretch. He could see the big top billowing and shaking like it was about to tumble over and blow away. The tent, no matter how unsecure, was a sanctuary from the storm. It was the only shelter he could see. If the tent could stand the wind, then he had a chance, too. If he reached it, he wouldn't die alone. For some reason, that mattered more now than it ever had.

Sonny stopped the truck in front of the big top and sighed with relief. He had no idea if he would be welcome or not. Frances Avalon, the bearded lady, had seemed a suspicious sort, but she had said he should stop by, so there was some hope in that. His larger concern was getting out of the truck and making it inside without causing any harm to Blue. Sonny could shield his eyes against the storm. The dog was on his own to survive such a storm.

The truck rocked back and forth with so much force that Sonny feared the wind was going to carry it away. It felt like the ground underneath of him was going to swallow him whole. This was as bad a duster as he could remember.

"Come on, Blue," Sonny said, as he grabbed the rope that he used for a leash. It had a slipknot fashioned at the end that served as a collar. The dog drew back, melted away from Sonny, but relented when he said, "I'm not leaving you here. You're coming with me. Now, come on." Sonny's voice was calm, peaceful, with no tension in it at all.

Sonny slipped the rope around Blue's neck and pulled it so it was snug, not tight. The dog didn't look happy, but he didn't offer anything vocal, a growl or otherwise, to ward Sonny off.

A quick search of the tent allowed Sonny to see the entrance flap, tacked down with a few stakes.

The wind tried to rip the truck's door off the hinges when Sonny opened it. He caught the handle to keep the damage to a minimum. Sand pelted his bare skin without regard to its tenderness. It felt like he was being stung by a squadron of invisible hornets.

He ran straight to the flap, pulling Blue along with him without any regard to the truck. It would survive or it wouldn't.

A strong tug allowed enough room for him to hurry inside the tent. The wind helped, pushing Sonny from behind, causing him to stumble forward. He was able to keep himself from falling with a little bit of luck. When he stood straight, he made sure that Blue was still attached to the leash, that he was okay, able to see. He was. Then Sonny focused on the center of the tent. A hundred surprised eyes stared back at him.

All of the circus people were huddled together in the center of the tent.

He slipped his hook into his pocket as quick as he could.

The flap banged against the outside edge of the canvas like a bird's wing readying to take flight. A radio played somewhere inside the tent. Happy clarinets tooted back and forth, accompanied by a cheerful woman's voice assuring anyone within earshot that everything was going to be all right. That type of music had been playing every hour of every day since the Depression had started, and now it was background noise. Nobody believed that happiness would ever return, no matter how much prefabricated cheer blew out of the radio speakers.

Sonny wondered where the electricity was coming from since they were out in the middle of a field, too far away from the Harmeson place to plug into anything. But an energy source was the least of his worries. Candles used to fascinate him. Electricity scared him. It was black magic as far as he was concerned, silent and invisible, so powerful it could kill a man with a simple touch. The world was addicted to the fear of the dark, turning night into day, into battling darkness with false light. They wouldn't win, but Sonny wasn't going to be the one to tell them.

"Who are you?" a short man wearing a dull white Henley undershirt said, as he stepped out of the crowd of people. They all looked like a flock of colorful birds gathered to fly south for the winter. The tall man, Paul, was easy to see, but the rest of the people were so close together it was hard to make out any real detail about them. A couple of dim lights hung overhead, and they swung with the wind, causing the light to strobe and flash like it would if a lightning storm had snuck inside the tent.

A buzz of new energy emitted from behind the crowd, low and disturbing. Sonny looked to the ground to make sure he wasn't going to get electrocuted, then faced the man who spoke, readying to introduce himself. An unlit cigar stubbed out of the short man's mouth. He was bald as the day he was born. Sonny didn't like the hard look on his face.

"His name is Sonny Burton," a familiar voice said. The crowd shifted and Frances Avalon pushed her way out of the crowd like she was making a grand entrance. She came to a stop next to the short man without any expression on her face. "And this here is Milton Stein, our ringmaster and manager," she said, offering both hands at the man, presenting him to Sonny in as loud of a voice as she could muster. The wind competed with Frances, whistling around the big top with renewed fury, but it didn't drown out her booming voice.

Sonny relaxed a bit. He was grateful to be inside, pleased that Frances was there.

"The man from town," Milton said. It wasn't a question. The ringmaster followed Sonny's lead and relaxed a little bit himself. "Igor, go tighten the entrance before we all blow away."

Milton Stein wore black tuxedo pants, frayed at the hem, with a shiny stripe going down the side of each pant leg. Dust sat on top of his black boots, making them look brown, and he was in need of a shave. His face was as stubby as a fresh-picked cotton field, assuring Sonny that there was no performance planned anytime soon. *Who would come out in this weather anyway?*

A man twice the size of Milton, and as bald, hurried out of the crowd and headed to the waving flap, then did what he was told. Sonny assumed the man buttoning down the canvas was Igor. He looked like he was made of all muscle, no fat showing on him at all. His arms and legs looked like oversized tractor tires. There was not one hair to be seen on any of his exposed skin; light danced across him, making him shine like he was plugged in somewhere. He wore a ribbed white undershirt, short pants that had suffered too much bluing, and work boots that looked like they had been bought in the last century. He might have been the strong man or an alligator wrestler if they had those kinds of creatures in this circus. Sonny hadn't seen any alligators in the parade.

Frances and the ringmaster walked toward Sonny in unison. It was a walk that looked like it had been made together a million times before. They were the same height and moved together from feet to fingers, rehearsed like two drum majors leading a marching band.

Blue stood at Sonny's right calf with his hackles raised. The dog didn't growl or wag his tail. He was stiff, standing at attention, ready to be released to attack or inspected by an approaching general.

"I didn't expect to see you so soon," Frances said.

"He can't stay here," Milton said to Frances. She ignored him. Everyone else remained silent with their eyes fixed on the three people, but mostly on Sonny.

Done with securing the flap, Igor hurried back to where he came from. Sonny could see Paul, standing above everyone else, looking off in the distance with the same sad, amused, uninterested face he wore in town.

"You can stay here as long as you need to," Frances said. She swatted Milton's arm with her left hand. It was then that Sonny saw the wedding ring. The ringmaster wore a ring, too. It looked like Frances's. Sonny assumed the two were husband and wife even though their last names were different. It felt like he had walked into a different world. A place where he didn't have any footing at all.

Milton frowned and pursed his lips. His eyes were filled with words that were forbidden to escape his mouth.

"Nobody's going anywhere in this storm, Milton," Frances said. "Don't be an idiot and don't be rude. This man stood up for us in town. He could have kept on walkin' and minded his own business, but he didn't, did he?"

"No, he didn't." If Milton Stein wore any authority when he walked to Sonny, Frances had stripped it from him in a matter of seconds. It looked like it had happened before, too. "Thank you, Mr. Burton, for being kind to my wife. I'm sorry if I was rude." Milton stuck his hand out for a shake.

Frances nodded at Sonny, urging him to pull his hook out of his pocket. He hesitated, then offered the metal appendage to Milton without breaking eye contact with him.

The ringmaster didn't flinch. He shook the hook like it was a hand. Sonny stiffened what was left of his right bicep to provoke as much tension against the man's fleshy hand as he could. He could see a look of approval from Frances out of the corner of his eye. She was the real ringmaster of the circus, not Milton. She didn't need to announce the title to anyone. She wore it like an invisible cape that gave her confidence and power.

"Nice to meet you," Sonny said, withdrawing the hook. "I'm sorry to barge in on you, but I wasn't going to make it home in this storm. This is the first place I saw that I could take cover in." He looked to the ceiling, then back to Milton and Frances. "Aren't you afraid this thing is going to fall on you?"

Frances smiled and stepped forward a bit. "Well, that has happened before. This ain't our first duster." Her Southern drawl was deeper, more pronounced, relaxed.

"It's not," Sonny said. "But I wish it was our last."

A loud chatter sounded from behind the crowd, drawing

Sonny's attention away from the bearded lady. No one else inside the big top seemed to pay attention to the noise. He followed the sound above his head and focused on a monkey the size of a human toddler climbing down the center pole of the tent.

"That's Charlie," Frances said. "Don't pay no attention to him. We let him have the run of the place so he doesn't become agitated. He has a bad attitude about cages."

"Aren't you afraid he'll escape?" Sonny asked.

Frances cocked her eyebrow. "You think we should be afraid of everything, Sonny Burton? Most of us here aren't scared of much, and the things we are afraid of are the things you can't see. Like ignorance and hate. Charlie understands the rules. He ain't stupid enough to set foot outside the tent without bein' on a rope. He don't trust the outside world any more than we do."

"I'm sorry, I didn't mean to offend you."

"You didn't. You don't have a grasp on us is all," Frances said. "We was gettin' ready to sit down for our noon meal. Care to join us?"

Sonny looked back to the monkey, who was almost to the ground. Somewhere from behind the crowd of circus people, an African cat grumbled. He wasn't sure if it was a lion or tiger. Then he saw the elephant for the first time as the crowd broke away and moved toward a long table that sat in the middle of the ring. The elephant was lying on the ground, resting, not bothered by the duster at all.

No bleachers had been erected for a paying audience to sit in. The tent served the members of the troupe, all of them, including the animals, as a sanctuary, a place to ride out the storm. Sonny realized that the tent was more than a performance hall, it was their home. All of them, and he'd walked in the front door like he'd had a right to. He couldn't help but to feel ashamed.

"I don't think I'll be going home yet," Sonny said, listing his ear toward the ceiling, taking in the roar of the unrelenting sandstorm as it pelted the canvas and tried to rip it apart. "If you don't mind."

"We're happy to have you." A smile grew on Frances's face. "You can sit next to me. Come on . . ."

Charlie the monkey leaped from the pole to the ground, broke into a full run, and jumped into Frances's waiting arms like it was the most normal thing in the world, then they all walked to the table. No one grumbled about making room for one more.

CHAPTER TWELVE

A steam generator the size of two Brahman bulls sat atop a large wagon. The metal engine clunked along at a slow pace with belts and pulleys in no hurry at all, attached to three dull copper disk dynamos with cords snaking off them in all directions. The machine was the heart of the circus, pumping electricity into an unexpected place, creating dim lighting, and who knew what else, inside the tent. Sonny assumed the faster the machine went, the brighter the light would be. It was the first time he'd ever seen a portable generator. What struck him about the light, the inside of the tent, and all of the people it housed, was how unfazed they were, humans and animals alike, by what was happening outside. The wind whistled through the tent and the canvas trembled, threatening to collapse. It sounded like a runaway train was careening toward the big top. But no one seemed to mind or care, and Sonny now understood why they were all huddled in the middle of the tent: they had gathered for their noontime meal like it was an ordinary day.

A long table greeted Sonny as he followed after Frances. Charlie clung to her like a hairy baby, and Milton remained at her side. Blue tagged along on a loose leash, curious about the people, but not venturing far from Sonny's ankle. The dog was leery of Charlie and kept his distance from the monkey.

The meal was no banquet or feast. The table had no centerpiece and didn't suggest any elegance at all. Beyond the table, an oversized pot steamed over an easy fire; a thin wisp of smoke spiraled upward, exiting a hole at the top of the tent. Sonny didn't catch a whiff of the chicken soup until he was almost upon it. He figured it had to be watered down to feed so many people.

"Come on," Frances said. "New friends eat first." She motioned for Sonny to go to the front of the line. Igor and two women, identical to each other with long, blond trusses and dancers' legs, stood out of the way, allowing Sonny first dibs on the soup.

He felt awkward, out of place, but didn't want to insult Frances or the circus people any more than he already had. A stack of bowls sat on a folding table next to the pot. He dipped out a helping of soup, making sure not to spill a drop. It was more broth than soup. There were only a few carrots and occasional slips of green floating on top. There was no meat to see. It must have sunk to the bottom of the pot or didn't exist at all.

With the bowl balanced in his left hand, he tugged Blue back to the table and sat down. He stared at the thin soup and waited for the others to join him before he took a taste of it. His stomach grumbled; a reminder that he hadn't had a thing to eat all day. Aldo had roused him out of bed, and everything had gone from bad to worse from there. But he waited, restrained by manners and respect. The last time he had enjoyed a decent meal of any kind was in Edith Grantley's kitchen. He'd only eaten canned meat or beans since arriving back home.

A few loaves of French bread dotted the table. Crocks of butter were scattered between the bread. There were no drinks offered. Bread and soup, nothing more. That was all there was for this meal. The way Sonny saw it, even as hardscrabble as the offering was, it was a lot more than most people were going to welcome for their noontime dinner.

Blue settled down at Sonny's feet, fading into gentle obedience. Sonny watched the rest of the people get their bowl of soup and find their place at the table. He recognized the fat man from the parade. The man was even more obese than Sonny had first thought. His legs looked like they weighed two hundred pounds apiece as he shuffled to the steaming pot of soup. It was a surprise that the man could walk at all, that he could stand upright, and care for himself in any way. The flesh on his arms hung like sheets on a clothesline, swaying in the wind every time he took a breath.

The temperature inside the tent was cool, but not cold. Still, the fat man's face was red from the effort of walking; sweat beaded on his massive forehead. Sonny had never seen a man the size of this one. He wondered how he got that way considering his soup bowl was the same size as everyone else's.

There were a variety of men and women waiting with trained patience in the soup line, all strangers to Sonny. A few midgets, the tall man, and the rest looking as normal as they could. Some, though, wore physiques that suggested they worked daily at staying fit. Sonny wondered if the trio of black-haired men in undershirts with arms that looked like they were sculpted from Italian marble were acrobats or trapeze artists. He looked to see if there was a swing hanging from the ceiling. There wasn't. Another sign that a performance wasn't planned anytime soon.

There were a few women among the men, all dressed in casual clothes. Some of them even wore pants, but most of them wore skirts or dresses. None of them had makeup on, or fancy feathers in their hair. If Sonny didn't know where he was, he would have thought that this was a normal soup line. Normal except the midgets, the fat man, Paul, and the monkey, Charlie. There was nothing normal about their presence. Everyone chatted in low voices, with their words obscured by the wind and subdued mood. Time passed, and his stomach protested at every tick of the clock.

Frances joined Sonny at the table. She had sent Charlie somewhere else; the monkey had vanished. Milton was right behind her. He sat down opposite Sonny.

"You didn't have to wait for us," Frances said.

"I appreciate your hospitality."

"It's the least we could do. We wasn't gonna send you away hungry."

Sonny cocked an ear to the side of the tent. "Sounds like it's letting up a bit."

Frances and Milton listened, then nodded together with their chins dipping at the same time. Sonny wondered if they knew what they were doing, or if they had been together for so long that they mirrored each other without realizing it.

A few more people sat down at the table. No one waited for anyone to say anything, grace or otherwise, before they started eating. They didn't fuss over Sonny, either. They accepted that he belonged there, though more than a few stole suspicious glances his way when they thought he wasn't paying attention. He was.

"You better get some bread before it's all gone," Milton said to Sonny.

Sonny looked down the table and there was a quick grab going on by almost everyone that sat down.

"I'm fine," Sonny said.

"You don't like bread?" Frances asked.

"I like it as much as the next man, but I figure I'm taking someone else's helping the way it is." Sonny still hadn't taken a taste of the broth in his bowl.

Frances stood, reached down the table, grabbed a loaf of bread, tore off the end piece, and handed it to Sonny. "Nonsense. You're our guest. We share what we have. It's how we survive. Little John won't mind you takin' a little bit of the leftovers." She nodded her head to the fat man. He was chewing a chunk of bread slathered in butter. Little John. Ironic. Humorous. Maybe he once was little. Sonny wondered what the fat man's real name was.

Sonny took the bread and set it down next to the bowl. "Thank you."

"You haven't never been around folks like us, have you?" Milton said.

Sonny shrugged. "Not like this. It was my job to shut down the circus on Sundays, not get to befriend the people who played in them."

"Frances said you was a Ranger. That how that injury happened?" Milton's eyes were hard and penetrating, focused on the hook. Sonny didn't think the ringmaster liked him, but he appreciated the direct question instead of having to digest another stare.

"Don't be rude, Milton," Frances interjected.

"It's all right. I don't mind," Sonny said. "I get stares all of the time. Though most everyone around Wellington is aware of what happened by now. Bonnie Parker shot me, got me in the arm before her and Clyde ran off an abandoned bridge and crashed their automobile. They got away. I didn't. The wound got infected with gangrene, and that was that. Leave it and die. Take it and see what kind of life I could live. I wasn't ready to die, so I let them take it. I'm still not sure I made the right choice."

"Well, those two got theirs, I'd say," Milton said. "They came through our doors once. Laughed and guffawed like anyone else. They were really generous, paid extra to have us show them around. Bonnie was real taken with Charlie. Tiny little thing she was. And with such a bad limp, too. I feared Clyde was gonna take out his gun and kidnap the darn monkey. That would have been a fool thing to do. Charlie don't take orders from no one but Frances. He loves her. Bonnie would have had a fight on her hands, and one of them would have come to a bad end. Probably Bonnie. Monkeys bite somethin' fierce, and that ain't a pretty sight."

Frances took a slurp of broth, watching Sonny as close as she could. "I'm sure he's had his fill of Bonnie Parker, Milton," she said, after she swallowed deep.

"I'm making conversation, Frances. For God's sake, I can't even do that right?"

"Don't mind him, Sonny. Storms make Milton more nervous than he is."

"I'm not nervous."

"If you say so."

"I say so."

"They cost us time. And money," Milton said. "They cost us more money than we have."

Sonny knew better than to put his nose somewhere it didn't belong. He buttered his bread and took a bite. The bread was fresher than he thought it would be, and the butter was rich, bright yellow in color. He wondered what kind of cream it had been made from. He followed the bite of bread with a spoonful of soup. Like he thought, it was weak, and didn't taste like chicken at all.

"Well, none of us like these storms. We had anticipated that we'd be down to the gulf by now," Frances said. "We was gonna take some January time. Nobody wants to see us perform in the winter, and we need a rest. Bad luck and bad weather has beseeched us somethin' awful this year. So, here we are, running late and behind in our travels. Some days it's a wonder we're still together at all."

"Only because of you," Milton said.

Frances blinked and a smile danced across her chubby face. The beard hid a lot of emotion, but it couldn't restrain the quick flash of pride.

"I wondered why you were passing through this time of year," Sonny said, as he took another bite of the bread. He liked the butter. He wanted more of it but restrained himself. "One thing after another is all. Moving these huge beasts ain't easy," Milton said.

Frances looked upward again. "Sounds like the wind has stopped. We'll have to clean everything and hope the trucks start." Then she went back to eating. They all did, allowing the silence to settle around them and comfort them the best it could.

Sonny was standing next to the open flap, preparing to go home, when he heard the rattle and grumble of an engine approaching. He stepped outside, with Blue at his side and Frances and Milton close behind, to see who was on the road.

The sky had cleared as late afternoon fell toward evening. It looked like the sandstorm had blasted all of the color out of everything. The sky was white, or faded gray, depending on the direction you looked. East was the darkest, with the storm still evident, marching away like a wall of tired Confederate ghosts. West was pale as Little John's flabby skin. But it was south that interested Sonny. He looked from the sky to the ground and spied a familiar car speeding toward the big top.

"That's the sheriff," Sonny said. "Heading this way." He stopped, with the shadow of the big top covering him in dim, dusky light. "You don't have anything to hide, do you?"

Frances stiffened as she fixed her eyes on the police car. "I told you, they always come along. It don't matter if we're clean or dirty, we might as well surrender without a whisper."

Sonny looked past her, took in the sight of sand drifted alongside of the tent, then looked to his truck with the west-side tires buried halfway. None of them were going anywhere soon. The was no running for any of them. Not like Sonny would have left Frances there to face Jonesy on her own.

The sheriff's car slowed, pulled off the road, and came to a stop next to Sonny's truck. Jonesy got out, jiggled the sand out of the cuffs of his pants, and put his faded brown campaign hat on. "I didn't expect to find you here, Sonny," he said, coming to a stop in front of the trio.

Blue wagged his tail, expecting a treat of some kind from Jonesy. None came. The sheriff ignored the dog.

"Might as well tell you," Jonesy continued. "This concerns you, too."

Sonny drew back and took a deep breath. He didn't like Jonesy's tone and rigid stance. The foul mood Sonny encountered earlier in the day at the office had only grown darker. "Is there a problem?"

"Sure is. Heck Kilbride's gone missin'. None of you would know anything about that, would you?" Jonesy said.

"Why would you think we would have any information about someone we've never heard of?" Milton said.

"There was an altercation in town between Sonny, the woman here, and Heck." Jonesy doffed his hat. "Ma'am," he said, then continued on. "Heck left downtown and hasn't been seen since. He should be home, but there ain't no sign of him anywheres."

"And you think we did somethin' to him?" Frances said. "Because he called us freaks and told us we weren't welcome in his town? Don't you think that happens everywhere we go? There's a Heck Kilbride in every burg we've ever pitched a stake in."

Jonesy crossed his arms. "Don't go gettin' all haughty with me, lady. All I care about is what happens here in Collingsworth County. Your problems in other places ain't my concern."

More noise from the road made it to them, causing Sonny to move and see three more automobiles heading toward them.

"That'd be my deputies to help in the search," Jonesy said.

"We got reason to believe Heck's here somewhere."

"I bet you'll find him in a tavern somewhere," Sonny said. "Or in his car stuck in the sand alongside the road, caught in the storm on his way home. I think you're jumping the gun here, Jonesy. It's been hours, not days."

"Doesn't matter what you think, Sonny Burton." Jonesy uncrossed his arms, dug into his back pocket, and produced a piece of paper. He held the legal documents as if to show it off. "I've got a search warrant and I intend to look over every inch of this place." Then he handed the paper to Milton, who took it, without looking to Frances for approval.

Sonny stared at the sheriff, tempted to tell him that he didn't recognize him at all, but he held his tongue. He didn't want to make things any worse than they already were.

CHAPTER THIRTEEN

Edith felt the blood drain from her face as a cold chill ran down the back of her neck. She was facing in the opposite direction. The line of windows that looked out from the booths gave view to the road. The parking lot was behind her. "Does he have on a white straw cowboy hat?"

"How'd you know?" Stella said.

"An unlucky guess."

"Are you in some kind of trouble, honey?"

"I think I might be."

"Don't you worry none. Glenn served in the war. He don't tolerate no shenanigans in this here establishment. Whatever the trouble is, he'll handle it."

"I thought this fella was only a bum," Edith said, fighting the temptation to look over her shoulder to see if the man was the same cowboy who had talked to her in Corsicana. "Is he still there?" It was a whisper. Edith was having trouble catching her breath. All kinds of trouble were fluttering around in her throat. A scream paralyzed by fear. A cry for help stopped before it could start. A rage that wanted to yell as loud as possible. But nothing could take flight, escape her mouth. Her fingers felt like shattering icicles.

"Yes," Stella said. "He's still there."

Glenn rang a bell and slid Edith's club sandwich onto the pass-through shelf. "Order's ready," he called out.

"Keep your pants on, Glenn, we got a situation here," Stella snapped over her shoulder, then slid into the booth across from Edith so she could see out into the parking lot. "So, what is this, a jilted ex-boyfriend, or what?"

"I told you, I thought he was a bum. He was standing by my automobile when I came out of the gas station restroom. He came out of nowhere. Tried to talk to me, made me feel really uncomfortable. He was crouched like a beady-eyed lizard and I felt like a fly about to be snatched out of the air."

"Oh, honey. I get 'em all. I've been pinched, grabbed, and felt up more times than I'd like to count. Men are all hands, sometimes. So, you ain't never met this fella?"

"I told you. I thought he was passing through, a hobo, or a worker at one of the factories around where I stopped." Edith's hand trembled and Stella reached out to calm her. The waitress's hand was warm; a soft, white blanket of hope. "Thank you. He must have followed me here. I've been on the road for hours. I didn't think he would come after me. Never thought about it one time. The gas jockey called him off me, and I slipped into the automobile and sped away. I thought I was done with him, that it was a passing thing. An incident I'd left behind me. I drove and drove because it's all I knew to do."

Stella pulled her hand off of Edith's, and said, "Well, it ain't over, 'cause he's comin' inside. Glenn, you best grab that billy club of yours. I think you might need it."

The bell tinkled and Edith froze, willing herself not to move, not to shiver, not to show one sign of fear or acknowledgment that danger had welcomed itself into the café. As far as Edith could tell, she was trapped. There was no way she could escape through the front door or make it to the kitchen by the opening in the counter without passing the cowboy. She held as still as she could, wishing she were invisible, but knew that was impossible.

"May I help you?" Stella said, as she stood up from the table and headed to the front door. She was confident, unwavering, acting like she had when Edith had walked into the café.

"No." The man's voice was unmistakable. Footsteps approached and he stopped at the end of the table Edith was sitting at. "We meet again." He sat down across from her without asking permission, if she minded, if the table was taken. He smelled of cigarette smoke and cheap gin and wore a Cheshire smile on his dirty face.

"I was leaving," Edith said. She reached down to grab her purse, then started to slide out of the booth. Stella hovered close, but there was no sign of Glenn.

The cowboy smiled, then matched her movement. He was missing a right incisor and one of his lower front teeth. They were all stained, decayed. His face was weathered, and his eyes looked like his black pupils were deep wells made of cold, hard steel mapped with red squiggly lines.

When Edith stood, the cowboy followed suit. "Can't you sit and visit a while?" he said, then reached out and grabbed her wrist, stopping her forward motion. Edith's face turned to paste, and the man's touch sent an electric shock wave through her body. It was a handcuff clasp. One more twist and the discomfort would have turned to pain.

"Hey, there," Stella said. "Leave her alone."

"You mind your own goddamned business." The cowboy hissed, taking his eyes off of Edith for only a second.

Edith saw Stella's intrusion as an opportunity to break free and yanked her wrist and arm back as hard as she could. The movement surprised the cowboy, got his attention as Edith's arm flew back, freeing her. She gasped and whimpered, teetered, but didn't fall over.

"Is there a problem here?" A deep male voice boomed throughout the café, from behind Stella.

Edith and the cowboy turned at the same time to see Glenn

standing at the end of the counter. He wore loose white pants, a tight white short-sleeved shirt with the sleeves rolled to his shoulders in perfect cuffs, exposing two blue ink tattoos. One was of a ship, and the other was a hula girl in the middle of a hip-shaking dance. His arms were muscular, carved of flesh-colored granite. He looked like a mean bull about to charge the skinny cowboy. A leather billy club dangled from Glenn's right hand, the grasp tight, the message clear. He knew how to use the club and would if he had to.

"No problem here, mister," the cowboy said. "I'm talkin' to this lady here is all."

"Do you know this man, ma'am?" Glenn said, ignoring the cowboy.

"No. I'm leaving." Edith moved toward the door, but the cowboy stepped in front of her, blocking the way.

The air inside the café was heavy and greasy, still, like all of the fans and movement had stopped; a sudden heat wave had come out of nowhere. Sweat beaded under Edith's lip. A sink dripped in the distance, and a machine of some kind hummed from the inside the kitchen, feeding off of electricity, causing one of the overhead lights to dim, threaten to go out, and leave them all in the dark.

"Let her pass," Glenn said, making his way from behind the counter.

Stella stood rigid, frozen; her eyes fixed on the cowboy. She was close enough to reach out and slap him, but she didn't attempt to interfere.

The cowboy stared at Edith, didn't move, either. "This is between me and the lady, here."

"There's nothing between us." The words escaped Edith's mouth unbidden, relieved for the escape. She couldn't have stopped them if she had wanted to. "What do you want from me?"

The cowboy smirked, then allowed the gesture to roll into a wicked, hateful smile. "Your automobile, your fancy shoes, your life. I want one second of the freedom you have is all, lady. Ain't that enough for a man like me to want in this life?" Then he slipped his right hand into the pocket of his denim pants, producing a knife that with the flick of his wrist revealed a four-inch blade. The snap of polished steel echoed through the café like Glenn's voice had; a crack of thunder after a lightning strike that caused everyone but the cowboy to jump inside of their skin.

"Stella," Glenn yelled, "don't!"

But it was too late. Stella kicked the cowboy in the knee. An act that the man didn't anticipate, didn't see coming in any way. It was a hard kick and dropped the cowboy to the floor. He fell backward, past Edith, crumpled into a ball, grabbing his knee, yelling in pain.

"Run," Stella said to Edith, jumping back out of the way, allowing Glenn to rush the man. The knife was still in the cowboy's grasp. Caution was called for. An injured snake was still capable of biting. "Run, now, honey."

Edith hesitated, feared leaving the waitress and cook with the cowboy, but she knew this would be her only chance to flee. She took it without another second's hesitation. The door flew open at her push, and as she exited the café, she heard the cowboy shout at her, scream at the top of his lungs, "I'm comin' for you, lady. I'm comin' for you."

Ennis, Texas, disappeared behind Edith in a cloud of dust, fear, and dread. It took thirty miles for her heart to stop beating so fast, for her to calm down as much as she could, for her to realize that a decent person would have gone straight to the police, would have gone for help. Instead, she'd run like a thoughtless, frightened child, thinking only of herself and her own safety.

The realization almost made her slow the Pierce and turn around and go back. Almost. But she didn't slow down, not one mile per hour. Instead, she pushed the accelerator down, getting as far away from Ennis as fast as she could. She had left the bloodstains in her parlor by fleeing, this was no different. Other than it was. Those people, Stella and Glenn, had been nice to her, had come to her aid, and what had she done? She'd left them to face the cowboy on their own is what she did. Guilt replaced her fear, and another wave of tears washed out of her.

The last thing she had expected when she'd stopped for a bite to eat was to be followed inside by the cowboy. She still couldn't rationalize his motive and couldn't even begin to understand why he wanted *her life*. She was an old widow on the road to see a man who wasn't aware that she was coming, who she thought she loved. Everything she owned, had worked for, hung onto through the ugliness and uncertainty of the Depression, was behind her. The only things of value she held now were her hopes, dreams, and the 1928 Pierce Arrow that Henry had given her. If Edith had thought the cowboy would have left her alone, she would have given the automobile to him. Not without regret and hesitation. The Pierce was a show of love not prosperity. At least to her. The world, and the struggling men in it, held a different view. They saw Edith as rich, as a person of means, and maybe that was true. Truer than she'd realized when she had left on her journey north. She wished she could stop, find a telephone, and call Sonny Burton. Tell him that she was on her way to him, that his silence had provoked her to make the journey to Wellington alone, to find out once and for all if she mattered to him. A letter would have sufficed. A postcard. Anything. But nothing had come, and now she had put her life on the line, all in the name of love, of the promise of something better waiting for her in the future, miles away from all that she knew. Any fool would have turned around and taken the back roads back to Huntsville. But she didn't. Edith kept driving north with her sights set on Fort Worth.

She looked in the rearview mirror every ten seconds, and when she saw an automobile or truck behind her, she pulled off the road on the closest exit, found a place to park, hiding the best she could. There wasn't a lot of traffic on the road, so that helped, and she'd recovered the Smith & Wesson from under the seat and put it on the passenger seat. The gun was within reach, loaded, and ready to fire if the need arose. The cowboy had a weapon and wasn't afraid to use it, or show that he was going to use it, but Edith had evened the field with the gun. Except, she hadn't used the gun. She hadn't thought about it then. All she had wanted to do was get as far away from the café and the cowboy as she could.

As she drove and played hide and seek with the traffic, Edith worried more about Stella and Glenn. She could only assume that the muscular cook had restrained the cowboy and called the police. She hoped the wicked man was in jail where he couldn't hurt anyone or come after her like he had promised to do. The fact that two strangers had saved her life did not escape Edith. It was the second time in recent months that she had found herself in harm's way that was no cause of her own other than being in the wrong place at the wrong time. *Had the world gone mad?* she wondered. Did this desperate age change good men into bad? Or bad men into evil men? It was hard not to consider such a thing. The ills of the world were like a spreading disease, waiting for her at every turn. She feared her luck was running out, that she wouldn't escape so easy again. Strike three, you're out.

CHAPTER FOURTEEN

Sonny watched the sheriff poke into haystacks, peak behind curtains, and search the staging area behind the circus ring without finding one trace of Heck Kilbride. Frustration chewed at the corner of Jonesy's mouth and rage burned in his bloodshot eyes. Each step he took ended with an angry thud. He grumbled and huffed like a wolf in a fairy tale, but no matter how hard he looked, how hard he tried, his search came up empty. Sonny stayed out of the way and offered no comment. Instead, he watched every move the sheriff made with dread and confusion.

Frances followed along, shaking her head every once in a while, staying silent, too, as they went. She wore her resignation like a familiar old coat but offered no resistance. No one did. Milton had gone off with the deputies, so did two of the acrobat-looking men. It was like they all had assigned roles, which they probably did, now that Sonny considered it.

After a long stretch of invasion of the performers' quarters, Sonny, on the other hand, ran out of patience and the investment in peace to stay quiet any longer. He had been acquainted with Hiram P. Jones, Sheriff of Collingsworth County, Texas, for longer than he cared to remember and had called Jonesy a friend for almost as long, but enough was enough. Whatever was going on here extended beyond the reach of friendship and professional respect. This looked like abuse of power to Sonny, a rare show of bullying from Jonesy. The invasion of the circus was beneath the man and the office.

"What are you looking for, Jonesy?" Sonny said, as they were about to make their way to the animal cages.

Jonesy stopped with a scowl. "I done told you. I'm lookin' for Heck Kilbride."

Frances stood next to Sonny, eyeing the sheriff with a different kind of suspicion and annoyance than Sonny. She remained silent, too, but it was hard telling how long that would last. From what Sonny had seen, the woman liked to be in charge of everything within her sight. Her rage was obscured by the beard on her face, but not hidden.

"Heck's not here, Jonesy." Sonny made no effort to hide his feelings. "Why don't you tell me what the hell is really going on?"

The sheriff didn't flinch, didn't allow a change of attitude to show on his face or in his bulldog stance. "I hear tell you was at Sugg's not so long ago, Sonny. About the same time this one stopped to get gas in her truck. You two travelin' together, are you?"

"No, of course not. It was coincidence, a matter of timing. We left the square at different times."

"And where's Tom Young's cow? The one that was in the back of that truck?" Jonesy said. It sounded like he was in court, wearing a lawyer's suit instead of a police uniform, cross-examining a murder suspect.

Sonny looked to Frances to answer the question. The cow sure wasn't in the soup. Sonny knew that much.

"I'll be happy to show you what's left of that cow, Sheriff." Frances pushed past Jonesy and motioned for both men to follow her. "And the receipt, too, if you care to believe that it's real and not faked."

Jonesy started to say something, but to Sonny's surprise, he didn't say a word. He followed after Frances, matching her pace, allowing her the lead. He rested his stubby hand on the grip of his holstered government-issue Colt.

They entered a separate tent, an extension of the big top, and were confronted with the sour odors emitted by a close collection of animals. The tent smelled like a barn that hadn't been mucked out in a week. But that wasn't the case. All of the visible cages were clean and well cared for, as were their occupants, even if they were a little thin. There were dogs, white horses, monkeys, a lion, and a tiger, all caged, with the two camels and the elephant chained at the back, standing still as an artist's model.

Jonesy trailed after Frances, who had stopped in front of the lion's cage. "He has part of the leg." She put her hands on her hips and narrowed her eyes. "Good enough for you, Sheriff?"

Sonny stood back as Jonesy peered into the cage, making sure to stay back far enough so the mean-looking cat couldn't reach out and take a swipe at him. The smell of raw meat and blood overtook the straw and smell of the barn. It was like Sonny was suddenly cloaked in the aroma of death, and he realized that all of the smells had accumulated in the fabric of the canvas over the years; it was the tent that smelled so bad, not the cages.

"How can I trust it's a cow?" Jonesy said. "Could be Heck from where I stand."

"You think Heck had a leg bone that thick?" Frances said. Her hands were still anchored on her hips, and her stance had become stiffer with the question. "That cow will last us a few days. More if we have to stretch it. But we're not in the business of workin' with hungry cats, Sheriff. Hungry humans are easier to deal with. You can fire them, but you can't let a lion loose to fend for itself, now, can you?"

"Probably not a good idea." Jonesy looked in the cage as close as he could. It was clear he still had his doubts about whether the bone belonged to Tom Young's milk cow or not. From where Sonny stood, he thought Frances was telling the truth. The bone looked too long to belong to anything other than a cow or a horse.

"You've seen everything, Jonesy. Heck's not here," Sonny said. "But you knew that. I'm sure you knew that. You were using Heck's disappearance as an excuse to poke around for something else if I was to guess. Now, why don't you tell me what that is, or quit this charade you're playing."

"You sure do think highly of your deduction skills don't you, Sonny?"

Sonny leaned back like he was avoiding a punch. He was surprised by how venomous the man's response was. "I'm sorry, Jonesy. Look, if you have nothing else for me, I'll be going now." He tipped his hat to Frances, then started to take his leave. "If you're not going to end this charade, I am."

"I didn't tell you that you could leave, Sonny Burton," Jonesy said.

Sonny kept on walking. "Arrest me, then," he said over his shoulder, more determined to leave the smell of blood and deceit behind him than he had been when he'd first arrived.

It only took a couple of minutes to clear the tires of the sand that had piled against them. Once he was certain that he could flee the circus, Sonny jumped into the cab of the truck and settled himself behind the steering wheel. Blue greeted him with a wag of the tail, but there was no more show of affection than that. Sonny wouldn't have tolerated a lick of any kind, and Blue wasn't the kind of dog to offer one.

Regret shimmered through Sonny. He had left Frances to face Jonesy on her own without offering so much as a thank you for her hospitality. There was no way he was going back inside. All he could do was hope that the bearded lady would understand his decision to walk away from the sheriff. He wasn't too worried about Frances, though. If anyone could handle themselves in a tough, uncomfortable situation it was the bearded lady, the real iron fist of the circus. She had shown her strength from the start and had obviously experienced a one-on-one with the law more times than Sonny knew. If Jonesy didn't watch himself, he'd become cat food himself.

Sonny started the Model A, put it in reverse, and gave the engine a good dose of gasoline. He narrowly missed one of the deputy's cars and found his way to the road. He hesitated for a second, deciding which way to turn. Left would take him home. Right would take him back to town.

He decided that going back to town made sense. Home was a desolate cave, void of any life or answers to the questions that had collected at the forefront of his mind. Town might not give him any leads, but it was a start. He felt a strange urgency to find out what was going on with Jonesy. More than he had this morning. The sheriff had made things personal. Accused Sonny and innocent people of some kind of nefarious wrongdoing. Frances, nor anyone he had met inside the big top, seemed capable of hurting anyone, not even Heck Kilbride. It was amazing that something hadn't befallen the town bully before now. But one thing was for sure, Jonesy had made Sonny angrier than he'd been in a long time. Enough to rekindle the investigator in him. He thought that had been buried with Billy Bunson. He thought he was done poking his nose into places it didn't belong. Maybe that would never change. Maybe it couldn't.

He pulled out onto the road and gunned the engine, leaving a thick cloud of fresh dust behind him. Tires didn't squeal on dirt. Which was a shame. Sonny would've liked the truck to have let out a yell for him.

The truck rattled and protested as Sonny brought it to speed. Even Blue looked at him with concern, like, "what are you doing?" He paid the dog no mind. His jaw was clenched, and his left hand was gripped on the steering wheel. He swore he could feel tension in his right fingers. If only that were true. He could use two fists right now.

Sonny parked the truck on the north side of the courthouse this time. He wanted to avoid the entrance to the sheriff's office and go as unseen as possible as he made his way to the basement, to the small Texas Ranger office housed next to the boiler room.

He kept his hat on inside the building, tipped it down, as he looked to the floor, avoiding glances, doing his best to hide his identity—even though that was impossible. Almost everyone in the building knew Sonny or knew who he was. He'd spent the better part of the last decade as a Company C Texas Ranger in this part of the panhandle. Most of the Rangers were out of Lubbock, but there were offices scattered about in towns like Abilene, Amarillo, Childress, and beyond. Texas Rangers were hard to miss. They carried a history on their shoulders and in their hearts that showed regardless of whether they wore a uniform or badge.

Sonny made his way to the door of the office, took a deep breath, and pushed inside. His son, Jesse, sat behind the desk, staring at a paper in his hand. Another desk sat empty. It was for the secretary, who was nowhere to be seen.

"Pa," Jesse Burton said. "I wasn't expectin' to see you out on a day like today. That was a hell of a duster. You all right?"

"As all right as I can be." Sonny allowed his shoulders to drop, relieved to be on familiar ground.

Jesse favored his mother Martha's side of the family. He was shorter than Sonny and stockier, too. His hair, shorn short like a military man's, was blonder than it was brown. There was no mistaking his son's German heritage, or the fact that he was neat, ordered, and for the most part, lacked a sense of humor.

Jesse was all business, which as it had turned out for him, served him well as a Texas Ranger.

"Second time today I was in this building," Sonny said as he took off his hat.

"You get caught in the storm?"

"More than one the way it looks now."

A puzzled look crossed Jesse's face. "How so?"

Sonny looked around the small office and noticed a stack of boxes in the corner. All of the pictures had been taken off the walls. "I'm not interrupting anything am I?"

"Not much." Jesse returned his attention to the paper in his hand.

Now that Sonny focused on his son and the cramped surroundings, he saw that Jesse's desk was sparse, too. "What's going on?" Something didn't smell right.

"Amarillo. That's what's goin' on. I'm leaving for Amarillo Friday."

"They're moving the office?"

Jesse allowed the paper to slip from his hand. It fell flat as a brick on the desk. There was no air movement inside the office. There never had been. It was a steamer in the winter when the boiler next door was cooking, and cold as a morgue in the summer, which, depending on a man's constitution, was either a comfort or a cellblock in hell. To Sonny it had been the latter. Hell. He'd preferred to be outside on the back of a horse, going from one place to the next. Those days were long gone. Jesse, on the other hand, had taken to office work and liked seeing the world from behind a desk. Another difference between the two of them.

"So, you're moving, too?" Sonny said.

Jesse shrugged. "I haven't got my orders yet, but the office is. Out with the old, in with the new. Ma Ferguson and her ways are gone, and Governor Allred is cleaning house. I can't say I blame him. I tried to avoid the Ferguson politics as much as I could, which was one of the reasons I was okay with stayin' here. I wanted to be as far away from Austin as I could get. But the taint of favoritism followed me, regardless. Most folks thought I got my position because of you and your misfortune. Not one person bothered to ask me how long I'd been a Ranger elsewhere before I came here. No one but Jonesy. But he would, wouldn't he?"

"You can count on Jonesy to ask a lot of questions."

Jesse scrunched his forehead, forming a brief washboard of misunderstanding. "What's going on, Pa? Why are you here?"

"Naw, I don't want to bother you with it." Sonny turned to leave.

Jesse stood with a concerned look on his face. "You don't have to go. I was gonna run by your place to tell you what was goin' on, but now I don't have to."

"You got your own problems. No need to hear mine out."

"It's usually me comin' to you." There was a new warmth in Jesse's voice. Sonny knew he had been an absent father in his son's life for a lot of years, especially the early ones when Sonny was on the trail, riding with the Rangers from one conflict to the next. Resentment had been a common wall built between the two of them. But that wall had started to crack over the last couple of years. Once Jesse came to Wellington and took to be the Ranger there, they'd had the chance to spend more time together, develop some respect for each other's strengths, and had learned how to forgive their weaknesses. Sonny could hear things in Jesse's voice now that he'd never heard before and knew the sincerity that settled on his son's face was real.

Sonny made his way to the chair in front of Jesse's desk and sat down. He adjusted himself, tugged on the prosthesis to get it in place so he would be more comfortable. Jesse didn't notice, or care. He sat back down behind the desk. The boiler in the next room clanked and groaned, offering its own comment on the situation. Both men ignored the contraption. It was warm as a summer day inside the office. Perspiration had already started to collect on the back of Sonny's neck.

"You heard Heck Kilbride is missing?" Sonny said, all adjusted and as comfortable in the chair as he could be.

"I did, but I think it's a little too early to be alarmed."

"Me, too. I'm happy you feel the same way. Jonesy doesn't. He saw fit to ferret out the local judge, Millard Kaine, and get himself a search warrant to poke around the circus that's parked outside the Harmeson place."

"I heard they went through town. He out there because they stole all of Tom Young's cows?"

"Cow. And they bought it." For Sonny, there was no hiding his frustration at the dishonesty of gossip spread about like fertilizer on a garden. Turned out that fertilizer was manure. Pure manure.

"How are you so sure of that?"

"That's what this is all about," Sonny said. "Jonesy, that is. Not the cow, or the circus."

"Okay?" Jesse was still confused, unclear, but interested.

"I better start at the beginning."

"That might help."

"Aldo Hernandez was on my doorstep this morning. He asked me if I would talk to Jonesy about his cousin, Rafael. It seems Rafael was going to the CCC training camp."

"Unusual for a Mexican, isn't it?"

"That's what I thought. But it gets more interesting. Aldo said Rafael was with those boys because Jonesy wanted him to be there to get some kind of information."

"He was there as a snitch? Another odd choice."

"Agreed. Whatever the reason, Jonesy and Rafael were asking for trouble."

"And they got it."

"You're aware of this part?"

"I do but tell it to me anyway."

Sonny drew in a breath and continued. "Rafael had some tequila, and they all had some drinks. Rafael passed out, but when he came to, Leo Dozier was lying next to him with the tar beat out of him. Everybody said that Leo and Rafael got into a fight, but Rafael didn't remember it. Now get this, they take Dozier to the hospital, and Rafael is charged with assault and battery and taken to jail."

"Seems cut and dried to me. How many witnesses?"

"Six, I think."

"No need for a jury trial."

"Maybe. But Rafael, of course, didn't have bail, so he's still behind bars. Now, Aldo knew that Jonesy had put Rafael up to this, so he asked me to talk to Jonesy, see if I could convince the sheriff to be lenient on Rafael, or get him out of this mess altogether by telling the judge what was going on—what he was after."

"Seems reasonable," Jesse said. "I'm kind of surprised you got yourself involved in this."

"Aldo and I have a history. He's my friend."

Jesse didn't need to do anything but stand there.

"Now, get this," Sonny said. "Leo Dozier lost his spot in the CCC. Clyde Jones took his place."

"A relation to the sheriff?"

"No other," Sonny said. "When I went to talk to Jonesy, he was defensive, in a mood like I've never seen. He pretty much told me to get out of his office. I asked him if he was involved in something, and that set him off even more. I'm not sure I'm dealing with the same man I've known all of these years."

"I thought you and Jonesy were friends."

"That makes two of us." Sonny wiped the sweat from his

neck with his handkerchief. "I left the office and intervened in an argument between Heck Kilbride and Frances Avalon, the bearded lady from the circus. Her and Paul, the tall man, were in town getting supplies, and Heck, of course, told them they weren't welcome here."

"You had a busy morning."

"You could say that. Then the storm came, and I took refuge at the circus. They were kind enough to offer me a meal, until Jonesy showed up, saying that we were all under suspicion in Heck's disappearance. You would have thought the place was teeming with killers, and I was no more than shit on the sole of his boot. He wore hate and anger in his eyes like it was a shiny badge all to itself.

"Jonesy's never been the kind of man to throw his weight around. That's one of the reasons I've held as much respect for him as I have. He had that search warrant and his badge as a key to the kingdom, so there was no arguing with him. I fear there's more to this than meets the eye. Something's got a hold of Jonesy, whether it's an illness, or a bad situation, I can't say for sure. A bad situation is more my guess, but I'm at a loss."

Jesse stood from behind the desk, walked over to the hat tree, plucked off his white Stetson, and put it on square.

"Where are you going?" Sonny said as he stood.

"Well, if Rafael Hernandez is still in jail, then we need to go talk to him."

"You don't need to get involved in this."

"Too late," Jesse said, heading for the door. "The minute you said you had a problem, I was involved."

CHAPTER FIFTEEN

Jesse walked straight to the entrance of the jail and asked the matron, Peggy Anne Birchway, if he could see one of the prisoners. Peggy Anne looked like she shared Jesse's lack of a sense of humor. Her face, caked with heavy tan foundation, looked as solid as a board cut from an oak tree. Her eyebrows were drawn on, black as pitch, and her uniform, a brown dress cut below the knee, was starched so heavy that when she breathed the fabric rattled. She would have faded into the wall, being as brown as she was, but her hands, arthritic and gnarled, were as white as a surrender flag. Sonny had known Peggy Anne ever since he had started working out of the Wellington office. She didn't acknowledge his presence, looked through him like he wasn't there, or worth the time to say hello to.

"Which prisoner would that be, Ranger Burton?" Peggy Anne said. It was more of a demand than a question.

Sonny flinched at the sound of Ranger Burton. He had answered to that title for so long his tongue was trained to respond on hearing the two words spoken together. He swallowed and made sure he was a good foot behind Jesse, stopping his response mid-throat. It was an unnatural position. He might as well have been hanging upside down.

"Rafael Hernandez," Jesse said.

Peggy Anne opened a ledger and pulled her finger down the page slow as a snail. "Looks like you're too late. He was released an hour ago."

"You're sure?" Jesse said.

"As sure as I'm sittin' here, Ranger Burton. Why would I say that if it wasn't true?"

"Who signed him out?"

"Sheriff Jones. Says so right here." Peggy Anne tapped Jonesy's signature on the ledger.

"All right," Jesse said. "I guess that settles it."

"It does," Peggy Anne said. "Anything else I can do for you?" She didn't mean it. Sonny could tell the only reason she asked was because she had to.

A newspaper laid on the desk next to the ledger. The *Leader* was open to page two, the Personal page. Next to the gossipy section was a triptych picture of a young colored boy that looked like a mug shot. The other two pictures were of the boy, crumpled on the ground, dead, and of a crowd gathered around a tree. A title sat atop the picture as if it were an everyday occurrence: *As Troops Faced A Lynch Mob.*

Sonny looked away from the picture. He hadn't had time to read the paper, but he knew the story before he read it. The colored boy had said something to a white person, presumably a woman, that was deemed out of line, and was lynched for it. Sad to say, but Sonny had seen the results of more than one lynch mob in his tenure as a Ranger. Hate and prejudice were a way of life, with nothing, including the law, strong enough to change it. Rafael was no colored boy, but he was a Mexican, one short step up from a colored in some men's eyes and one step down in others. Which was one of the reasons why Jonesy's choice to send Rafael into the CCC camp seemed out of the norm. Boys that went to the CCC camp were considered to be the best of the best, and Anglo almost a hundred percent of the time. If the story that Aldo had told Sonny was true. If Rafael *was* a snitch for the sheriff. There were a lot of ifs that didn't make a lick of sense.

"No, thank you," Jesse said. He turned to Sonny, shrugged, and headed back toward the office.

Sonny wasn't sure he wanted to follow after Jesse. He wanted to get out of the courthouse as quick as he could. It felt like the walls were closing in on him and the floor was made of eggshells. Every step he took threatened to shatter underneath him. But he wanted to talk with Jesse, see what he thought, even though Sonny knew what he was going to do next. He was going to the hospital to talk to Aldo.

Jesse was halfway down the hall before Sonny caught him. "Slow down," Sonny said. "Where are you off to?"

"Out to the Hernandez place."

"You think Rafael's going to be there?"

"Where else would he be?" Jesse said.

"If it was me, I'd take a one-way ticket out of this county, or at least, lay low until whatever's going on blows over."

"Maybe," Jesse said. "You see the paper today about the trouble down in Shelbyville?"

"The lynching?" Sonny said. "No, I haven't read it yet. I saw the picture on Peggy Anne's desk."

"That kind of trouble could find its way here. A man don't have to be a colored to get himself hung from a tree. Rafael's lucky he found himself in jail."

"Maybe, too lucky."

"What do you mean?"

"Who arrested him?"

"I don't know," Jesse said. He took a deep breath and squared himself with Sonny. "You really think Jonesy's got a dirty hand in all of this?"

Sonny looked down the hall to make sure they were alone. "We should go outside. We don't need our suspicions echoing through the halls."

"You're right. I need to lock the office. I'll meet you outside," Jesse said.

"I'm parked outside the north entrance." Sonny headed off down the hall without saying another word and made his way outside the building.

He waited outside the door, amazed at the cloudless sky and the calm breeze. The temperature was mild, and the light was tilting toward gray as evening came on. The sandstorm was a bad memory. It didn't take Jesse long to join him. No one else went in or out of the building, and the traffic around the square was sparse. Most of the businesses were closing down for the day. Somehow, the day had slipped away from him.

"I think the Hernandez house is the best place to start," Jesse said, with the Stetson on his head, and a shiny chrome Colt .45 on his hip.

Sonny cast a glance the opposite direction. "I'm going to go talk to Aldo."

"Do you think that's a good idea, Pa?"

"What do you mean?"

"Getting involved. Do you think you should get involved in this, especially if Jonesy's in some kind of trouble?"

"That's why I should get involved. I can ask questions you can't, go places you can't."

"How do you figure?"

"You wear a badge. I don't."

"For now. I'm not sure what's gonna happen come Friday."

Sonny smiled. "Nah, you're a lawman, Jesse. Whether you're a Ranger for the rest of your days is out of your control. But no matter what happens, you'll be making right out of wrong. I'm sure of it."

"Thanks, Pa. That helps."

Sonny turned away from Jesse, anxious to be inside his truck. He knew his son was standing there staring after him, wearing a prideful smile, but Sonny wasn't going to turn to see it. He didn't want to be disappointed if it wasn't there.

Sonny pulled to a stop in front of the hospital. Blue stood in the seat, ready to get out of the truck. "We'll go home soon, boy," Sonny said. "You stay here." He opened the door, straightened himself the best he could once his feet hit the ground, and headed to the front door of the two-story building. A second of hesitation grabbed him before he entered. Sonny had avoided the hospital as much as he could since the amputation. But there was another reason, too. He had only seen Betty Maxwell a few times since she had returned to work, and that hadn't been long enough to speak to her at length. The woman had always caused him to go dry in the mouth, even before he'd lost his arm. It wasn't that he pined for her in any way. Betty Maxwell was a good twenty-five years younger than he was. She *was* a beautiful woman. There was no question about that. It was her attitude, her personality, that confounded Sonny. She was direct as an arrow, took no pity on anyone who felt sorry for themselves, and demanded they do the best they could. In other words, she challenged him like no other woman had ever dared—until he'd met Edith Grantley. Now that he thought about it, Betty was a lot like Frances Avalon. Both women ran the show, even though most men looked right past them.

With that thought, Sonny pushed in through the door, not surprised to see Betty Maxwell sitting behind a desk, exactly where he'd expected to her to be.

"Well, if it isn't Sonny Burton," Betty Maxwell said, allowing a smile to come to her face. She was dressed all in white, from her shoes to her nurse's cap, her perfect brunette hair piled atop her head. "What brings you in today? Nothing the matter, I hope."

"Hello, Betty. It's good to see you," Sonny said as he took his hat off. "No, nothing's wrong. I feel fine most days."

"And the other days?"

"Fair to middlin'. Everybody has their days."

"I guess they do. But everything feels all right?" Betty motioned toward the prosthesis, toward Sonny's right arm. "We can make some adjustments if we need to. Or replace the thing if it's grown uncomfortable. Stumps shrink. There was a salesman in here from out east not so long ago, sayin' they were working on a lighter model. One that moves around easier, with more attachments instead of a hook."

"Now, what are you suggesting, Nurse Betty, that I go around wearing a Yankee arm? What would folks around here think?"

"They wouldn't be able to tell the difference unless you told them."

Sonny smiled at her dry, deadpan response. It was another reason he liked her. She treated him like he was a normal man. That and the strength she had showed when the time had come to show it. "Is Aldo around? I'd like to speak to him, if I could."

"He left right after the dust storm settled down and we could see across the street. A phone call came in for him. Something personal, he said. He had to leave as soon as he could."

"He didn't say what the trouble was, did he?"

Betty leaned forward on the desk, and Sonny stepped toward her so only a few feet separated them. "You heard about Rafael, didn't you?"

"I did," Sonny said, dropping his voice to meet Betty's low volume. There was no one in the waiting room, or anywhere else to be seen. The doctor was nowhere to be seen, and he wasn't going to ask where he was at. "He got out of jail about an hour or so ago."

"About the time Aldo left," Betty said.

"Did they meet?"

"Aldo doesn't say much about his personal business. Both of

the men involved have been here, otherwise I wouldn't be able to tell you anything."

Of course, they were. Where else would two men who'd been in a fight go other than the hospital? "Is the Dozier boy still here? I'd like to talk to him."

"No, Doc took a look at him, cleaned his bruises and scratches, and sent him home. To be honest, Rafael looked to have taken the worst of it, but the sheriff wasn't having him stay here. Rafael was taken to jail as soon as the bandages were on."

"And the Dozier boy could walk out on his own?"

"He had bruises, some cuts, and broken ribs. He isn't gonna be workin' at his daddy's wrecker service anytime soon. Good for him it's January."

"He was set to go to the CCC camp and spend the next six months away, like the rest of the boys. Now he's not. Wouldn't have mattered. Clyde Jones took his place. But you knew that, too."

"It had to be Clyde."

"Why do you say that?"

Betty looked down the hall both ways to make sure they were still alone. "Now, this is a rumor, mind you. Those things go around here like ants to watermelons in the summer. You like watermelon, don't you?"

"As much as the next fella," Sonny said.

Betty stood and walked over to Sonny so they were shoulder to shoulder. When she started to talk, it was no more than a whisper. "Clyde's daddy is runnin' buddies with Vince Kilbride."

"Heck's daddy."

"That's right," Betty said. "Those two have been causin' trouble around here since they was kids. Now Heck and Clyde have taken over where their daddies have left off. Now, this might be true, but I heard Clyde had it in for Leo for somethin'

138

involving one of them Harmeson girls. The details are slim, but I'd be curious if Heck was around them CCC boys when that fight broke out, or if he put Clyde up to it."

"Me, too," Sonny said. "Jonesy should have checked into that if he knew about the trouble between them boys. This is the first I've heard of it."

"There was an easier feather to pluck from the looks of things."

"Rafael."

"Makes sense, don't it. That's the way things work around here."

"Them Harmesons are fine people. I can't see them involved in all of this," Sonny said. "They bring me some eggs every now and then, check in on me like good neighbors do. I don't keep track of their girls, though."

"I don't imagine you do."

"I had a run-in with Heck this morning."

"I heard tell," Betty said. "You was protectin' some cow thieves is how it was told to me, but that didn't sound right, so I didn't believe it. I didn't say a word to anyone else about it."

"The circus people bought that cow fair and square."

"I'm sure they did, but if I was them, I'd get out of here as soon as I could. Their feathers are the same color as Rafael's. Different is what they are, easy to blame anything on that goes wrong."

"I imagine they'll be on the road soon," Sonny said. "You heard Heck's gone missing."

"Now that I haven't heard, but the storm slowed things down around here. Folks had to cancel appointments for another day. Heck's probably out on the county line road, stuck in the sand, passed out from a bender if you ask me."

"Me, too, but the sheriff thinks different." Sonny took a deep breath and considered what Betty had said about Clyde and

Heck. "I'm surprised Clyde got picked to go to the CCC camp."

"You and everybody else. But if your last name is Jones around here, then it shouldn't come as no surprise at all."

"Jonesy's been an honest, decent man when I've had dealings with him."

"You haven't lived here all of your life."

"No, I haven't, but I'm a pretty good judge of character."

"Well, Sonny Burton, here's some advice. I'd stay out of this mess if I was you. You got better things to do with your time than make something your business that's got nothing to do with you. Trouble enough has found its way to your doorstep." Betty focused on his arm again, then headed back to her desk. "Maybe you should let Jesse take this on. He's more than capable."

"He's got problems of his own right now."

"We've all got problems of our own right now."

"You're the second person today who's told me to mind my own business."

"Who was the first one?"

"Sheriff Jones."

CHAPTER SIXTEEN

Cecilia Braun stared at Edith like she was an aberration who had appeared out of the late evening fog. The arthritic woman was twenty-four-years older than Edith, in her early eighties, and showed every year of her age from head to toe. She was stooped over, leaning on a cane carved of hickory to help keep her vertical, with uncombed frazzled white hair, and skin as leathery and wrinkled as a haggard dog's brow. A thick red and gold night coat, that looked more like a faded tapestry than evening attire, hung from her thin frame. Any softness or beauty in the old woman's face had been lost to time, weather, and a rigid stance on life. A familiar hardness was reflected in her hard, yellowed eyes. "I wasn't expectin' no visitors this evening," she said. Her voice was frail and horsey. She offered no hint of recognition or that she was happy to see Edith at all.

"I'm sorry to barge in on you unannounced, Aunt Cecilia, but I had no place else to go. I should have called ahead, announced my arrival, and asked permission to stay, but there was no time. I'm sorry to disturb you. I truly am."

"You're like your mother. Flighty, unaware of anyone else around you, and you lack proper manners. What if I had plans or was hosting a shindig?"

The house was dark and dusty. It didn't look like there had been a party held there since the turn of the last century—even though Edith knew that wasn't the case. "It's been a long time, Auntie. It's good to see you," she said, ignoring the personal attack. She had expected it. Cecilia and Edith's mother had been competitive sisters all of their lives. They were either vying for their parents' attention or trying to outdo each other in one way or another as they grew older. When one of them had a child, the other did, too. If one of their husbands built a house, the other would build one that was bigger. Children, houses, number of horses or automobiles, it didn't matter. They were always one-upping each other or trying to—and then sending long letters about their accomplishments or finding a way to rub each other's face in their perceived victory. Cecilia took it harder than Edith did when her mother died. There was no one left to challenge, no one to measure herself against. Her aunt had never got over her anger that her sister had gone and died on her, leaving her alone in the world in an oversized house that she had no need of, and from the looks of things, could not care for on her own. The house was starting to show the wear of age with flaking paint, rotted boards on the porch, and shingles tossed about in the yard like worthless poker chips.

The old woman leaned in toward Edith and studied her close. "Have you grown, child?" Her eyes were foggy and glazed over, in need of glasses that were nowhere to be seen.

Edith smiled, warmed by her aunt's words. She let her guard down, felt compassion for the old woman. "No, not for a long time."

"You were tall and slender. Benefits of not bearing children."

The smile faded from Edith's face. It seemed her family was quick to point out her failures, her tragedies, no matter how distant in the past they were. Her aunt, her sisters, even her mother when she was alive, held it against her that she didn't bring a child into the world to carry on the lineage. She should have known better than to have felt sorry for Cecilia. She knew she should have left her feelings locked in the automobile. "Do you mind if I come in and stay the night?"

"The night?"

"Yes, I'll be on my way first thing in the morning. Surely you have a bed to spare. I won't be a bother, I promise."

"Of course, I have beds. There are nine of them." Cecilia looked past Edith into the coming night. A slight gust of wind wrapped around their legs, appearing out of nowhere as if to encourage the old woman, or remind her that the house was lonely, a weight around her neck, and all that waited for her was silence and the tick tock of mortality echoing in the grand foyer. "Tell me," she said, "can you cook an omelet like your mother used to? I've been craving a decent breakfast like the ones she cooked for me. Can you do that?"

"Why, yes, I can. I most certainly can," Edith said. Her mother had taught her how to cook all of her recipes; omelets, beet biscuits, chicken croquettes, and corn fritters being her most favorite.

"Well, come on in then. It won't hurt if you stay one night. But only one night, mind you. I can't be bothered with someone underfoot, you understand. There's not enough to go around as it is."

"Yes, ma'am. Just one night. I promise." Edith leaned down and picked up her small suitcase, which held her clothes and the Smith & Wesson. She glanced over her shoulder to make sure she wasn't being watched. Satisfied that the cowboy wasn't hiding in the bushes spying on her, or following her, for that matter, she walked across the threshold and entered the cavernous Victorian house that had been built in 1891. Her uncle had been a successful businessman at the Fort Worth Stockyards. He'd dealt in cattle in one way or another and had a knack for reading the markets. The house was in the best part of Fort Worth, sat on three-quarters of an acre, with nine bedrooms, a wraparound porch, and a porte cochere that was set off by a circular drive in front. A four-stall carriage house stood beyond the arched entrance. Edith had helped herself to an empty stall and stowed the Pierce Arrow out of sight.

A Juliette staircase welcomed Edith in the entryway; two opposing curved staircases with a balcony in the center that overlooked the oak double-doors and white marble floors. Edith and her sisters had played on the stairs long ago, in what seemed another age. The entryway had looked like the mouth to a giant cathedral then, and that hadn't changed. There *had been* a lot of parties held in the house. Edith and her family had been guests at more than one of the shindigs, as Cecilia had called them. But that all changed when death came calling for her uncle, like it had Henry, on a normal day, unannounced, unexpected, changing the world into a different place for everyone. Her aunt had not accepted widowhood any easier than Edith had.

"Not a thing has changed," Edith said.

"Everything changes. This house used to be alive. Now it creaks and groans so loud I think it will fall down on me while I sleep. It will someday. Me and Old Ben, my colored boy whose been lookin' after things, are all that's left of any of us. You remember Old Ben? Him and his wife, Bessie, held this place together, though I wouldn't never say that out loud in polite company. Can't give coloreds too much credit or folks get suspicious of you. Bessie done died on us, too. Old Ben is as blind as a cave-dwelling dog, and about as useless. But I can't toss him out on the street now, can I? Who would build my fires for me? Are you cold?" Cecilia craned her neck again like she was inspecting Edith for a second time, to make sure she was who she said she was. "You aren't in any trouble, are you?"

"Why would you ask that?"

"Why wouldn't I?"

Edith didn't answer. She just stood there with her suitcase in her hand, waiting for her Aunt Cecilia to finish her litany of questions and show her some hospitality. That took a while, no matter the occasion, whether there was an invitation or not. The ornate grandfather clock ticked behind her, and the blanket of night covered the outside of the house. The crystal chandelier that hung overhead had been electrified, but only half of the lights burned and offered any light. Her Aunt Cecilia's world was no different than Edith's: dim and growing dimmer by the minute. Both women had their own reasons to fear the dark.

Sleep didn't come to Edith like she'd thought it would. The room was drafty, and the night air had a chill to it that would not go away. A thin layer of dust had congregated on the top of the bed and every other piece of furniture in the room, including the floor, quilts, and sheets, smelled musty and were brittle to the touch. Edith's footprints tracked across the dull hardwoods. They were the first sign of human existence in the tight room in ages. Mice scrambled through the walls, scratching and sniffing, disturbed by the interloper. More dust had been added to the floor when Edith had shaken the quilt of debris and wiped off the rotting sheets with her handkerchief. It wasn't a pleasant room, though it had been at one time when the brass bed had been shiny and the floral wallpaper was new, not faded and peeling like it was now. There had been a staff, six coloreds managed by Bessie and Ben, to keep everything neat and clean in the massive Victorian. Those days were a memory as fragile as the sheets, as desperate as the floor under Edith's feet. Still, the room was a better place to sleep than in the Pierce, hidden off the road, fearing every sound was the cowboy come to keep his promise. She could only hope that the cook and waitress in Thompson's Café had subdued the man, kept him contained until the police had arrived. She could only hope she wasn't being preyed upon.

Edith stared out of the corner window in the dark, the bare

overhead bulb switched off, watching the street in front of the house for any movement, any shadow that looked like it might be a threat. The Smith & Wesson was within reach, sitting on top of a small, wobbly writing desk, in wait. The gun was close by, inches away from her hand. Her fingers were magnets aching for a new appendage to attach itself. Cold steel warming in her hand gave her peace and comfort. She hated that feeling.

Satisfied that the night was silent, that there was no madman lurking in the bushes, lying in wait to enter the house and do her harm, Edith sat down on the single mattress, put her face in her hands, and breathed as deep as she could. There were no tears. Crying wouldn't help. She knew that. Nothing would help except moving forward, arriving at her destination. She was too far from home to turn around, and too close to Wellington not to finish her journey. It would be foolish to stop now. All she wanted was to be with Sonny, feel his warmth, the safety of his presence, the comfort of his purpose. Sonny knew the world she had found herself in. He would know what to do, what to say, how to keep her fears subdued. *He would protect her.* That thought provoked the first tear to ease out of the corner of Edith's eye, and she knew she could not tolerate any more tears to manifest and multiply. She had to do something. So, she stood and squared her shoulders like she was getting ready to walk into a boxing ring, then exhaled as deep as she could, forbidding the tears to drop to the floor. The mice in the walls went quiet. The wind outside settled. Silence engulfed the ten by ten bedroom that felt more like a tomb, or a trap, from which there was no escape.

"No one can protect you," she said aloud, soft like she was whispering in a baby's ear. "Sonny can't save you. No one can. You have to save yourself." The whisper fell to the floor without disturbing any dust, but it echoed in the room and found its way back into Edith's heart, finally allowing her some rest. The day had exhausted her.

Walking into the kitchen was like walking into a different house. It was bright and cheery, the walls painted a fresh yellow, the color dimmer than the Pierce, but still bright, a shock to Edith's eyes. The smell of brewing coffee greeted her nose. A blue enamel pot sat on the eight-burner stove, the lid jiggling with pressure. The clatter was regular, in time, like a clock's tick. An old black man, Ben, his hair a field of pure white cotton balls, stood hovering over the stove with his back to the kitchen door where Edith stood. Some of the best meals she'd ever eaten had come out of this kitchen.

"Have a seat, Miss Edith. I'll have your coffee ready in a minute. You still take it with a drop of cream?" He hadn't turned around, signaled in any way that he was aware of her presence. It was like he had eyes in the back of his head. The man's voice, strong and healthy, startled Edith. She jumped inside her skin.

"Yes, Ben, that would be nice. You have a remarkable memory."

Ben grabbed the handle of the coffee pot, faced Edith with a wide ivory smile, and poured the steaming hot coffee into a waiting pink-and-white Wedgwood china cup. "My memory is not as good as it used to be, Miss Edith. It is a great pleasure to see you again."

Ben spoke with an elegance that warmed Edith's soul. His voice reverberated through her own memory like background music in the house. Never harsh, always calm, with an expected perfection that would never be equal to his employers, but as refined, if not more.

Edith walked to the preparation table that sat between the stove and the door. She looked at his deep brown eyes and searched for a sign of blindness that her aunt had spoken of the night before. His eyes, like her aunt's, looked clouded and yellowed with time, but Ben didn't seem hindered by the lack of sight.

"It is a pleasure to see you as well, Ben. How are you these days? Aunt Cecilia told me you were blind and riddled with the affliction of old age."

He was dressed for the day, and wore a white long-sleeved starched shirt, black pants with a perfect crease, and black shoes to match that looked like they had been dipped in lacquer. Ben was shorter than Edith by a good six inches and did not look too frail other than he was a little hunched over, his arms skinny as a cat's leg. His face was clean-shaven, free of wrinkles or any other presence of a lethal ailment.

"Ma'am thinks everyone is almost blind because she is," Ben said, dropping his tone so his words were a shared secret between the two of them. He had called Aunt Cecilia *Ma'am* and nothing else. That had not changed.

"I was sorry to hear about Bessie," Edith said.

Ben smiled wistfully. "She has gone on before me to prepare the way. We sang her home in a beautiful ceremony. I was sorry you weren't at her funeral. You would have enjoyed it."

"I'm sorry, I wasn't informed." The offer of an invitation to Bessie's funeral caused a warm smile to flash across Edith's face. She knew the funeral would have been held at the Allen Chapel A.M.E. Church on Elm Street, a tall, square yellowish brick Tudor Gothic Revival style building that she had stood outside of as a little girl on a stolen Sunday morning, listening to the singers wail their praises to heaven. The music was joyful and made her tap her feet on the outside pavement. She'd told Old Ben how moved she'd been by the expression of faith she had heard. She hadn't been allowed to step foot inside the church but found her way there out of curiosity. It was one of the few times she'd faced a tongue lashing from her father after he'd discovered where Edith had disappeared to.

Ben handed Edith her cup of coffee. "Just how you like it." He waited for her to accept the cup and take a sip before he said, "I hear you're in some kind of trouble. Is there anything I can do to help you?"

"What kind of trouble is it that you think I am in?" Edith said, as she sat the cup on the table.

"Ma'am said trouble is all. That's not true?"

"Not entirely. But I didn't tell her anything of the woes that follow me. She would have had plenty to say, said it was foolish for a woman to be on the road all alone these days. I might have agreed with that. The world *is* a dangerous place. I knew that, was shown it in a horrible way before I left Huntsville, but I wasn't aware that madness and evil had taken over every corner of every town along the way. I would have made this journey anyway if someone would have told me. There is something I need to understand about where I stand in the world."

"That does not sound like the kind of trouble I feared you were in," Old Ben said.

"What kind of trouble is that?"

"I feared you'd lost everything like the rest of us have. It sounds like you're searching for something instead of leaving something behind."

"Maybe a little of both," Edith said. "Maybe a little of both."

CHAPTER SEVENTEEN

The headlights of Sonny's truck sliced through the early darkness like a sharp knife cutting through tender beef. Swirls of sand had drifted across the farm-to-market road that led out of Wellington, slowing Sonny's trip home more than he would have liked. Blue stared out of the window, stoic, quiet, content to be inside instead of in the bed of the truck, suffering the weather. The window was cracked about an inch from the top, allowing a cold breeze to circulate air inside the cab, helping to keep Sonny awake. It had been a long day in town. Not what he had planned on at all. It could have been longer if he would have gone out to the Hernandez place, but when it came to that fork in the road, Sonny had chosen to take everyone's advice and stay out of whatever it was that was going on. Jesse was more than capable of handling himself anyway. The boy had proven himself in tough situations more than once.

Sonny had to slow the truck again to navigate another wall of dust storm residue piled in the middle of the road. There was nothing left for a lot of poor dirt farmers to toil in, to make a living with, but there were still productive cotton fields dotted around the county, allowing some farmers, like the Harmesons, to carve out a living, if it could be called that. January was hard on everyone, but farmers saw the worst of it, living off of last year's crop if there was any profit at all, and hoping for a better crop in the year to come.

The truck lurched through the pile of sand, and Sonny sputtered on toward home. He slowed again as he passed by the circus, curious if Jonesy had found what he was looking for, if Heck Kilbride had shown himself, proving the sheriff wrong and Sonny right. The way things were, Jonesy wouldn't admit to being wrong if Heck Kilbride tapped him on the shoulder and asked him to dance.

A dim glow emitted from inside the big top, making the giant tent look like an eerie jack-o'-lantern at Halloween, beckoning fearful thoughts and spooky dreams. Sonny thought about stopping and talking to Frances and Milton, but he didn't. He'd had enough of other people's troubles for one day the way it was. He pressed on, taking notice of the Harmeson house as he passed by. It was a typical two-story farmhouse with a chicken coop and a couple of barns dotted around the property. The house, like most of the rest of the houses in the county, was in dire need of a whitewash, but that would have been a waste of time and money as long as the dusters roared across the land peppering the siding with enough force to skin the wood down a layer or two. Nobody had enough time or money the way it was to make things look nice.

Sonny didn't want any trouble to befall any of the Harmesons. They'd struggled enough. But it was hard to tell what would happen, or what had happened with one of the daughters. Sounded like a typical falling out to Sonny. A girl in a middle of two boys, Clyde and Leo Dozier. Only Clyde was no normal boy, and Leo had lost his spot in the CCC camp and taken a good beating from the sound of it. And Rafael Hernandez had somehow gotten himself stuck in the middle of everything. All Sonny could do was hope that the mess would work out and drive on home. Everyone was right. He didn't need the trouble. But it wasn't that easy for him. He felt guilty about leaving everything behind, about not being able to help Aldo. That was the worst of it. Leaving things undone wasn't his way—at least in the past, when he had been whole, a Ranger, a man with a purpose. He was none of that now.

Once he was at home, Sonny stopped the truck, shut off the engine, and opened the driver's door. Blue jumped across his lap and dashed outside before he could say stop. He wouldn't have anyway. The dog had been stuck inside the truck most all day without a complaint of any kind.

Blue barked and skittered about on his three good legs, sniffing all of his familiar places. If anything had been out of place, he would have alerted Sonny right away. There was little to steal. No chickens to filch, no goats to run off with. Anything worth taking was inside, and the value of whatever it was only meant something to Sonny: letters, pictures, his pa's Peacemaker, that kind of thing. His house was bare of trinkets, collectibles, and money in the mattress. He had a little money at the First National Bank. He trusted it as much as any other. Most all of the banks these days posted their financial conditions in the *Leader*. Transparency they called it, so people could see for themselves what solvency meant. A thief would have been mighty disappointed if they broke into Sonny's house expecting a haul of some kind. Even the icebox was thin of food.

Stiff from the day, Sonny pulled himself out of the cab, stood as tall as he could, and grabbed the box of food from the Vallance Grocery. He balanced the box in the crook of his prosthesis and held onto it with his good hand.

The cold night air struck him in the face and invaded his lungs as he nudged the truck door closed with his side. He coughed, unprepared for the drop in temperature. A shiver ran up his spine and he wished he had a glove for his left hand. The hook was forever cold, one less thing to worry about keeping warm. At least he couldn't feel the steel appendage. Winter nights in the Panhandle could get freezing cold with the offer of snow throughout the season. None of that kind of weather was in the forecast. A blizzard would have been welcome if it would quench the thirst of the dry ground.

Sonny didn't move away from the truck. He stood there in the darkness, allowing his eyes to adjust, watching Blue celebrate his freedom and relief at being home. Sonny wished he could share in the joy. Coming home, even when Martha had been alive and Jesse was a boy, had never been easy, or welcoming.

The star-studded sky reached over his head and went on for as far as the eye could see. It was a massive black dome of nothingness, splattered with pulsing silver dots. There were no clouds to be seen and the moon had not risen yet. Whatever roamed the earth stayed silent, kept to itself. There were no dogs barking, no coyotes yipping, in the distance. Even the wind was weak, like it had lost its voice. The dust storm might as well have blown every living thing into the next county or beyond. Sonny was confronted with an empty house, an empty life with him and Blue to assure each other that they were still alive. *There was a benefit to living in town,* Sonny thought to himself. A benefit to the sounds of commerce, or people's troubles, even if they were confounding, like Jonesy's sudden turn to anger and mistrust, or the circus folks all gathered together to share a meal of weak broth and the commonality of never being home, being perpetual strangers, looked down on as less than, or worse, as freaks. At least they weren't alone. At least they all had someone, even if they didn't get along, like Frances and Milton. Feeling sorry for himself was something new to Sonny, or maybe he had never admitted it to himself or anyone else, that he allowed such a thing. Maybe he had been judging his own life harshly, as empty and pointless, for longer than he cared to admit. Maybe there were worse things than being alone, but Sonny couldn't think of anything—and that surprised him.

Sonny made his way to the mailbox, navigating his way in part from memory, and the rest with vision that had settled into the night. Canned meat, pork and beans, and peas all clanked together, rising into the cold air, then riding on it, announcing that there was something moving in the night. Blue followed along, crunching on the dry ground, wading through piles of sand without any trouble at all. Disappointment greeted Sonny when he found the mailbox empty. He yearned to find another letter from Edith, but there was none. There was nothing but a thin layer of dirt in the bottom of the box. No correspondence, no bills to pay, nothing with his name on it. One more reminder that he lived on the edge of the earth where few dared to tread.

"Come on, boy, let's go inside and get us some dinner," Sonny said to Blue. The dog wagged its thin tail and followed Sonny to the door.

The house smelled of fried Spam and fresh baked biscuits. A small Franklin woodstove sat in the front room with an easy fire blazing inside it, warming the house the best it could. The bedroom was the coldest room in the house, leaving Sonny to cover himself with a pile of quilts on long winter nights. Other nights, he fell asleep in the soft chair next to the stove with his clothes on and his shoes on his feet. There was no one to rouse him, to offer him comfort in the feather bed. On this night, though, he was wide awake as the clock ticked toward the darkest part of the hour. There was nothing worth listening to on the radio. Some new program called *The Intimate Revue* with a fella named Bob Hope. Singing, jokes, and Chevrolet commercials held no interest to Sonny. The Atwater Kent radio was turned off. His mind was still rooted in the day, toiling over the events like a laborer set on meeting a quota of some kind. The troubles in town and at the circus were a ditch he couldn't quit digging no matter how hard he tried to stop.

Blue lay in front of the Franklin, comfortable and satisfied after a bowl of table scraps, and what remained of Sonny's dinner. The wind outside had intensified, battering against the house, forcing its way inside through the cracks around the windows and under the door. It was either weather, sand, or insects trying to get inside, trying to take over the house no matter the season. Keeping them all out was a constant battle, one Sonny would have surrendered to if he could have found it in himself to live with bugs and dirt. The remnants of life with Martha held on strong. He wasn't near as neat as she was, but he couldn't tolerate living in a mess, either. He might not have had much, but there was no call to live in filth; he wasn't dirty as his dead wife used to say, he was lazy. Sonny saw it another way. He wasn't ambitious, had never had any desire to be a leader of men. He had preferred to ride alone. It had been that way since he was a child. An only child. His mother had died in childbirth and his father had never remarried and had more children like most men did when their wives died. Maybe he was like that, too, a one-woman man, regardless of the gauge of happiness. Though he couldn't say there was a lot of love shared between him and Martha. Their union was more a duty than anything else. They had agreed to be married, and so they were until the day she died.

Agitated, Sonny walked to the window a dozen times, looking toward the Harmesons' place with a window or two aglow, dim and uninviting. It was like looking at a ship far out at sea, or in Galveston Bay, a place he had been to more than once in his life but had no inclination to return to.

He couldn't see the big top from where he stood, either. There was no out-of-place giant pumpkin on the horizon, no sign of it at all. He wondered if they'd left under the cover of night like Bob Suggs had suggested they would. It would have served them well, getting out of Collingsworth County, leaving

Jonesy to his own problems, and not be blamed for anything else that they didn't do. He hoped nobody's chickens or cows had gone missing after the storm. The bearded lady and the tall man would be accused of stealing them, too.

Sonny wasn't sure what he was looking for. Answers about Heck, Leo, Rafael, and the Harmeson girl, or something else. Something that still didn't sit right. The change in Jonesy. The rumors swirling around town about the circus people. Jesse leaving for Amarillo, and the closure of the Ranger office in Wellington. His distress was all of that, and more. He didn't like being attached to the trouble that involved Heck Kilbride, and he felt protective of Frances Avalon and the rest of the circus folks. They had made him feel comfortable. That had been a surprise. He would have never thought he would have felt like he belonged around people like that, but he had.

He tore himself from the window and walked to the middle of the room. He had no desire to turn the radio on and fill the house with pointless noise from some variety show or more bad news, if he could get any good reception at all. It was too early to climb into bed, though the day had made him feel like he had been dragged through the trenches. He was by himself, which was no different than it ever was, only now, for some reason, Sonny was uncomfortable inside his own skin. Blue was not enough company. He needed something more than the dog's devotion and constant presence. He needed another human being. More than anything else, he needed someone he could talk to, someone he could trust, someone he could be himself with. That was a rare need. The circus had stirred something in him awake, but it was more than that. As much as he liked those people, he knew they would move on. Edith Grantley, on the other hand, was in Huntsville waiting to hear from him, waiting for him to show up and pick up where they had left off.

There were a lot of miles between Wellington and Huntsville, and Sonny wasn't about to jump in his truck at this late hour and tackle that drive in the dark on an impetuous whim. The second he thought about such a thing, doubt crept into his mind and soul. He was a one-armed old man with nothing in front of him but a single lane road to death. Whatever waited for him beyond that was anybody's guess. Sonny held little sway in religion, in the words of revival tent preachers, who were as itinerant as circus performers, and less reliable. Heaven was for the hopeful, and in his life, seeing all the evil, harmful things humans could do to each other as he had, he'd lost that hope in people one drop at a time—like an empty crankcase leaking oil until the engine locked and quit running. There would be no trip to Huntsville on this night. Maybe never. No time soon for certain. With Edith on his mind, he made his way over to the desk that sat next to the radio, grabbed the latest letter from her, and ran the envelope under his nose. There was still a hint of her smell, or the scent she had applied to the paper, he wasn't sure which. The letter was the first thing that had given him any real comfort since he had returned home.

He knew that the best thing he could do was sit down and write Edith another letter. Writing the last one had comforted him, made him feel connected to the woman. He didn't want to lose that feeling, even though it was a foreign and uninvited feeling.

Sonny Burton
RR #1, Box 78
Wellington, Texas
January 15, 1935

Dear Edith,

    I have decided to make friends of this Olivetti. I am not deluded enough to think that I will ever become a master typist with only five fingers and a pointed hook, but it seems worth the effort to practice on this contraption so I can communicate with the ones who matter to me.

I apologize if this letter is a quick follow-up to the one I wrote to you yesterday. A lot has happened since then, and of all of the people in the world, you were, and are, the only one I want to share my day with. I was tempted to jump in the truck and drive to you, but that would have been foolish at this late hour. It is also too late to bother the Harmesons to use their telephone to call you, though I may attempt that in the morning. It would be a comfort to hear your voice on this weary night. So, I am left with this, typing a letter one mark at a time, hunting and pecking like a chicken for feed on the dry ground. I hope you don't mind.

I have told you that I have not been much of a letter writer in my life, so this act is not natural to me. It seems that you have that effect on me. I wasn't much of a dancer, either, until I met you. For some reason, the thought of that night still makes me blush like I did when I was a boy. That I lay in your arms, too. I haven't felt young in a long time. I regret leaving you in Huntsville by yourself. You have your house and your boarders to keep you busy, but I wish more than anything that you were here by my side. Is that too forward? I think you asked me the same question.

I was reminded more than once today that I am not from Wellington, and that has distressed me more than I thought it might. I have lived in this house, in this county, for a long time. I have tried to live a quiet life here. It was my refuge on returning home from France. Not long after separating from the army, I rejoined the Rangers—what else was I going to do?—and they sent me here. Duty drove me here, and I have been here longer than I have been anywhere else in my life. It felt like I had roots here. Like I was something more than a stranger passing through town. I was a one-man operation for most of those years, like the Rangers in Abilene, Amarillo, and other towns covered by Company C. In those days, I was no different than most fellas who had returned from the war. Solemn, stunned, and haunted by the sights and deeds of slaughter. I saw the worst any man could do to another, all because governments could not get along and settle peace between them. I have begun to wonder if man is at his most natural when he is fighting another man.

It was to Wellington that I came, along with Martha and Jesse, to live out the rest of my life. I had nowhere else to go. I wanted to be a part of this town, but I guess in the end, to be from a place you have to be born there, have your people buried in the cemetery there, and have been a child there. None of that applies to me in Wellington, except one. Martha is buried here. I visit her grave on Decoration Day and no other. I will never be able to claim Wellington as my own, and that realization has been slow in arriving. It dawned on me today.

I think that is one of the reasons why I hesitated to stay in Huntsville. Not only did I have a house in Wellington, but I knew little of what is in that city. It would be starting all over again, and in the end, the result would be the same as it is here. I would be an outsider in Huntsville, too. There are as many ghosts in your house as there are mine. What happened with Billy will always be there, and I'm not sure I could live with that day after day. And the same would be true for you here. My life with Martha is everywhere you look. Her ghost is in the choices of furniture, in the dishes she kept, and in every nook and cranny of this house. I have yet to clean out her wardrobe.

Her clothes still hang where they were the day she died. How could I expect you to come here and make a new life for yourself, with me, with my past, in a place I do not truly belong?

I am sorry if I am rambling on. It is late into the night now. It has taken me hours to write this much to you, but after the day I have had, I felt like I must confront my melancholy and share its existence with you—though I have done that before. You saw my gray mood, my anxious moments, as I paced in your parlor trying to outthink Billy Bunson. I was at a loss, and I let you see that side of myself—because you wanted to see it. Because you cared enough to watch, to be there for me in a way no other woman has been in a long time, if ever. I should hesitate in saying such a thing to you, but I don't. We are both deep into the winter of our lives. The days are short, and the nights are long. We do not have time to address a cordial reality. Our time together showed me that. I am a fool for driving away, for leaving you behind. I wish it wasn't true. I want you to understand that I see that now.

My day, dear God, my day has been long, lonely, and confusing. I wish you were here. That need and that want surprises me. I hope you are there when I call you. I would like nothing more than to hear your voice and dance under the moon.

Sincerely,
Sonny

CHAPTER EIGHTEEN

The scream of an ambulance's siren stirred Sonny from a deep sleep. At first, he thought he was dreaming, stirred by the memory of the passing circus, but a rapid series of eye blinks told him that this was no dream; the scream was a siren. He was awake, lying on his back in his bed, staring at the ceiling, with his ears tuned to the distance. His stump was cold, exposed to the open air from the lack of a shirt. A thin blanket had been kicked off onto the floor sometime during the night. Sleep had come to him in fits. The siren's wail had a distinct, recognizable series of notes to it. Two high, one low, repeated over and over again. The siren was mounted on top of a black panel truck that also served as a hearse for Wellington's deceased. The wavering shout kept rolling through his eardrums but was distant and fading.

Blue stood at the window, the curtains pushed aside by his long nose. He growled low as his body held still, muscles tense, his head moving side to side like he was trying to see across the field, to see what was going on. The siren was far away, but close enough to penetrate the walls of the frame house. Sonny didn't live on the edge of the world like he had thought. One day there was an elephant outside his front door, now there was an ambulance—which could not be good news for someone. Harm had come visiting close by. Too close.

Sonny sat in the bed, triangulating the wavering sound in his mind, figuring out where it was going. It didn't take long to figure out that the ambulance was heading towards the Harmesons or the big top, if the circus people were still camped out there.

He jumped out of the bed and made his way over to the window, joining Blue in his curiosity, in his fear that something was wrong. A slight rise in the land prevented him from seeing anything other than the Harmeson farmhouse. He was too far away to tell what was going on. If he wanted to be sure, he'd have to go find out for himself. He had a phone call to Edith he wanted to make anyway.

As he turned to start getting dressed, the siren stopped, and silence returned to the house. The windup clock on the nightstand said it was seven-thirty in the morning, but it ran a few minutes behind, or wasn't reliable at all if Sonny forgot to wind the damned thing. It didn't matter what time it was anyway— something was going on and he needed to find out what that something was.

The first thing he did was slide on the prosthesis. Everyday use had made the contraption easier and quicker to put on. The movements through the straps was almost mindless. Tightening the buckles once they were closed was the hard part, especially when Sonny was in a hurry. Everything came together in a rush, allowing him to feel a little more normal, able to put on his ribbed undershirt, then his long-sleeved work shirt. He had another little contraption to help him button the buttons, a dowel rod with a small hook on it that allowed him to slip the buttons through their holes. His speed at that task was improving, too, but he knew if he had two hands, like most men did, he would have already been dressed and out the door. It was a good thing nothing was on fire inside the house.

"Come on, Blue," Sonny said, after dressing and pulling his boots on. The dog was still at the window. He wagged his tail and did what he was told, following Sonny on his heels.

Sonny reached for his latest letter to Edith, which was already in an envelope with a three-cent stamp on it, and stuck it in his breast pocket. He didn't like to be in a hurry, but something deep inside him told him that he needed to be. Like that something told him he would need his father's 1873 Colt Army Revolver. He snatched the pistol off the table and headed out of the room. His coat and hat hung by the door, and he captured them with his hook as he passed and stuffed the Colt in the coat's deep pocket. Cold, morning air welcomed him as he exited the house. Blue barked and sped past Sonny, then found a place to hike his leg on one of the clothesline poles.

Sonny kept moving, his eyes focused on the Harmeson house in the distance. There was nothing to see, nothing to hear. No smoke, no sirens. Silence had returned to the house and the fields that surrounded it. If there were birdsongs welcoming the day, Sonny couldn't hear them. Nothing stirred. The ambulance had drawn every living thing's attention to it. Coyotes hunkered down in the bushes and the crows watched from the treetops, hoping for an opportunity to feed.

Sonny threw down the tailgate on the truck and Blue took a run, angling toward his target with the full power of his three good legs. The bad one slowed him a bit, but the dog had learned to compensate for his disability and used it for balance. He yelped sometimes when he jumped and landed, but not this time. He was as ready to go as Sonny was.

Sonny closed the tailgate and hurried to the cab of the truck, settled himself inside, and started the hand and foot dance that was needed to start the Model A. The motor fired right away, and Sonny tore out onto the road—forgetting to put the letter in the mailbox for Clifford to post. "Dag gone it," he said aloud, when he realized halfway down the road that the letter was still in his pocket.

It didn't take long before the Harmeson place came into

view. He was relieved that the ambulance wasn't parked in front of the simple farmhouse. Sonny almost slowed and considered the possibility that he had been dreaming when he'd heard the siren. But he kept going, maintaining his speed even as he passed by the vacant, sleeping big top. The ambulance wasn't there, either. Another relief. And no one was milling about, which Sonny found odd at first. Any normal crowd of people would have been curious about the siren. But the circus folks were not normal people. The law and services of proper society—like ambulances—brought trouble to them, not rescue, as far as Sonny knew. They were looking out of the tent's creases and holes, like the coyotes watching from the brush.

As Sonny came over the rise past the circus he slowed down. The road was blocked with the ambulance, a brown and tan sheriff's automobile, and another automobile that looked like Jesse's vehicle.

At first, Sonny didn't see anything unusual. Fallow cotton fields sat on both sides of the road for as far as he could see. Wind breaks populated with pecan groves, oak mottes, and lines of tall, dormant cottonwoods stood against the horizon. Closer to Sonny was another small collection of trees, a few more live oaks with wide branching arms reaching out from thick trunks, along with some smaller hardwood trees, hickories, and some wild cherry, situated alongside a dirt path, wide enough to get a truck down, that led to the old Dickerson family cemetery. Tilted pioneer gravestones bleached white by their years under the sun, almost unreadable, poked into the distant sky like a mouth full of decaying teeth.

Sonny pulled in behind Jesse's beige Plymouth sedan as his mouth dried into sandpaper. He took a double take to make sure he was seeing what he thought he was seeing: A man hanging from the tree, his feet a good fifteen feet from the ground, his neck twisted to the side. There was no question that he was dead. This was no page out of the newspaper, but a real lynching come to Collingsworth County. It wasn't the first hanged man Sonny had ever seen.

"You stay here," Sonny said to Blue as he angled himself out of the truck and headed toward a small crowd of men, looking at the hanged man like it was a horse that had somehow got itself stuck there.

"What are you doin' here, Pa?" Jesse said, as Sonny approached.

Jonesy stood next to Jesse, along with Hal Buckworth, the ambulance driver, coroner, and one of the two local morticians. Buckworth was tall, dressed in his normal work clothes, black trousers, white shirt, and a long black overcoat, and no hat. His hair, about the color of Jesse's Plymouth, was untouched for the day. He looked put together about as much as Sonny was, called out of bed by the tragedy before them. Buckworth should have been more used to it than Sonny, but it didn't look like it. The mortician's shirt was buttoned wrong, off-kilter; he hadn't noticed, or hadn't taken the time to button the shirt the right way if he had.

"Heard the siren," Sonny said. "I feared it was something at the Harmeson place or something gone wrong at the circus tent."

Neither Jonesy nor the coroner made any motion to welcome Sonny into the crowd. Both men ignored Sonny, gave off an air like they didn't want to acknowledge his presence; noses to the wind, still eyeing the hanged man like they couldn't believe what they were seeing.

"It ain't the circus," Jesse said.

"Unless they's involved," Jonesy interjected. He couldn't help himself and the tension in his face and on his shoulders said as much.

Sonny exhaled, appreciative this was the sheriff's worry and not his. Jesse's, too, if Jonesy asked him to be involved. That was the way things worked with the Texas Rangers. The county sheriff had to ask for their assistance. Unless the new governor had changed things. That was possible for all Sonny knew. He wasn't paying any attention to Ranger business these days unless it involved Jesse.

He looked at the hanging man, since he was closer now, doing his best to figure out if he knew who it was. That didn't take much figuring. The man had sun-bronzed skin that would stay brown no matter the season. Black oily hair hung forward, bangs obscuring eyes frozen into a stare. His clothes were threadbare, and one of his shoes was off; his toes pointed to the ground. Even from a distance, Sonny knew the man, and he found that to be unfortunate. This man was kin to Aldo.

"That's Rafael Hernandez," Sonny said. "How in the hell did they get him up there?"

"Hard to say, but you're right. That's Rafael," Jonesy said, turning his attention to Sonny.

"He was safer in your jail." Sonny took his hat off, held it against his chest in respect for the dead, then looked to the ground instead of at Jonesy. A bit of anger showed a sign of life behind his ears. He felt the heat in them instead of the cool air he'd expected.

"Why in the hell do you think he was in jail? I was tryin' to keep him safe. Then you and Aldo started poking around making a fuss. I had no choice but to put him back out into the world on his own."

"Don't go blamin' this on me," Sonny said, putting his hat back on, taking a step toward the sheriff.

Jesse put his arm out and stopped Sonny's forward motion. "Pa," Jesse said in his stern Ranger voice. Sonny would have been proud any other time, but not now. He didn't push past Jesse, but he balled his fist on his left hand. His right bicep tensed, too, but the hook showed no sign of emotion or action. It never would.

"I was protectin' that spic, Sonny Burton," Jonesy said. "Regardless of what you think. I'm as upset by what I see as you are. If not more." The sheriff was tense as a little cow dog going after a bull's ankle.

Hal Buckworth stood still, the tails of his black overcoat waving in the breeze, minding his own business. It looked like he was trying to figure out how to get the body down from the tree and hadn't come across an acceptable method yet.

Sonny exhaled and looked away from Jonesy. The only reason he decided to back down was his personal history with the sheriff. Sonny had liked Jonesy. Respected him. But the situation that had erupted over the past few days had made him question how well he really knew the man and his morals. The fact that Jonesy admitted that he was protecting Rafael helped Sonny to see there was more going on, like he had thought there was. "You couldn't keep Rafael in jail forever. Not with Leo Dozier walking around with a few scrapes and bruises. It would have been different if Rafael would have killed Dozier, but he didn't. It was plain as day that you were holding Rafael for another reason."

"I needed more time to figure out what Clyde was doing," Jonesy said. "Clyde and Heck Kilbride. I knew they wasn't out to do no good, and I had to be careful how I went about findin' that out, you old fool. Once you stuck your nose in this, I knew you'd get Jesse involved, then who knew what would happen? It would have been out of my control. The last thing I needed was the whole town seein' that I asked a Mexican to snitch on my own family. That'd be the end of me with my family and my position as sheriff. Who's gonna vote for a man who betrays their kin with a spic?"

"They're going to figure it out now," Sonny said. "Seems to

me this worked out the way it was meant to anyway. Clyde's at the CCC camp. That was most likely their aim, wasn't it? Sending in Rafael worked out for them. Dozier didn't get hurt too bad. But this? This doesn't look good for Heck."

"He disappeared remember," Jonesy said.

"If that's what happened. Sounds like one of Heck's sleight of hands to me," Sonny said.

"I'd normally agree with you, Sonny. This lynchin' makes Heck's disappearance suspect, and when he does show his face, he better have one hell of an alibi. But there's more to it," he said, motioning to Jesse and Sonny. "Clyde never arrived at the CCC camp. Nobody can tell us where he's at, either. I got one dead man, and two men in the county missin'. Clyde went missin' before Heck did. You and the folks on the square was the last ones to see Heck before he disappeared. He headed out of town towards home and that was it. There ain't no sign of him nowheres. He ain't buried in no sand mound from what I can tell. I got men all over the county lookin' for them both. And now this."

"Why in the hell did you send Rafael into that hornet's nest in the first place?" Sonny said. "You had to be certain that no good would come of it."

"I done told you," Jonesy answered. "I set a snitch on my own family. Rafael was the last person they would suspect was workin' for me. You're aware how those things go, Sonny. Rafael got himself in a little trouble a few years back, and me and him worked out a deal. I let him walk free, but he had to give me the goods from inside the Mexican side of town. I didn't have no way of hearin' what they was doin' over there. Any of them. I needed a way in, and the opportunity with Rafael presented itself to me. That worked out fine for a time. He told me some things that helped me keep the peace. When I started gettin' a drift that Heck and Clyde was plottin' somethin' I figured . . .

well, you know what I figured. I didn't want them boys to fear I was on to them."

"About a snitch in position in the CCC camp?" Sonny said. "That doesn't sound like something you'd risk getting Rafael beaten for. You had to speculate that it was a possibility he'd get hurt. Especially with Heck Kilbride involved. That boy's a class A bully. There's more to this, Jonesy. What were Heck and Clyde planning that got your attention?"

The sheriff rocked back on his heels and looked past Sonny. The rumble of a couple of automobile engines greeted Sonny's ears at about the same time. The ambulance and the collection of the four men had started to draw a crowd.

Sonny glanced over his shoulder to the road. Two black Model A Fords had pulled off the road to see what was going on. He didn't recognize the drivers, couldn't see them well enough to determine who they were for sure. It didn't matter. Word would get out about the lynching soon enough.

"We got to get on with this, Sonny, before a crowd starts to draw," Jonesy said. "But to be honest with you, that question you asked ain't none of your business. You gave all them rights away when you hung up your Ranger hat. If I need Jesse, I'll ask, but from what I understand, he's on a short leash these days. So, I might be on my own with this, and that's all right with me. It has to be that way, don't it? I got myself into this mess, so I need to get myself out of it."

Jesse and Sonny stood shoulder to shoulder, staring at the sheriff, put off again by his reluctance to involve them in police business. Sonny was perplexed, and he could tell Jesse was, too.

"We better get that man down from there," Hal Buckworth said. "You got any ideas how we can do that, Sheriff Jones?"

CHAPTER NINETEEN

After breakfast and a warm bath, Edith packed her suitcase and readied herself to continue her journey north. Old Ben and her Aunt Cecilia were standing in the entryway waiting for her as she descended the Juliette stairs. They looked like human-sized salt and pepper shakers, black and white, a pair that looked like they belonged together. Edith would never utter a thought like that out loud, but there was no denying what she saw. She was happy Old Ben and Aunt Cecilia had each other in their old age. It would be awful living in the rambling Victorian house all alone. Edith hesitated to leave, considered packing the two of them up and depositing them into her boardinghouse in Huntsville, but she knew that would never work. Cecilia would never leave her house, and Old Ben would be lost, too, in a new city unsure of where he belonged.

"I'm sorry to see you go, Miss Edith," Old Ben said as Edith came to a stop before him. He handed her a white pail that had red ladybugs painted around the center of it. A wisp of steam escaped from under the lid. It was latched closed but had no way to be sealed.

Edith set her suitcase down and took the offering. The smell of warm biscuits emanated from the pail comforted Edith and brought a childish smile to her face. "I wish I could stay longer, Ben, so we could have ourselves a proper visit. Maybe another time."

Cecilia stood silent as a hoot owl trying to hide in the daylight with her jaw set hard. Edith prepared herself for a scathing review of her plans, of how she was dressed, of something mined from the past that would play at the present to wound her.

"You'll be comin' back through now, won't you Miss Edith?" Old Ben said.

"Yes, probably sometime. Maybe soon. Maybe not so soon. It depends on what happens."

"You sure you're not in no trouble?"

"No, I don't think so. Not any trouble that I can't handle myself."

"I hope you're right," he said. "You never did say where you're headin' to, Miss Edith?"

"You were sweet to worry about me." Edith reached for her suitcase with her free hand, ignoring Old Ben's question with blatant intention. "I really should get on the road. I want to be off it before dark. Thank you for your hospitality, Auntie. I appreciate the bed."

Old Ben stood back as Edith leaned into her aunt and pecked her on the cheek with a quick kiss. The woman smelled of lavender and talcum powder.

"You can stay as long as you want," Cecilia said. "I don't want you to leave." She took hold of Edith's wrist and held it tight, making it clear that she meant every word she'd said.

The gesture was unexpected considering Cecilia had been firm about Edith staying only one night. Edith gasped a little, almost dropped the pail of biscuits. She blinked her eyes to make sure it *was* her aunt standing before her.

"I'm afraid I won't see you again," Cecilia continued, her voice genuine, breaking on her last word.

"Oh, Auntie, you'll see me again. I promise," Edith said, regaining her senses, though her eyes glazed at the show of emotion, of honesty, from Cecilia.

"The length of the days grows shorter by the hour," the old

woman said. "Your mother made promises she couldn't keep. Don't be like her now. You never were. You have been your own person. I liked that about you."

Edith pulled her wrist away from her aunt. "I should be getting along. Don't worry. I'll head back sometime, and I'll stop again. I keep my promises." She didn't hesitate any longer. She walked to the door. Old Ben hurried and opened it for her.

Edith walked out into the bright morning sunlight and didn't look back.

She headed west out of Fort Worth toward Denton. From there she'd head to Wichita Falls, and then to Wellington. She had never been this far north before. Edith figured she had about two hundred and fifty miles to go before she reached Sonny's home. Driving between thirty and forty miles an hour, depending on the road conditions and stops, she should arrive six or seven hours later, before nightfall. She didn't want to drive after dark, all things considered. She did worry, though, about the cowboy and his whereabouts. She was afraid of almost everything, unable to enjoy the simplest vistas or sunsets like she had hoped she would be able to. The sight of the land was all new to her. She hated the cowboy for what he had taken away from her, like she hated Billy Bunson for the death and destruction he'd caused in her house. The only way she was going to feel safe was to be in Sonny's presence. If he'd have her. She worried about that, too.

She stopped before leaving the proper limits of Fort Worth and had gas put into the tank so she wouldn't have to worry about finding a station anytime soon. The attendant was helpful, cleaned her windows, checked her oil, all the while Edith kept a keen eye out for the cowboy, or anyone else who might cause her trouble. No one did. She was back on the road without a hint of any concern at all. The automobile smelled of biscuits and dry sliced ham. She'd bought a cold Dr. Pepper to help wash down the food Old Ben had packed for her. Lunch would come later alongside the road with a nice relaxing view.

The ride gave way to less and less houses the farther north Edith drove. The land was flat, and before long, a long lake stretched out to the east of her. She skirted it but was taken by the shacks and the smoking chimneys that accompanied them. It didn't seem like there had been a heavy western migration from this part of Texas, but Edith imagined that making a living might have been easier near a large body of fresh water. Fish and other forms of meat could be caught or trapped, not bought, by resourceful people. People who had lived by the lake all of their lives knew how to survive whatever the world threw at them. The sight of a community that seemed to be working and thriving calmed Edith, gave her a little bit of hope that everything was going to be all right in the end. Everyone was trying to escape the Depression, but there seemed no end to it. The whole world was in the same state as her Aunt Cecilia's house: crumbling down around her. Except this little enclave. It was like she was driving through a different world. She hoped so.

Edith was sad to see the lake district fade away in her rearview mirror, but drove on through the day, taking in the sights, trying to leave her fears and regrets behind her. Her Aunt Cecilia's show of desperation on her departure had caught Edith off-guard. There had been no personal attacks, no grudges from the past to make her feel bad.

Cecilia had almost begged her to stay—which had never happened before. It was like her aunt had realized where she was in her life, how fragile the world around her was, that her own mortality was at stake. Edith had realized that, too. Not once, but twice in a matter of weeks. She would have liked to have stayed and visited. Gone to church with Old Ben regardless of

173

what people thought or said and made her way around Fort Worth to see the sights. Her memory of the city was that it was stately, wealthy, but she was able to breathe there. Maybe that's what she wanted to remember, or how she wished it was when she had been a child. But the visit was not to be. She had little time to waste. She had to face Sonny and get on with her life one way or the other. With him or without him. There was no in-between. Of course, Edith longed for them to spend whatever time they had left in their lives together. She wanted that more than anything. But only if Sonny wanted her in his life, too.

Denton came and went, and she was back out into the country surrounded by open January fields, and a crisp blue sky that seemed to go on forever. The road turned to hardpan, and she had to slow down to about twenty miles an hour, weaving around sinkholes six inches deep. She was relieved that it was dry out, not raining. The drive would have been slower, more precarious, maybe impossible to make. There had been some luck to be had on this trip. Edith hoped it held out until she arrived in Wellington.

The smell of food permeated the comfortable interior of the Pierce, and Edith was tempted more than once to pull over and eat her lunch earlier than she normally would have. But she restrained herself, keeping her foot and desire on the accelerator. She wanted to get as far away from Fort Worth as she could. The engine rumbled and purred, and the automobile seemed like it was built for long road trips; tires gripped the road like passionate lovers and the engine rumbled with power and lust. Edith was disappointed in herself for not taking more drives.

The sun reached high overhead, beaming down through a cloudless sky, allowing her to see a good ways into the distance. Some stretches of the hardpan road were smooth for miles, while others were pockmarked with holes of varying depths. For now, the road felt like it had been made for racing, and she drove at a good speed. There was nothing ahead of her to give her any concern. The road reached all of the way to the flat horizon, urging her on. She looked in the rearview mirror expecting to see the same thing, lulled by the monotony of the miles she'd put in. But there was something there. A truck raged toward her, driving fast, leaving a cloud of dust behind it like it was on fire.

Edith gripped the steering wheel tight, and flicked her vision to the road, then to the mirror, then back to the road. Her nerves turned hot, tense with dread and concern reawakened from a light sleep. The truck kept coming toward her like it didn't see her, wasn't slowing down at all. She was tempted to go faster, to try and outrun the truck. The Pierce had a capable engine, more powerful than most Model A or T trucks. The truck behind her looked newer, so it was a Model A or a Chevrolet. Either way, she was sure the Pierce was more hare than tortoise. But, she reasoned, there was nothing to fear, at this point, to try to flee from other than her imagination. There had been little traffic to contend with.

She looked into the rearview mirror again, trying to see if there was one person in the truck, or two. It was close enough to tell now. The truck was twenty yards behind her. As far as she could tell there was only the driver, and there wasn't much detail to be had. Direct rays from the overhead sun bounced off the windshield glass, making it look almost black to Edith. All she could see was the figure of a man. Her heart raced even faster, and her foot fell heavy on the accelerator.

The truck more than matched her speed. It came within inches of the Pierce's rear bumper. Sweat dropped down from Edith's forehead and she could hear her heart beating like a bass drum, reverberating throughout the interior of the automobile. Whether it was true or not, she felt as if her worst fear had come true: the cowboy had found her on an empty stretch of the road.

She glanced in the mirror again to determine if she was right, if she could make out the wicked face she had left behind in the Ennis restaurant. The bright sun didn't help. Neither did the shadow from a visor that had been bolted across the roof of the truck. It looked like a panel truck of some kind, a delivery vehicle for some kind of business. There were no markings that Edith could see, and she still couldn't make out the face of the driver. She wasn't sure if it was the cowboy or not. After returning her eyes to the road, she reached over and pulled the Smith & Wesson from her purse and situated it next to her right leg.

The roar of the engine inside the Pierce was double what it had been. Edith couldn't hear herself think and her heartbeat had been washed away by the mechanical grind of two engines competing with each other. When she looked into the mirror again, the truck was gone. A quick glance to the side told her that the truck was edging alongside her. The Ford radiator was even with the rear of the driver's side door of the Pierce.

Edith tightened her grip on the steering wheel even harder, certain that the driver of the truck was going to try and run her off the road. She wasn't going to let that happen if she could help it. Her entire body was tense as a rubber band pulled back as far as it could stretch without breaking.

The truck matched her speed, was even with the Pierce. Edith looked over, expecting to see the cowboy but saw a little boy instead. A redheaded freckle-faced boy of about twelve was waving and laughing like a clown on the other side of the truck's passenger window. Her shoulders drooped, air fizzled out of her lungs, and she laughed out loud. It wasn't a happy laugh, but a hard laugh. "You fool, Edith," she said, relieved and ashamed for making such a terrifying assumption.

She pulled her foot off the accelerator and allowed the Pierce to slow. The panel truck kept going, leaving her in the dust. It was a dirty green truck with the words *Argyle Bakery* scrolled in fancy writing on the side. Edith's laugh matched the boy's, who had disappeared in a brown cloud along with the bakery truck.

A minute or two later, the truck was a good distance ahead of Edith, and she had calmed down, was done with chastising herself for being afraid of nothing. She relaxed and took a glance over to the lunch pail. It was time to pull over and take a break, eat some lunch, and gather herself to make the rest of the drive to Wellington.

A sudden bump startled her attention back to the road. The steering wheel lurched from Edith's grip as the Pierce jumped hard to the right. She pulled back to the left, overcorrecting, sending the rear of the automobile out from behind her. Another bump rattled her, but she was holding on tight, braking and trying to dodge any more holes in the road. There wasn't another automobile coming from the opposite direction. The Pierce was sliding sideways, covering both lanes like a bad bet on a roulette wheel. Force and gravity controlled the vehicle now, and there was no avoiding any of the potholes. A deep one caught the rear tire and righted her, sending the Pierce into its normal lane. Edith slammed on the brake pedal as hard as she could and came to a sliding stop.

The engine stuttered, then died with a gasp of steam belching from the radiator. Edith put her head on the steering wheel, doing everything she could to steady her pulse. A million scenarios zoomed through her head: all of them bad, ending in injury or death. And none that were true. Only what could have happened. Once she was calmed down, she opened the driver's side door and stood out of the Pierce.

There was no one around. The land was flat and dry, crusty brown, dead to anything that grazed. No houses or barns stood in watch nearby. She was in the middle of nowhere and had no idea how far the next town was, or how far the next place she could walk to was to get help if she needed to. A steady wind blew across the fallow fields, pushing at her with a temperature much colder than she'd felt when she left Fort Worth. Edith shivered as she walked around the automobile, looking for any damage. There was none that she could see until she rounded the other side of the Pierce, and then she didn't see it, she heard it. The passenger side front tire was hissing, losing air and deflating as she stood and watched. A quick look around told Edith again that she was on her own, that she would have to get herself out of this mess.

She started chastising herself all over again, questioning why she had taken the journey in the first place. As the tire sent out its last gasp of air, a wave of anger rolled over Edith. Anger at Sonny, not at herself. If he hadn't left, she wouldn't be standing by the side of the road, staring at a flat tire. If he had answered her letters, she might have stayed in Huntsville, not been so desperate to drive hundreds of miles to find out where she stood with him. If he would have called her, she could have asked him if she could come to Wellington. All were good reasons to be angry, but she realized none of them would help her get down the road. She was going to have to figure out how to change the tire herself. The argument with Sonny, real or imagined, would have to wait until later.

She decided to calm down and eat the lunch Old Ben had packed for her before she did anything else. Getting her nerves calmed down and regaining her strength seemed like a smart idea. Without thinking, Edith opened the passenger door. The bump had jarred the pail and turned it on its side. The tin rolled out onto the ground before Edith could catch it. The lid spiraled off as the pail rolled and the biscuits and dried ham scattered in the wake.

Edith stood there and watched as her lunch scrambled in the dirt. The sight almost made her cry, but she restrained herself, found her core, and decided not to let the situation get the best of her. The last thing she was going to do was eat dirty food. Not today. Not after everything that had happened.

Edith slammed the passenger door closed, walked to the rear of the Pierce, and stopped, knowing full well that she couldn't stand there and wait for someone to come and help her. She had to help herself.

Spare tires were mounted on both sides of the runabout, and there was a tool kit stowed in the rumble seat compartment. Although Edith had never changed a tire on an automobile, she had spent many years working in her father's foundry; mechanical work had come easy to her. Systems made sense to Edith and instinct told her why and where things like nuts, bolts, and washers fit together. Her first attempt at removing the spare tire on the driver's side failed. The bolt was too tight for her to loosen. She tried the other side and found success. The bolt holding the tire to the steel body spun right off. From there, she rolled the tire next to the flat, then set about figuring out how to use the jack. It seemed easy enough, and in a matter of minutes she had the Pierce's tire off the ground. Only one of the bolts holding the tire gave her trouble, but she put every ounce of muscle she had into the turn and forced the bolt loose. Then she pulled off the flat tire and replaced it with the spare, tightening each bolt as she went.

Edith was proud of herself, and stood back to admire her work, then caught her breath and started to think about getting back on the road. She heard a rumble in the distance, then saw a cloud of dust rising toward her. Another vehicle was heading her way at high speed. She thought to be afraid all over again, then relaxed herself by closing her eyes to see the laughing boy pass by. Her fear was like her anger, a manifestation of her own inadequacies.

She stood at the rear of the Pierce and watched the vehicle

and cloud of dust get closer. The engine sounded like the buzz of a wasp diving through the air with the intention to attack anything that got in its way. But that didn't put her off and send her running for the safety of the interior of the automobile. There was nowhere to run. Nowhere to hide. Nowhere to be safe. If there was any hope in being rescued, she had to stand tall, and use whatever feminine wiles she had left.

The oncoming vehicle was another truck, but unlike the last one, this wasn't a panel or delivery truck. It was a rusty old Model T with its engine wound out as high as it could go.

Edith stood in wait as the sound of the truck's engine slowed. She squinted her eyes, trying her best to see the driver, but the truck were still too far away to make out any detail. But that didn't stop her. She stayed focused on the driver, but as the truck got closer, she still couldn't tell much. The dirty windshield was the same color as the hardpan, and it was a wonder that the driver could see out of it.

To her relief, he slowed down and pulled over behind the Pierce. She still couldn't make anything out, not until he stood out of the truck and put on his frayed white straw hat.

It was the cowboy.

CHAPTER TWENTY

The elephant stood steady under Rafael Hernandez's body while Igor sliced the rope. Sonny stood with Jesse, Jonesy, and Hal Buckworth with their necks craned in unison, hoping that the strongman didn't let Rafael's limp body fall to the ground. Frances and her husband, Milton, were in charge of the elephant. Milton held a chain that was tied around the beast's neck like a giant leash, while Frances stroked the elephant's long trunk, all the while whispering soft words that none of the men could hear. The elephant flapped its sheet-sized ears, nonplussed by the task at hand. Sonny wondered if the elephant had ever been used to retrieve a hanged man from a tall tree before. He wasn't going to ask.

"I'm against this," Jonesy said to Sonny.

"You didn't come up with any better ideas."

"I could have shot through the rope and dropped him, is what I could have done." The sheriff squared his shoulders and jutted his plump chin out as far as it would go. "Them circus folk don't need to feel useful. They could have used that elephant to hang Rafael. You think of that, Sonny, before you went askin' for favors?"

"You see any elephant footprints under that rope when you got here?" Sonny said.

"Nope. But that don't mean nothin' now, does it? Circus folk could have worked some of their tricks. It's what they do. Trickery and deception."

181

Sonny ignored the attitude. "You should be grateful the circus was still here and willing to help out."

"If you say so."

"I do."

Igor eased Rafael's body over the back of the elephant as gently as he could, then slid down and straddled the beast's wide haunches, holding onto the dead body so it wouldn't slide off. Milton knickered the elephant like he would a horse, and slow-walked it toward Buckworth's waiting ambulance.

Jonesy pursed his lip as the elephant walked by. The earth under all of their feet vibrated from the beast's effort. Sonny was wide awake this time, not roused from a sleep, left to question whether what he was seeing was real or not. There was no question that Rafael was dead, and the giant gray beast was walking him home.

"You going to go tell Rafael's family? Or do you want me and Jesse to do that for you?" Sonny said to the sheriff as they fell in behind the elephant.

Jonesy eyed Sonny, annoyed at first, then allowed his mind to think past whatever was standing in the way of his common sense. "That'd free me to find out what's going on with the search for Heck and Clyde. You mind doin' that, Jesse?"

"If that's what you need," Jesse said.

Jonesy bit his lip on the side of his mouth for a long second. "You can make sure your pa gets home and minds his own business is what I need. But since him and Aldo are close friends, I don't see how that's gonna happen. I ain't fool enough to believe he can help himself any more than you can when it comes to stickin' his nose where it don't belong. But," Jonesy said with deep emphasis and came to a stop, "that's as far as your involvement in any of this goes. You understand? The both of you? You go tell them Hernandezes that Rafael's body is at

Hal Buckworth's funeral home and they should come and get it."

Sonny and Jesse stopped alongside the sheriff, while Hal Buckworth followed the elephant. He felt the weight of the Colt in his coat pocket shift, a gentle reminder it was there.

"I understand," Jesse said. "Pa?"

"Sure," Sonny said. "I don't want anything to do with any of this." He meant it, too, though he already felt like he was knee-deep in a swamp trying to trudge his way out of the muck.

"I mean it," Jonesy said. "I'll throw the both of you in jail if you go off the rails on this. I got enough to worry about other than you two actin' like the law in this county." He pursed his lips again, then twisted his waist, and spun around with a solid step.

Sonny watched Jonesy stalk off to his automobile, shaking his head. "Seems awful funny to me," he whispered to Jesse.

"He's not himself these days, that's for sure." Jesse looked to the ground, then to what was left of the dangling rope. The noose was still wrapped around Rafael's neck, while the rest of the rope hung from the thick live oak branch, dangling in the wind as a reminder of what it once was.

"Did he even look around for any sign of what might have happened here?" Sonny said.

"Said he did before I came along, but I agree, he didn't seem too interested in searching for anything solid. It was almost like he was resigned that this was going to happen, that Rafael's death was no surprise to him."

"So, Jonesy got here first?"

"Yes."

"How'd he come upon it?"

"Said Leddie Harmeson called it in."

"Leddie? The mother?" Sonny said. "That seems odd. If any of the Harmesons was going to call this in, I would have figured it would have been the old man, Peter."

"I'm telling you what Jonesy told me."

"And, you?" Sonny said. "How'd you hear about this?"

"I was heading out to see you."

"First thing in the morning?"

"Yes. I wanted to tell you that I'm not going to Abilene when they move the office."

"Where are you going?"

Jesse shrugged his shoulders, and said, "To the breadlines. I'm out of a job. Word came down from Governor Allred himself. My services are no longer needed. Come Friday, I won't be a Ranger any longer." All of the air seemed to go out of Jesse's face. He turned pale as a fresh bleached sheet, and his words cracked like he couldn't believe he was hearing what had come out of his mouth.

Sonny wasn't expecting to hear those words, either, but he wasn't surprised. Ma Ferguson's time in office as governor had left a stain on almost every government organization in the state of Texas, including the Rangers. Maybe the Rangers more than most. There were men in the organization who didn't belong there, were friends of friends who had made political donations of one kind or the other. Jesse was not one of those men. He was a Ranger from head to toe, inside out, had blood that ran red with Ranger history. There was no cause to let him go that Sonny knew of other than he had served under a veil of corruption and the new man was doing nothing but cleaning house.

"I could give Frank Hamer a call," Sonny said. "He might not have much pull with this Allred administration, but I could ask him to put in a word for you."

Jesse's whole body went rigid. "That's the last thing I want you to do. You don't need to do anything, Pa. It's like you said, I'll find my way to another badge sooner or later. This isn't the end of the world."

"You look like it is."

"I never thought I'd have to worry about such a thing. I thought I'd be like you and be a Texas Ranger all of my life. It's all I've ever wanted to be, and now I have to figure out what I'm gonna be next."

"Well," Sonny said, "You got two girls that miss you."

"Yes, I guess you're right."

Hal Buckworth had rolled a gurney next to the elephant. Milton and Frances held the beast as still as they could as Igor lowered Rafael's body down to the mortician. A few more automobiles had stopped alongside the road to watch the spectacle. Sonny was surprised a reporter from the *Leader* hadn't showed face yet. They'd missed their chance for a second-page picture like there had been from that lynching down in Shelbyville. The morning was young, so that might have been an explanation for the reporter's absence. That, or something else was going on somewhere else around Wellington that had taken their attention.

With the body laid out and covered on the gurney, Buckworth pushed it to the ambulance. Neither Frances nor Milton offered to help. They stood silent along with the elephant, who had shown no interest at all in any of the commotion. The beast was tame as a fat gray cat.

Sonny watched the gurney in silent reverence, allowing the conversation between him and Jesse to drift away. Jesse seemed thankful not to have to talk about himself any longer, which was something Sonny understood.

Once Buckworth loaded Rafael's dead body into the ambulance, Sonny made his way to Frances and Milton. He tried not to pay any attention to the elephant, but the size of the beast made it impossible to ignore. One wrong move, or one flick of anger from the elephant, could turn into a catastrophe. A raging bull elephant loose in the cotton fields, stomping out the life of every human in its path. No warning, no chance to get away. His tombstone would read: Here lies Sonny Burton, one arm lost to Bonnie Parker, flattened in the end by a stray elephant.

"Thank you for helping out," Sonny said to the twosome. Jesse had followed along and stood at his father's side as wary of the elephant as Sonny.

Frances, who had opted for an ordinary overhead white smock instead of a glittery red blouse, said, "It was the least we could do. Most folks don't see us as neighborly, but you have reason to. I'm surprised you're not sheriff of this county instead of that beady-eyed trash can who looks at us like we're lower than the sidewalk he walks on."

"I've got no interest in local politics. Besides, Jonesy's not a bad man, he's going through a rough patch."

"We're all in a rough patch," Frances said. "That don't give a man with a badge the right to be mean. I want to say something more about him, but I won't." Even with half of her face covered with a black, hairy beard, it was easy to see that her face was boiling red.

"I'm not sure how we would have got him down without your help, Frances," Sonny said, doing his best to turn the subject away from Jonesy. "I've been wondering how they got him there in the first place."

"Pretty easy, if you ask me," Milton said, stepping forward. "No different than hoisting a heavy bag of flour to a loft. A couple of strong men could have easily pulled that body that high."

"But he was alive," Jesse said.

"You sure of that?" Frances looked to Jesse, then to Sonny. "He could have already been dead when they hanged him. Did the sheriff check into that?"

Jesse and Sonny both shrugged.

"Why would someone hang a dead man?" Sonny said.

"Why hang any man and leave him to be found?" Milton said. "Whoever did this wanted to make a statement to the Mexicans, or someone closely associated with 'em. They wanted the body to be found is the way I see it."

Sonny drew in a deep breath, then looked back to the severed rope swaying from the tree. As far as he knew Milton and Frances weren't aware that Jonesy had used Rafael as a snitch. Maybe they were right. Maybe the lynching was a message to the Mexicans. Or maybe it was a message to Jonesy. Jonesy sure was in a hurry to get away from the lynching. If Sonny was a betting man—which he wasn't—he would have bet a hundred dollars that Heck Kilbride and Clyde Jones had something to do with killing Rafael. Sonny had no proof of that. It was a feeling since they both were missing. It would explain a lot.

"We'll be leavin' soon," Frances said. "We need to get back on the road, away from whatever is goin' on here. We've been dragged into it too much already by bein' accused of stealin' cows that we paid for fair and square. Now this, right down the road from us, makes me and Milton a slight bit nervous. The wind's gonna blow back on us yet, you wait and see. I didn't like how that sheriff came into our place yesterday turnin' over every rock lookin' for something that wasn't there. And I didn't like how he looked at us today, his feathers puffed like a cock rooster struttin' around the farmyard with spurs as sharp as razors, ready to run us off any second. He's up to something, that one is. You mark my word, Sonny Burton. And he's gonna try and pin all of this nonsense on us, or one of us, you wait and see."

"How can you be so certain?" Sonny said.

"Because," Frances answered, with a quick pull to the end of her beard, "it's happened before."

CHAPTER TWENTY-ONE

Sonny settled himself into the passenger seat of Jesse's Plymouth, and Blue did his best to get comfortable in the plush backseat. The dog looked unsure of where to sit, turning around like he was winding himself up to start or finish something.

Jesse chewed on a toothpick and stared down the road, watching the elephant ease its way back toward the big top. "You sure you want to go out to Aldo's? I can handle this if you'd rather not, Pa."

Sonny kept an eye on the elephant, too, then turned around to the backseat and told Blue to lie down in a tone that allowed for no argument. "Not right away," he said to Jesse, settling himself forward in the passenger seat. "I'd like to stop by the Harmeson place on the way."

"Jonesy said not to get involved in this, and I think we better heed his orders. Something tells me that he wouldn't hesitate to throw us in jail if we don't play by his rules. The last thing I need on my record right now is an arrest I'd have to explain."

Sonny tapped the letter to Edith that was in his breast pocket. "I got a phone call I'd like to make to Huntsville. The Harmesons' place is the closest phone around."

"I think that's a bad idea," Jesse said.

"If Jonesy is knee-deep in this mess with Heck Kilbride and Clyde Jones, then you need to be aware of it. You're still a Texas Ranger and he doesn't have total control over what you do."

"Until Friday. Unless I get fired before then for doing

something I shouldn't do."

"Well, then, you'll have a few extra days to figure out what you're going to do next."

Jesse started the Plymouth and put it in gear. "Thanks, Pa, for keeping me on the straight and narrow."

"Better late than never."

"If you say so."

"I do."

Jesse drove along, overtaking the elephant, then passing by. Milton led with the rope loose in his hand. Frances gave a half-hearted wave. She looked lost in thought in the rearview mirror. Sonny and Jesse stayed silent as they passed, but Blue let out a low growl.

It didn't take long to get to the Harmesons' house. Jesse pulled into the yard alongside a green farm truck that Sonny knew to be Peter's.

"Why don't you stay here and let me do what I have to do, Jesse," Sonny said. "That way if anybody steps on any toes it'll be my tail that Jonesy grabs ahold of and not yours. You're right, you don't need this kind of trouble."

"That's mighty considerate of you, Pa."

"The Harmesons might be a little nervous around a Ranger, all things considered. My guess is Jonesy already had a talk with them, but that's only a guess."

"You're probably right. I'll keep an eye out for trouble. What are you lookin' for, Pa?"

"I'm not sure other than I heard tell Leo Dozier and Heck both had something to do with one of the Harmeson girls. Now, it's funny that Dozier boy got into a fight with Rafael and lost his spot at the CCC camp to Clyde Jones. Then Heck *and* Clyde go missing—and Rafael's left hanging in a tree right down the road from the Harmeson place."

"You think the girl is hiding something?"

189

"Don't you?"

"It makes sense once you put everything together like that. The only thing that doesn't come into play," Jesse said, "is the circus."

"I don't think they have anything to do with this," Sonny answered.

"They made some trouble in town with Heck."

"They didn't do anything other than be in the wrong place at the wrong time. Heck was being a bully like normal. He saw an opportunity to get some attention and that's what he did. They're nice people, Jesse. I broke bread with them while we were riding out the storm. Nothing seemed out of the ordinary—other than the obvious."

"A woman with a beard and a man that stands eight feet tall."

"Exactly. They're passing through and nothing more."

"You seem sure of that."

"I am."

"Okay," Jesse said, tapping his fingers on the steering wheel. "I don't like this, but I'll stay out of it and let you go see what you can find out."

"That's the best idea you've had so far." Sonny looked over his shoulder to Blue, and said, "You stay here, boy. Do your best not to bite Jesse. I won't be long." He turned back to Jesse and smiled as he reached to open the door with his left hand.

"The feeling's mutual, Pa. I don't like that dog any more than he likes me."

"That's the truth if I ever heard it."

Sonny got out of the Plymouth and made his way to the front door of the simple farmhouse. It opened before he made it to the first step of the porch. Peter Harmeson stood in the doorway with a dour look on his long, unshaven face. He was a skinny man, about fifty, with brown hair graying on the edges. He was wearing a white ribbed T-shirt, work pants, boots that weren't tied. The laces hung limp and threatened to trip him when he walked. Winter allowed for days that didn't require early outside work, but Sonny was surprised to see the man so unprepared for the day. He looked near sick, paler than normal if that was possible.

"I thought I heard another automobile turn into the drive," the man said.

"Sorry to disturb you, Peter," Sonny said, standing rigid on the porch. "I'm sure you've had enough excitement this morning."

"Too much for my likin', but I should've known trouble was comin' my way when I gave that bearded lady the permission to stay on my ground."

"I'm not sure they had anything to do with what happened this morning."

"It was still a mistake. Ain't been a quiet night's sleep since they pitched camp. Those lions and tigers growl and holler into the deep hours. I'm surprised you haven't heard 'em at your place."

"I thought it was the wind I was hearing."

" 'Fraid not. They's a noisy bunch, and if I had any steel in my spine at all, I'd go tell them to get on down the road and be done with it. But I got other troubles."

"I talked to Milton, the ringmaster, and his wife a little while ago. They said they were leaving soon."

"Well, that's a bit of good news. Now, what brings you to my doorstep, Sonny Burton? If it's eggs you're after, you'll need to go fetch 'em yourself. My girls are preoccupied at the present."

"I'm sorry to bother you with my own personal needs," Sonny said. "But I was wondering if I could use your phone. I need to make a call down to Huntsville."

"This got anything to do with that lynchin'?"

"No, sir, it doesn't. I don't have anything to do with the law anymore."

"What's that, then?" Peter said, jerking his head toward Jesse sitting in the Plymouth.

"That's my ride. My son, Jesse."

"What's become of your truck?"

"Wouldn't start," Sonny lied.

"Huntsville, you say?"

"Yes, sir. It'll be a short call and I'll reverse the charges, so there won't be any cost to you."

"If'n it was anybody else but you, Sonny, I'd send 'em packin', but you're a good neighbor, so I can't see cause to tell you no. Come on in," Peter said, as he stood out of the way to welcome Sonny inside the house.

Sonny stepped inside the door and was greeted by the smell of coffee mixed with frying bacon. Soft morning light filtered through the bare window in the sparsely furnished front room. A dormant brick fireplace captured the far wall. The grate and ash can were empty, and a pile of seasoned logs sat on the floor, ready to be burned at the first complaint of cold. A Philco radio cabinet sat on the opposite wall next to a floor lamp, with a scattering of five chairs around it. There were a few pictures on the wall; a landscape with a lone white cow in a green field and a frame of Jesus next to a wood cross, reminding Sonny that Peter and his family were papists. The wood floor and the rugs on it were clean, as was everything else in the room, but Sonny wouldn't have expected anything else. Every time he'd stopped at the Harmesons' for one thing or another, everything had been in its place.

The clatter of cooking came from the kitchen at the back of the house along with a low murmur of voices.

"We're havin' a late breakfast," Peter said, embarrassed by the late hour in the morning that food was being prepared.

"The phone is in the same place it was last time you was here. Hep yourself."

Sonny still stood silent, past the open door. "I've been thinking of getting a telephone of my own."

"Worst thing I ever did," Peter said.

"Why's that?"

"The world trudges inside your house uninvited is why. No offense, I ain't sayin' that about you, Sonny. But the thing rings at will, no matter whether we're sleepin', eatin', or prayin'. Has no manners at all. Brings bad news, and when you talk, you have to wonder who's a listenin' to your conversation. A private word is lost. A man is best to stick to writin' letters, like you obviously have." Peter pointed to the letter sticking out of Sonny's pocket.

Sonny's face flushed red, and that surprised him. The correspondence with Edith had not come to him naturally, and neither had the words he'd shared with her. He would have been embarrassed if anybody would have had access to what he had said to her. Peter's revelation was something to think about when he was on the telephone. "I hadn't thought about the downside of a telephone in the house. It sure would come in handy if you needed help, though."

"It would, it does, and it did," Peter said, "But I still regret havin' the blasted thing in the house. The girls nipped at my heels for ages before I gave in to them. I should have knowed better." He shrugged and cocked his head to where Sonny knew the phone was. "But that's my burden to carry. You go on and take care of your business. I'll stand here and bellyache all day long if I got someone who'll listen to me."

This was an odd view of Peter Harmeson for Sonny. Images of a hardworking family man were more common than the half-dressed recluse who stood before him; Peter patching shingles on the roof, manhandling a mule and a plow in cracked, dry earth, or steadying a Winchester Black Diamond twenty-gauge pump action shotgun to bead in a chattering squirrel for the morning gravy. Those were solid memories of the man whose house Sonny stood in. Peter Harmeson was like most of the men around Wellington, of the land, a survivor, and protector of his family. Instead, on this morning, he had found a man that was a cracked shell of himself, melancholy, and teetering on lost and confused. There was no mistaking that death had visited this house, but that was what Sonny found odd. Why would the Harmeson family find grief in Rafael Hernandez's death? Why did the house feel so tense and sad?

"I appreciate your hospitality, Peter," Sonny said. "I won't be long."

"Take as long as you need." Peter wandered off into the dimmer part of the house, creaking up the stairs to the second floor.

Sonny watched until Peter was gone, then made his way to the phone. It was a wood box attached to the wall mounted in between the kitchen and the front room, visible, and in earshot of anyone on the first floor of the house. Sonny figured the phone had been placed there on purpose so Peter and Leddie could keep tabs on the conversations that occupied their three daughters.

There was, also, no way Leddie and two of the girls, the youngest one, Nora, and the oldest one, Regan, could overlook Sonny's presence at the phone from their spots in the kitchen. There was no sign of the middle girl, Ida. All of the girls favored their mother, broad shouldered with alabaster skin and ginger hair that looked like it had been touched by the sun and blazed with red-hot flames. All of the females had hazel eyes that changed color with the weather. Sonny assumed that on this day they were gray.

He nodded to the three of them as he grabbed the cold black

metal earpiece and leaned into the voice receiver, a tube shaped like a miniature phonograph speaker. The girls and their mother had stopped all of the motion of their cooking chores, and stared at Sonny in unison, expressionless, void of any emotion at all. Even on a good day, they were pale as chalk. They seemed to glow in the shadows of the kitchen as the bacon sizzled in a black cast-iron skillet the size of a serving platter. Two loaves of bread proofed on the counter not far from the woodburning stove. All three of them had on spotless aprons. Everything was clean in the kitchen, in the house; the floor would have been safe to eat off of.

The Harmesons went back to their kitchen duties. Cutting vegetables. Wiping counters. Putting pans away as quiet as possible. Sonny was well aware that his privacy was lost on the outside of the phone as well as on the inside. He would have to filter his words. The last thing he wanted to deal with was a rumor making its way around Wellington that he had a woman friend.

"Long distance, please," Sonny said, as the operator connected.

"Number please," she said, distant, like a bad cold had lodged itself in her throat.

Sonny gave the operator Edith's number, which he had memorized by heart, and waited as she dialed. All he heard on his end was a series of clicks, and then the buzz of the ring circling inside his ear like a lost bee. He held his breath and closed his eyes, waiting to hear Edith's voice, doing his best to conjure her image in his mind. The worry of the Harmeson house fell away from him as the phone continued to ring, and he held onto a mental image of Edith as hard as he could. He had never missed a woman so much in his life. Each day away from her had seemed like a lost century. Somewhere deep inside himself he wondered if this was what love was, if he had ever felt something like this before. And he knew he hadn't. Being away from Martha had never made him ache with this kind of longing. Days passed when Sonny had been riding with the Rangers, or fighting in the trenches during the war, without one thought of his wife back at home. He felt bad about that. Even now, he realized the difference, how it should have been—for them both.

"Grantley house," a male voice said after a long series of rings.

"This is Sonny Burton. Is Edith available?"

"Oh, hey, Sonny. This is Marcel Pryor. How are you?"

"Fair to middling. How about yourself?"

"Still working at the prison and holding down the fort here."

"Holding down the fort?"

"Well, I don't imagine she's had time to get there yet."

"Get where?" Sonny said.

"To Wellington. To you."

"Edith's on her way here?"

"Yes," Marcel said. "She waited for you to answer her letters, and when she couldn't take it any longer, she settled it in her mind to come to you and find out what was what."

"I sent her a letter," Sonny whispered, looking down at the other letter in his pocket.

"She didn't get it."

"I waited too long to answer."

"You did."

"When did she leave?"

"Yesterday morning. She was planning on staying with her aunt in Fort Worth. By my guess, if all is well, she should be there sometime late this afternoon or in the evening. I should have asked her to check in with me every once in a while. I've got be honest with you, I'm worried that I haven't heard from her. A woman on the road alone in these times. I guess I could have ridden with her, but I didn't think I could risk my job."

Sonny didn't respond. His ears felt warm and his heart raced. He wasn't sure what to feel. Blood careened through all of his veins. Even his invisible veins. He could feel the tips of his fingers on his right hand pulsing, even though he knew there was nothing there but a cold metal hook.

"You still there, Sonny?"

"I'm here. All right, Marcel. This isn't your fault. I'm sure she's fine. I'll keep an eye out for her. If something should happen and you need to get ahold of me, call this number. BH719. It's the farm down the road from me. Tell the Harmesons what the problem is, and they'll get a message to me as soon as they can. There's some trouble going on around here, so I'm out and about a lot right now, but this changes things. I wish I'd known what she was planning on doing."

"Can't help yourself, can you?"

"I guess I can't."

"Sonny," Marcel said. "She cares about you. You felt that, didn't you?"

"I did," he said. "I do."

CHAPTER TWENTY-TWO

Edith felt like a squirrel caught in a hunter's crosshairs. She couldn't believe what she was seeing. The cowboy had slammed on the brakes of the truck and jumped out of it wearing a victory smile on his dirty, twisted face. A short-blade knife hung from his right hand—the same one he'd pulled in the restaurant—and he looked the same as he had the first time she had seen him. Somehow, the cowboy had escaped from the café in Ennis unscathed. He was standing six feet from Edith, trapping her at the rear of the Pierce with the threat of the knife. She looked away, glanced to the passenger side door, knew that the Smith & Wesson was lying on the seat. Sweat formed on her palms as she refocused on the cowboy. She couldn't give him a hint about the plan that was forming in her head. She had to get to the gun. It was the only way she was going to escape.

"How did you find me?" Edith said, her throat dry with fear.

"You told that waitress where you were headin', lady. Ain't but one smart way to get to Wellington from there. I ran these roads in my gin-runnin' days. Besides, you stand out like a bumblebee in the desert drivin' this here fancy vehicle of yours."

"You better not have hurt them."

The cowboy chuckled and took a step toward Edith.

She screamed as loud as she could, then rocked off her heels and edged her way down to the door handle as quick as she could. The sudden scream stopped the man, backed him up the step he'd took toward her. She had surprised him, which was good, but she wouldn't be able to do it again. He'd be expecting it. A couple of crows that she hadn't seen in the field lit into the air, adding their nervous caws to the scream.

"You stop right there," Edith yelled.

The cowboy cocked his head to the side. As he did, the sun caught his dilated iron-black pupils, forging them with a glazed look that was empty of understanding. Edith wondered if he was drunk on something, or worse, a morphine addict. She'd seen that look in the eyes of broken men before. His condition—if she was right—might give her an advantage. She was going to need all the luck and forethought she could muster to outwit and survive this encounter.

She'd been able to escape the cowboy two times. Her gut told her that he was playing for keeps this time. There was no one around to save her or distract him so she could run. She was on her own in the middle of nowhere. This was the worst possible scenario. The one Marcel Pryor had insisted that she be prepared for. *God, what she wouldn't do for him to be at her side right now.*

Without any more hesitation, Edith yanked the automobile door open, reached in, and grabbed the pistol. When she turned around the cowboy was three steps from her. He stopped, holding an odd look on his face. It was like he was enjoying the confrontation. A laugh escaped from his lips. "You don't give quit. I like that in a woman. Someone who'll fight. Makes life more interestin'."

Edith's finger was wrapped around the trigger, but she hadn't cocked the gun. The cowboy knew that. She aimed it at his forehead. "You come toward me and I'll shoot you." The barrel of the Smith & Wesson shivered sideways, then bounced as her nerves vibrated from the inside to the outside. Her skin felt electric, and she could smell the stench of the pungent cowboy's body odor. She wondered if his smell would stick to her hair, if she would ever be able to forget it.

"Well," the cowboy said, licking his lips, "we got us a real standoff here, don't we?"

"What do you want with me?"

"I done told you. Your life. Your automobile. Ain't that enough?"

"I didn't do anything to you."

"Nobody said you did, but there's been plenty like you that have. It's my turn to take whatever I want."

Wind pushed across the open field and whistled through the Pierce's open door as it made its way to the other side of the road. There was no living creature in sight. No hawks circling overhead or mice foraging in the fields. It was like Edith and the cowboy were the only two living creatures within a hundred miles. She hoped for a traveler to come along. The bakery truck on a return trip. Would the redheaded boy continue laughing when they passed by, seeing her in distress, at the mercy of the cowboy, or keep driving? That would be worse, knowing someone didn't stop to help.

"I am going to walk to the other side of this automobile, and I am going to drive away. I have nothing more to say to you," Edith said. The cowboy stepped forward and Edith stood fast and steady, holding the Smith & Wesson toward him, then cocked it, rolling a cartridge into the chamber. "I will kill you if I have to."

"A lady like you wouldn't do no such thing. I bet you feed the hobos and put out dishes of milk for the stray cats. You've got a heart. You wouldn't kill a thing. Includin' me."

"I would and I will. Now, you can either stand right there or go back to your truck, it doesn't matter to me. But I am going to do what I said. I am going to walk around the front of my automobile, and I am going to drive away. If you follow me, I will lead you to the next police department I can find, do you understand? I will outrun you. You won't be able to catch me. I can drive this automobile and push it to its limits."

"You think awful highly of yourself, don't you?" the cowboy said, then stepped toward her.

Edith didn't answer. She pulled the trigger.

The shot exploded in a controlled burst of a spark and gunpowder. The striking smell rushed into Edith's nose, replacing the ugly smell of the cowboy, as she tried to control the gun's recoil. The bullet fled the barrel and did what she wanted it to: Knock the white straw hat off the cowboy's head.

He was stunned, had leaned over to try and avoid being killed. The color of his face matched the white hat and his eyes reddened with anger once he realized that she had missed on purpose. He started to lurch forward, but Edith cocked the Smith & Wesson again and set another cartridge into the chamber. "I won't miss this time," she said. "That was a warning. I don't want to harm you. All I want to do is get on my way and that is what I am going to do. But if you come at me again, I promise you I will put a hole between your eyes, and I will leave you for the coyotes to feast on—which is more than you deserve. Now leave me alone."

Edith backed away from the cowboy, keeping the barrel of the gun steady, pointed at him.

The cowboy howled with laughter and rushed her as she reached the passenger door. He waved his arms like a madman with the obvious intent of tackling Edith.

She pulled the trigger again, hitting him in the right knee where she had aimed. He was about to reach her. Killing didn't come easy. She couldn't stomach the thought of putting a bullet in his head. The orchestra of the gunfire and the shattering of bones echoed across the empty fields. Edith added her voice to the performance by screaming as loud as she could. It was a reaction, not something she'd meant to do. Her body took control and her rage and fear released itself unbidden into the air, draining energy and purpose from every cell in her body. Never in her life had Edith Grantley ever thought she would shoot a man. Even now, she couldn't bring herself to kill him. All she wanted to do was stop him from coming after her.

Bone, blood, and cartilage splattered out from the cowboy's knee. The impact of the lead had sent him back a couple of steps as a moan escaped his surprised lips. Pain exploded in his glazed eyes, followed by anger and rage. Instead of tackling Edith, he was wrapped up in himself, arms all tangled together as he tried to keep himself upright and moving toward his quarry. He stumbled forward hell-bent on inflicting terror upon her.

She pulled the trigger again.

This time, she caught him in the left shoulder. If he kept coming, she'd move to his head, and put an end to the cowboy once and for all. She didn't move. Her feet were planted to the ground like they had rooted a mile deep. A voice from far away inside of her head screamed at her to run, to get away, but she didn't listen. She knew better. Running only antagonized this man. Fueled him like it was a game. She was prey. Easy prey. Or so he had thought in his warped and muddled mind. But he was wrong about that. Edith was going to do everything she could to escape this maniac's grasp. He wasn't going to lay one finger on her if she had anything to do with it. All she had to do to break the Sixth Commandment was pull the trigger one more time. If hell waited for her for protecting herself, then so be it.

The second bullet had shattered the cowboy's clavicle at the joint. He staggered back, standing halfway vertical, grasping the wound with his right hand. The knife fell to the ground, thudding next to his boot. Blood rushed through his fingers, draining to the ground, promising to empty his veins before he could do anything about it.

Edith felt nothing now. Adrenaline had turned her own blood to ice. She couldn't tell that she was breathing, that her heart was pumping, that she was holding a gun. The Smith & Wesson felt like it had become part of her. She was one with steel and lead. Her tongue tasted of gunpowder and her nostrils were tainted with smoke. She wondered if this was what war had felt like to the men like Sonny who had fought overseas.

She cocked the gun again. Bullet number three out of six. She would empty the chamber if she had to, if he did not surrender to her power, if the cowboy did not leave her alone.

The man stumbled forward, landing on the wounded right knee. The pain and the force of the fall sent another scream from his mouth into the air, lingering before it blew off on the wind. Edith was sure no one heard it. Or at least no one that could help her.

The fall flattened the wiry cowboy, and if there was ever a chance for Edith to flee, it was now. She waited for him to settle to the ground. He was twisted into a pile of dirty clothes, blood, and Texas dirt. He didn't look human, but more like an armadillo, cast to the side of the road after being run over by a truck. Edith wasn't going to do anything until knew she was safe to run, that she wouldn't have to keep looking over her shoulder once she was on the road.

The cowboy closed his eyes and nothing on his body moved except the slight rise in his chest. He was still alive, still breathing, but he was hobbled.

Edith didn't waste another breath. Escaping was now or never.

She rushed to the driver's side of the Pierce, flung herself inside, switched the Smith & Wesson to her left hand, and started the automobile with her right. As soon as the engine fired Edith pressed her foot down hard on the accelerator and worked her way through the gearshift as fast as she could, like she was on the last lap of the Indianapolis 500.

A squall of dust spread out from behind the Pierce and she was twenty yards down the road before she could see that the cowboy had not moved, that he was still lying motionless in the pile where she had left him.

Edith didn't pay any attention to her speed or worry about attracting the attention of the police. Just the opposite. She wanted to draw out a hiding motorcycle cop. But there was none to be seen. There had been little traffic on the road all day long. Now that she knew what the cowboy was driving, she could keep an eye out for it in her rearview mirror. Only once did she think she was being followed. That had caused her to push the Pierce's engine to its limits, winding it out so far that the whole automobile juddered like it was going to break apart. Her fingers were gripped so hard around the steering wheel that she feared her skin would break open. Her stomach was weak and queasy as she replayed the encounter with the cowboy over and over again in her mind.

The sight of blood, the smell of the gun smoke, and the memory of the cold Smith & Wesson in her hands brought on a sick feeling that was foreign to Edith. Her life had never prepared her for such an event. It was impossible for her not to get angry with herself. When that met with resistance, or ran out, she turned her anger toward Sonny Burton again. He was easy to blame. It was his fault that she was on the road in the first place. It was his fault that her heart was breaking. His fault that she had to fend off a man who meant her harm. His fault . . . for not answering her letters, walking out and not taking her with him. This was all Sonny's fault for leaving her. The thought slowed her, forced her to pull her foot off the accelerator and glance into the rearview mirror. Thankfully there was no sign of the cowboy, or any other vehicle, causing her to pull off the side of the road.

Bile bubbled into her throat and almost escaped her mouth before she was able to get out of the Pierce. Before she knew it, Edith was on her knees, vomiting a combination of fear, anger, and self-pity. It was the self-pity that she hated the taste of the most. She had never been one to feel sorry for herself, and she had allowed that emotion to almost cripple her. That and anger. She knew it wasn't Sonny's fault that she was on the road. None of this was his fault. She had made the decision to go to Wellington uninvited. He had nothing to do with that. Still, there was another part of her reaction that she didn't understand. But that didn't take long to figure out. Once she vomited again and wiped her mouth with her sleeve, she caught a whiff of the gunpowder. She knew then that she had come close to killing a man, shot him twice and left him there to fend for himself—or die. *She had left him there to die so he would leave her alone.* Edith didn't know who that person was—the person who had pulled the trigger. The memory of blood exploding from the cowboy's knee almost knocked her off of her knees, but she stood fast, her head hung down, fighting the urge to collapse into a ball of tears with all of her might.

Time passed and Edith found it in herself to gather what strength she had left and made her way back to the Pierce. As she settled in to continue the drive, she caught a glimpse of herself in the mirror. Hair all a mess, makeup gone, skin pasty; she didn't recognize herself. A quick look over her shoulder told her that the road was clear, and without any more hesitation, she continued on with her journey. Only she had a stop to make that she didn't have before. She was going to stop and make a report at the nearest police station she could find.

Wichita Falls was the next town she came to, and it hadn't been too difficult to find the police. All Edith had to do was stop and ask. "North to Ohio Street," a white-haired, potbellied man at the train depot had told her. "Keep goin', veer right, then turn left on Ohio. You'll see the police station plain as day. It's a simple two-story brick building, with an overhang wide enough to park a couple of automobiles under."

Edith had thanked the man and drove on, finding the police station with no problem. Before she knew it, she was sitting in an office waiting for a policeman to listen to her story. She knew she looked a sight, but she didn't care. This was the right thing to do and she knew it.

"I'm sorry to keep you waiting, ma'am," a tall, mid-thirties man said. He wore a white shirt and a thin black tie that matched the color of his hair. There was no badge to be seen, but that didn't matter to Edith. The man carried himself stiff and businesslike even though he wore a boyish face.

"I don't mind." She sat in an uncomfortable straight-backed wood chair, knees together, and her shoulders even, though it took some effort not to let them droop.

"You have a shooting to report?" the man said as he sat down, staring at Edith like she was a white rhinoceros. "My name is Bill Spurling, by the way. I'm a junior detective here."

"Nice to meet you, Mr. Spurling."

"Bill is fine. Why don't you tell me what this is all about?"

Edith pushed herself to the edge of the chair, so her knees were almost touching the gunmetal gray desk. All of the papers on it were organized in neat stacks. She recounted her first meeting with the cowboy at the Magnolia station, then at the café in Ennis, and finally on the side of the road outside of Wichita Falls. "I had no choice but to leave him there and come here. Does that make me a bad person? A criminal?" Her voice broke and her throat quivered.

Bill Spurling sat back in the chair, still looking at Edith like she was the most unusual creature he'd ever seen. "No, no, relax. This man sounds like a bum with a vendetta against the world. I'll send a patrol car out to see what they find, and get in contact with the police in Ennis, too, in case there was trouble at this café you spoke of." He stood, moved around the side of the desk, and stopped next to Edith. "Why are you traveling by yourself in the first place?"

Edith wasn't expecting the question. "I, um, am going to see a man in Wellington." She didn't want to offer any more details. Instead, she stared past the detective at a framed black and white picture of FDR hanging on the wall. It was crooked.

"Okay, then. I hope it's important. Would you like some coffee while you wait?"

"Yes, that would be nice."

Spurling didn't say anything else, walked out, and closed the door behind him, leaving Edith alone in the small office to consider again what had brought her there. The office was small, limited to a desk, a couple of filing cabinets, and the chair she sat in. Two tall windows looked out over the street from the second floor. The morning had passed by faster than she thought it would, and she found that she was hungry, in need of eating since she had left the biscuits and dry ham that Old Ben had put together for her alongside the road. She would eat somewhere down the road—if she wasn't in any trouble, if she was able to leave.

If they found the cowboy dead, Edith knew she would have to answer to that in a more serious way than recounting her story to Bill Spurling. She looked at the door behind her and wondered if it was locked, if she was going to spend the night in jail.

The detective brought Edith coffee and didn't offer her any more information before he left again. Time ticked on, echoed by the wall clock that seemed to move in slow motion. It was almost an hour before Spurling came back. He closed the door behind him and sat down at his desk.

"Well, as it turns out, there was an altercation in Ennis. The cook was wounded in a knife attack by a customer. The description matches the one you gave me, so we're figuring it was this cowboy you spoke of. We don't have an identity yet, but we're working on that."

"The cook? Is he all right?"

"Needed some stitches. The attacker fled and there was no one to stop him. Sounds like it could have turned out worse than it did."

That means Stella, the waitress, was unhurt too, Edith thought, but didn't say. "Did you find him dead on the road?"

This time Spurling shook his head. "No, ma'am. All the patrol car found was a spare tire flat as a pancake. There was some blood in the dirt at the side of the road, but there was no truck, or any sign of this cowboy. He was gone by the time we got there."

CHAPTER TWENTY-THREE

Sonny stepped outside the Harmeson house, leaving the same way he came. Peter was nowhere to be seen and Leddie and the two girls were still in the kitchen, chipping away at their daily chores. He'd offered a solemn goodbye, then saw himself outside with the intent of heading to Jesse's Plymouth, but a sound to his left stopped him. It was a girl sobbing as quiet as she could.

The sound was easy to follow, off the end of the porch, into the side yard. A tall live oak sat between the chicken coop and a larger shed that Sonny knew to be a workshop for repairing whatever was broke around the farm. Ida, the middle girl, ginger hair and alabaster skin like the rest of the Harmeson girls, sat on a swing attached to the ancient oak, with her face buried in her hands, tears staining the dry earth underneath.

"You all right there, miss?" Sonny said, walking toward her like he would an injured cat—cautious so he wouldn't get clawed.

Ida looked startled. "Oh, I didn't see you there, Mr. Burton." She stood and glued her hands to her side after wiping her tears away the best she could. Her eyes were puffy and were going to stay that way for a while.

Sonny stopped before the girl, and could smell the lye soap, a mixture of animal fat, wood ashes, and water, radiating off the simple homemade blue dress she wore. Her feet were bare and speckled with a thick garden of freckles. The temperature was in the mid-forties, but Ida was dressed for summer instead of winter. "Aren't you cold?" he said.

"I'm fine, thank you for asking. I was just going inside anyway." Ida stared at Sonny's face, then let her eyes drop like everyone else did to his right arm, to the prosthesis, and let her stare linger there for a couple of long beats. A mockingbird lit on top of the shed and whistled, then flew off without offering another note.

"Are you all right?" Sonny said again, ignoring her stare the best he could. He didn't want to pry, but something had seemed off since he had arrived at the farm, and with Rafael dead, there were a lot of questions still to be answered. Not to him. He was only a concerned citizen, but if Ida knew something that could help, then he had no choice but to follow his instinct—no matter whether it made Jonesy mad or not.

"I'm sad is all." Ida stood stiff, doing her best to show respect because she was being spoken to, but she didn't look Sonny in the eye. Every time he tried to force her to make eye contact with him, she looked away.

"About Rafael?" he said.

"I figured that was why you was here." She sucked in a breath of air. "Does it hurt?" Ida said, switching her thoughts to follow her eyes. She couldn't look away from the silver hook that had taken the place of Sonny's hand.

"Thank you for asking. It hurt a lot when they first took it, but every day the pain of it gets less and less. A person gets used to such things as time goes by."

"I couldn't live with it. I'd die if I lost my hand." Ida wiped her face with the sleeve of her dress, ridding herself of the last wet spots of tears. "I hurt really bad inside right now, and I don't think that hurt will ever go away."

"I'm sorry you're hurting," Sonny said. He lowered his head and his tone at the same time.

"Nobody's in trouble, are they?"

"No, of course not."

"Then why are you here?"

Sonny twitched, stopping a shake of his head midway through. "I needed to make a personal phone call is all."

"But you know that Rafael is dead."

"Is Rafael a friend of yours?"

Ida stared at Sonny like the question had been conjured from magic. "He did some work for Pa every now and then. Everybody knows everybody in Wellington, Mr. Burton."

"You're right," Sonny said. By his guess, Ida was probably fifteen, the middle child, lost in the shadow of her older and younger sisters, stuck out in the middle of nowhere with no one to talk to, especially a boy. Rafael, on the other hand, was in his early twenties with a couple of little babies all of his own . . . so forming the theory that Ida was somehow sweet on Rafael didn't make sense even though that's how it looked. Other than one thing. Betty Maxwell had told Sonny that there was some kind of trouble between one of the Harmeson girls and Clyde and Heck. Everything came back to those two. The connection didn't surprise him, but the thought of them made him feel hollow inside. All this trouble between Heck Kilbride, Clyde Jones, and a Harmeson girl might have got Rafael Hernandez killed, but Sonny didn't couldn't figure out why or how. Not yet. "Rafael was a good worker."

"Was," Ida whispered. "It's true, ain't it? It's true. It was him that was hung in that tree by them circus people?"

"I beg your pardon?"

If there had been any color in Ida's face, it would have drained out as fast as her words disappeared on the wind. She recoiled from Sonny like he was going to reach out, snatch her away, and take her to jail right then and there. Her eyes darted from one side to the other looking for a way to escape the situation she'd put herself in by saying something she shouldn't have.

"Nothin', Mr. Burton. It was somethin' I heard is all."

Sonny stepped forward. "Who told you the circus people hung Rafael? Your pa? Your sisters?" He couldn't imagine it would have been Leddie, who had not said anything against the circus folk. Sonny had never heard her say one cross word against anyone in all of the time he had known her.

"I need to go inside, Mr. Burton," Ida said, stepping to the side of him so he didn't tower over her, so he was out of reach with the hook and his left hand.

He wanted to grab hold of Ida, but he didn't. "Who told you such a thing?"

"I promised not to tell."

"Of course, you did, but it's important that you tell me."

"He'll be mad."

"Heck or Clyde? Which was it, Ida? Heck or Clyde who told you, then made you promise not to tell anyone? Why would they do that, Ida?"

"It wasn't neither of them, Mr. Burton," she said. "Leo told me, but you gotta promise me not to tell him I told you he was here. There'd be a whole lot of trouble if Heck found out I was a talkin' to Leo Dozier. Clyde, too. Them boys got into a row, and the last thing I want is anyone else gettin' hurt because of something I done said that I promised not to."

Sonny sucked in a dose of cool January air and let what Ida had told him settle into the confusing mess he'd been trying to sort out. Before he could formulate another question, one that he thought would keep Ida talking, Leddie Harmeson stepped out onto the porch and called out to Ida, "You get in here right now, girl. Your sisters got enough work of their own to do." Leddie's voice was sharp as a knife and it cut right between Sonny and Ida, severing any further conversation they might have had.

"You've drawn this foolishness out long enough, Ida. Now stop it this instant."

Ida stared at Sonny, and whispered, "Please don't tell on me." Then she ran onto the porch and disappeared into the house without saying a word to her mother.

"My apologies for my daughter's behavior, Mr. Burton," Leddie said. "We've been covered in a pall of bad news on this fine day, and Ida is my most dramatic child. I hope you won't think bad of us by her rude behavior."

"Of course not, ma'am. Of course not. You all have a good day now and thank you again for allowing me to use your phone." Sonny tipped his hat and started to walk toward Jesse's Plymouth. But he stopped when he was even with Leddie Harmeson. "I should apologize to you in advance. There might be a call come in for me. I'm expecting to hear some news about a friend of mine who is traveling. If that call comes would it be a bother to take a message and have one of your girls run it down to my house and pin it on the door?"

Leddie looked away from Sonny, down the road toward his house. "Only because it's you, Mr. Burton."

"I appreciate that, ma'am." He started to walk away again, but the woman's voice stopped him.

"You mark my word. This will all come back to those squatters down the road. I warned Peter to send them on, but he ain't never seen a woman with a beard who talked all nice and full of promises. He couldn't tell her no even though I was against them stayin' on our land."

"What kind of promises?" Sonny said.

"She said she'd let him help feed the lion."

Sonny didn't say a word to Jesse until they were on the road, well past the circus. "That was an interesting stop." His words hung inside the interior of the Plymouth like the knock from an uninvited visitor.

Jesse didn't bite on the comment. He let it fly by, and kept his eyes fixed on the road. His jaw was set into a familiar position of anger. He was a mirror image of his mother when he was angry. Martha had been born in a bad mood and had stayed that way most of her life, and Jesse had been prone to be moody, too. But the tense air in the automobile surprised Sonny. "You're not interested in what I learned?" he said.

"You left me out there like I was a child, Pa."

"I had a phone call to make."

"You took long enough."

"I couldn't walk into the man's house without exchanging pleasantries."

"No, you wouldn't do that."

"You're angry with me because I took too long?"

Jesse didn't look at Sonny once. He drove at a higher rate of speed than normal. The four-cylinder engine wasn't pushed to its limit, but it was getting a workout. A long plume of dust trailed behind them. "I'm angry because you're investigating something that Jonesy told you not to. I'm on thin ice. I need to hold onto to my reputation as much as I can. There can't be a worse time for a man to lose his job than right now. I got mouths to feed like everybody else, and the last thing I want to do is have to put my hat out and beg for a living."

"I ain't gonna let you or your babies go hungry."

"No, I don't think you would. I appreciate it, Pa, but I hope it don't come to that. Surely I can find a job with a badge on my chest somewhere in the state of Texas."

"A man with your experience shouldn't have a hard time. We both have acquaintances who'll help out if we ask."

"I'm out of a job because of something I have no control over. I served under Ma Ferguson. That makes me a tainted man. There might not be anybody willing to put their neck on the guillotine for me right now."

"You've never been a Ferguson stooge. You've got a good reputation."

"Keep that in mind when we're at the Hernandez's. It's something Jonesy gave us permission to do. Not go around askin' questions. I need to keep what reputation I have, thank you very much."

"I was only asking that girl why she was so upset. That's what took so long. You would have done the same thing considering we watched a man taken down from a noose no more than half a city block away from that house. Something didn't seem right."

Jesse didn't answer. He held the steering wheel like he had a tight hold on a fish, afraid it would get away.

Sonny continued talking as he looked down the road. "The girl, Ida is her name, told me that Leo Dozier had told her that the circus people hung Rafael."

Jesse turned to Sonny as a thought concluded, then refocused on the road. "That would mean he was there after it had happened."

"Yes, and he made her promise not to tell anyone. Heck and Clyde would be mad at her if they found out."

"What do you make of that?"

"I think we should talk to Leo is what I think."

"We can't do that."

"You can't. I can do anything I want to. If you'd like, after we talk to Aldo and his kin, you can take me back to my truck and send me on my way. What I do after that won't reflect on you one bit."

"I'm not going to sit back while you run all over the county with trouble followin' after you. You're a stubborn old man is what you are, and one of these days someone is going to take offense to that."

"I think I can handle myself," Sonny said.

"Maybe so, but I ain't gonna let you out of my sight if I don't have to."

"Quit your bellyaching, then."

Jesse didn't say anything else. He kept his eyes on the road and his hands on the steering wheel, ignoring Sonny like he wasn't there—except the angry expression on his face had thawed into a half smile.

"The phone call was as much of a surprise as what I learned from that Harmeson girl," Sonny said after a half mile of silence.

"Why's that?"

"Marcel Pryor answered the call. He told me that Edith took off."

"Took off?"

"Yes, sir. She got into her automobile and headed north to Wellington."

Jesse let his foot off the accelerator, allowing the Plymouth to slow down. "Here? To Wellington? What on earth for?"

"To see me, you fool."

"You're smiling," Jesse said. "You must think it's a good thing that she's coming here."

"Yes, I think it's a good thing. A real good thing," Sonny answered, then relaxed into the passenger seat and didn't offer anything else about how he felt about Edith or her impending arrival. He didn't have to.

CHAPTER TWENTY-FOUR

Aldo's house sat off the road farther than the other two houses before it. The battered clapboard house strained to bear two stories and had been built late in the last century, around the time Sonny had been born, by a farmer or landowner with dreams as immense as the Texas sky. The house had been stylish at one time. Eaves with decorative hand-carved scallops along with a sturdy red brick foundation demonstrated early pride and excessive skill; both were in disrepair now, crumbling, fading, the wood rotting into termite dust. The house was sandblasted gray from the onset of dust storms and a lack of resources to employ any kind of disciplined maintenance. A barn with a sagging roof sat behind Aldo's house, square in the middle of an overgrown pasture. There were long brown blades of buffalo grass waving in the wind, long dead, but not brittle enough to break off. The pasture was empty of any animals that Sonny could see. What fencing remained was in as much disrepair as the house. A few bored pigeons bobbed and pottered about, near a boulder-sized hole at the peak of the barn's roof. And a tall oak tree stood next to the house. It was so close a squirrel could have skipped over to the roof and hidden an acorn under a shingle—if the tree was healthy enough to bear fruit—without any effort at all. The tree's leaves were gone, blown away by the previous autumn winds. The old oak looked like a palsied fairy tale giant standing guard over a decaying fortress and a couple of rusted Model Ts. There wasn't a single sign of hope to be seen as a few scraggy chickens pecked around the front yard, filling themselves with pebbles, wishing to find the shell of a dead beetle, or better yet, a snake burrowed in a shallow hole, sleeping the winter away.

Jesse pulled the Plymouth to the front of the house and turned off the engine. "You want me to come with you?"

Sonny looked at him, then to the house. "I think that's a good idea. I expected there to be a load of vehicles here."

"You thought he'd already heard about what happened to Rafael?"

"I did, or I do. Word travels fast. Especially among Mexicans. Come on, let's go see if he's home."

"Doesn't look like there's been anybody here around in ages," Jesse said as he opened the door to get out. "Does he have an automobile?"

"Aldo walks everywhere he goes. He doesn't drive."

"But he works at the hospital."

"He walks into town every day. Has for as long as I've known him. Ever since I lost this." Sonny tapped on the upper part of the prosthesis. The false arm was made of oak, steel, and straps sewed of strong, pliable cloth that wrapped around his back and held the thing in place. The tap echoed out of the Plymouth like a woodpecker testing its beak against the integrity of untouched wood.

Jesse stood out of the automobile and Sonny followed suit. It had been a while since he'd paid a call on Aldo, but the place didn't look much different than it had the last time he had been there.

The two of them walked onto the porch shoulder to shoulder, scattering the chickens as they went. Sonny knocked on the door. When he did, the door pushed open with a painful creak. The hinges were in deep need of oiling. He looked to Jesse, then dropped his gaze down to the government-issue .45 that sat holstered on his son's hip. He flicked his head, and Jesse's eyes registered an understanding right away. Jesse pulled the gun from the holster and slid a round into the chamber as quiet as he could.

Sonny pulled the Colt out of his coat pocket and stepped to the side to allow Jesse to sweep beside him. There was no announcement of their presence, no call to signal to Aldo that they'd arrived or were coming inside uninvited. Instinct and fear had pushed good manners to the wayside.

The open door gave Sonny a clear view to the front room. The Colt was cocked and loaded, leveled, and aimed. While the outside of the house had not changed since Sonny's last visit, the interior had. Aldo had made sure to keep a neat house inside even if the outside was too much of a challenge to care for. His daughter, Carmen, helped out with the cleaning chores, even as she raised a baby boy on her own.

Aldo didn't have much. Some rickety furniture, a few pictures on the wall, and a full-sized cabinet radio stuffed against the opposite wall. But now, all of the chairs and tables were turned over, tossed about for no good reason. Pictures were on the floor; the glass in the frames shattered and strewn about without regard to the sharpness. The front room looked like a saloon after a Saturday night fight.

Sonny followed Jesse inside the front room, stepping over a wood chair that had been broken into pieces. The appendage was not something he thought about using to protect himself any more than he had when he'd had a fist. The hook was there if he needed it, and he had used it before, even though that use had brought a heavy dose of regret with it.

Jesse walked to the middle of the room and stopped. Sonny stopped next to him. They both listened. Water dripped from the pump that was mounted to a wash sink in the kitchen. A mouse scratched overhead in the ceiling, navigating between the two floors of the house. Outside noise worked its way inside through the cracks in the walls. A steady persistent wind blew from the west, intent on bringing dirt and sand with it. The inside of the house smelled of spices and peppers foreign to Sonny's nose, cumin, paprika, cayenne, and stale cigarette smoke.

A moan echoed through the house, and for a second, Sonny thought that it was only the wind. But Jesse heard it, too. He motioned upstairs with the barrel of the .45 and headed for the stairs.

Sonny didn't follow right away. He stood still, allowing the Colt to drop to his side, trying to make sense of what he saw, of the mess that had been made of Aldo's home. There was no question that a disturbance had happened, and as much as that concerned him, it confused Sonny. Why would anyone want to hurt Aldo? What did he have to do with any of the recent events in Wellington? There wasn't any kind of connection that Sonny could think of, other than Aldo was related to Rafael, and they were both Mexicans. That was it. Aldo had given Sonny no reason to think he was involved in Rafael's troubles in any way. *And where was Carmen?* he wondered.

Instead of following Jesse, Sonny headed the opposite direction and eased into the kitchen hoping that he would not find the Mexican girl and her baby crumpled on the floor. His mind worked that way. Imagined things around the corner. Most of the time they weren't there, but sometimes they were.

The small room was as much a mess as the front room, but no one was on the floor, hurt and helpless. The cupboard was toppled over, and the contents, cans, boxes, and dishes were scattered across the floor. Sonny studied the kitchen, and he came to the conclusion that there hadn't been a fight in the house, or there might have been, but the primary cause for everything being scattered about was that somebody was looking for something. Aldo had possession of something that somebody wanted bad enough to bust into his house and turn it upside down. The question was *who* was looking for something, and what were they looking for?

Sonny made his way upstairs to join Jesse. There were only two bedrooms on the second floor. Both were sparse, furnished with only the most necessary furniture: beds, a chest of drawers, and wardrobes that held one or two changes of clothes.

Jesse was standing in the bedroom to the left of the stairs. "There's nothing here. I could have sworn I heard a person moan."

"It must have been the wind," Sonny said.

They were both talking low, but it was clear there was no one else in the house.

The bedrooms had been ransacked, too. The mattresses on the beds were turned over and all of the drawers had been pulled out and tossed. Clothes were strewn everywhere. A blue work shirt hung from a floor lamp. Socks littered the floor, singled without mates like they were pulled apart and searched. Sonny wondered if Aldo kept money under his mattress like so many people did these days. Was this a simple burglary? A desperate man stealing another desperate man's cash? Or something more?

"I've looked everywhere," Jesse said. "The other room looks like this one."

"If Aldo and Carmen aren't here, we need to head over to Rafael's house."

"Where's he live?"

"A little piece north, next to Aldo's sister, Maria."

Jesse turned to leave the room, but Sonny lingered a second longer. This had to be Aldo's room, not Carmen's. There was nothing to suggest a woman's touch to the room. It held a simple single bed with a wood crucifix nailed to the wall above the headboard. The only clothes on the floor were the uniforms

Aldo wore to work at the hospital. There were no knickknacks, no pictures. Nothing but clothes and the crucifix. At least that was still there—more for Aldo's comfort than Sonny's.

On his way out, Sonny peeked into the other room to make sure for himself that he didn't miss anything. Like Jesse had said, it had been tossed, too. He wondered if the person who did this found what they were looking for. In an odd way, Sonny hoped so. Aldo and Carmen had enough problems in their lives. He stuffed the Colt back into his pocket as soon as he stepped outside.

Blue was happy to see Sonny when the two men arrived back at the Plymouth. The dog wagged his tail and tried to jump into the front seat, like he did when he rode with Sonny in the truck.

"You should have left that dog behind," Jesse said, settling into the driver's seat. "Get back," he added, commanding the dog with a harsh tone. Blue's ears dropped, and he obeyed, but offered a slight growl as he retreated into the backseat.

"Your mother failed you when she wouldn't let you have a dog."

"I didn't want one."

"You should have had one."

"I wanted a brother."

"You would have been better off with a dog, and from the looks of how things turned out you're lucky you got neither."

"Says you." Jesse started the engine, put the Plymouth in gear, and pulled off of Aldo's land.

Sonny was troubled that they hadn't found Aldo at home, but there was no use staying around any longer. "Take it slow," he said to Jesse.

"What are you looking for?"

"Anything that doesn't look like it belongs. I feel like we're missing something."

Jesse dropped the Plymouth down a gear to a slow crawl.

"You want to turn around and go back?"

"No, keep on driving. I hope Aldo is where I think he might be. We'll see if he's aware that the house has been tossed and find out if he has any idea why that happened. Or who might have done it."

"And if he's not at Rafael's?"

"We'll keep looking for him."

Three small shacks sat next to the farm-to-market road, surrounded by empty cotton fields, full of stubble from last year's crop. A thick pecan grove sat at the north side of the compound, leaves and nuts stripped bare by the wind and the harvest season. To Sonny's relief, there were several automobiles and trucks surrounding the shacks. Two horses were tied to the porch rail, and a Studebaker wagon with a lone mule was parked amidst the pecans.

Jesse pulled the Plymouth in behind a rusty farm truck that was used to haul bales of cotton and anything else that could be grown and sold.

"They already heard about Rafael," Sonny said.

Jesse turned the engine off and set the brake. "Or something else is going on, all things considered and what we found at Aldo's house."

"We need to walk soft on this ground. These folks will be spooked the way it is. Two gringos come knocking on the door won't be welcome, no matter that both of our last names are Burton."

"You don't need to tell me that."

"I don't know what kind of relationship you have with these people. You and I both have known some Rangers who only see white when it comes to the world. Brown or black trouble don't matter as much."

"You should know me better than that."

"You're right," Sonny said. "I should know you better than that, but I don't." He grabbed the door handle, opened it, and stood out of the Plymouth. Then he opened the back door and let Blue out of the backseat. "Go on, do your business."

The dog hurried off to the nearest tree and relieved himself.

"You think that's a good idea?" Jesse said, appearing at Sonny's side.

"He won't go far. A dog's gotta breathe. Good, it looks like we've drawn some attention." Sonny motioned toward the first shack. Two Mexican men were heading their way. Sonny knew one of them, a relation to Aldo one way or another, an older man about Aldo's age who everyone called Rubo, but his real name was Reuben Jaurez. The other man, who was younger with a similar gait and hairline, was a stranger to Sonny.

"*Hola*, Rubo," Sonny said. He heard Frances Avalon admonish him in his memory for not extending the hook to her when they'd first met, as he took in the leery look on Rubo's weathered face. The Mexican's brown eyes were fixed on the hook. Sonny offered the man his hook, and Rubo took it with a surprised look on his face. Sonny had put as much strength into the handshake as he had when he'd had two hands. When they were finished, he let the hook drop to his side like he had in the past instead of stowing it into his pocket out of sight. He was no more a freak than Frances Avalon was, and he knew it.

"Hello, Mr. Sonny," Rubo said in broken English. "How are you?"

Both of the Mexican men looked at Jesse with suspicion. Three more men had walked out onto the porch of the closest shack. It seemed to be the hub of the place, where everyone was gravitating to.

"Fair to middlin'," Sonny said. "I'm looking for Aldo. Is he here?"

"You have not heard?"

"No."

"Someone broke into his *casa* and beat him pretty bad. It is a good thing that Carmen was in town."

"He's going to be okay?" Sonny stepped forward, but neither Rubo nor the other man moved. They blocked the way to the shack, which surprised Sonny.

"He is hurt bad. Aldo, he is a strong man, but no one can look inside him to see how much damage is done."

"Why not take him to the hospital? He works there. Doc and Nurse Betty'll see to it that Aldo gets taken care of better than anywhere else."

"We don't want to leave him alone there. We don't want him hurt. We've had enough of that in one day."

"You heard about Rafael, then?"

"The *funerario* stopped to tell Maria. He let her see the body so she would believe him. When Juan here went to fetch Aldo, he found him in a bad state. Town is too dangerous now. Our family is a target and we must protect ourselves no matter what it takes. Aldo will stay here, and we will look after him. He is our *familia*."

Sonny looked to Jesse, then back to Rubo. "You can trust us, Rubo. Aldo is my friend."

"We must be cautious."

Jesse stepped even with Sonny. "Is there anybody who would want to hurt Rafael or Aldo? Did he say who broke into his house? Who beat him? What they were looking for?"

"He cannot talk. Or has not."

"Did you call the sheriff?" Sonny said.

"Why would we do that?"

"Because it's the right thing to do. Jonesy needs to be aware that there was a crime committed here. He's the law."

"He is *gringo* law."

Sonny started to defend Jonesy, but he let the words slide

down his throat before they escaped his mouth. He understood why Rubo felt the way he did. Even a white man was lucky to find justice, and that was only if he lived on the right side of the tracks. It didn't matter how upstanding a sheriff was. "So, Aldo or Rafael didn't have any enemies?"

"No," Rubo said. "You are friends with Aldo. Rafael has a family and works hard when he can find it. I worried that he was walking into a nest of vipers when he told us that he was going to try and get into the CCC camp. That has something to do with this. I am sure of it."

"Did Rafael get into any trouble with the sheriff?" Sonny said.

Rubo and Juan glanced at each other, held a knowing look between them for a long second, then turned their attention back to Sonny. He wished he was a mind reader.

Rubo kicked a bit of dirt with the point of his cowboy boot. "Rafael was a, what you call it, a rounder? He liked *guera,* um, white girls, and one of them, they make trouble for him some time ago. We worried deep that he was going to jail, or something worse, but then it all went away, and Rafael went back to living normal. He wouldn't talk about what happened, and from then on, he no like the *guera* anymore. He settled down with Juan's sister and started having babies. We thought he had learned his lesson. We thought everything was okay."

"This girl," Sonny said, "can you tell me what her name is?"

Rubo and Juan shook their heads at the same time, but Juan's eyes betrayed him as he looked down the road, as far away from Sonny and Jesse as he could.

"I need you to tell me," Sonny said to Juan. "It won't come back on you, I promise. Me and Jesse will protect you like you're our own. Aldo means a lot to me. He came to me to see if I could help get Rafael out of jail. I did what I could, but it wasn't enough. I was too late. I couldn't help, and now I can. Tell me what you can, and we'll bring the person who did this to justice, no matter who they are."

"As a Texas Ranger, I promise you, there's no one that can hide from us."

Juan looked to Rubo for approval.

The older man gave it with a slight nod of his head. "Tell these men, it is all right. Aldo, he trusts Sonny Burton as much as he trusts me."

"I do not have a name," Juan said. "But the girl had hair red as a hot fire and skin the color of chalk."

CHAPTER TWENTY-FIVE

Bill Spurling stood from behind his desk, and said, "You're free to go."

Edith couldn't believe the words she was hearing. "But I shot a man. Twice. I shot him twice and left him there to die. I hope he's dead."

"We have no evidence of any of this, ma'am. And if and when we do find this fella, I got a feeling he got what he deserved. You were protecting yourself is all. Without any physical proof of the facts there's nothing for us to do but let you go. We have your report. That's enough for now."

Edith lowered her voice and clasped her hands over the top of her purse. The Smith & Wesson was stuffed inside it. "But," she whispered to the floor, "he's still out there somewhere."

Spurling walked around the desk and put a soft hand on Edith's shoulder. "I'm sorry, ma'am, we've put out an APB on this fella and his truck. The hospitals and local doctors have been alerted. We've done everything we can to find him. The best you can hope for is that this man crawled off to die like the animal he is."

"Drove off. He was in a truck. He would've driven off. Not crawled."

"If you say so." Bill Spurling's voice hit a patronizing chord, and his grip on her shoulder stiffened when he spoke.

Edith looked Spurling in the eye, and said, "You don't believe me."

"I believe every word you said, ma'am. It's rare when someone walks into a police station and claims to have a shot a man. I think that takes courage. The police in Ennis confirmed this man's existence, though they don't have a clue as to who he is or where he came from. Why wouldn't I believe you?"

"I must have done some eternal thing to bring this madness upon myself."

"Not many women like you are traveling alone these days, ma'am. Perhaps that's not such a good idea."

"You think I should go home?"

"I can't tell you what to do, ma'am."

"I'm closer to Wellington than I am to Huntsville."

Spurling pulled his hand off Edith's shoulder and made his way to the chair behind the desk. He leaned down and opened a drawer. "You say it's a .38 you're carrying?"

"It is."

He grabbed something, then placed a small box on top of the desk. "How many cartridges did you leave with?"

"Marcel said all I would need was a loaded gun, so that's all I have, minus the ones that I shot."

"You only have three, then," Spurling said, sliding the box toward Edith. "Take these. Reload your gun and please get to where you're going as fast as you can. I don't have to tell you that we live in desperate times. Men have resorted to any means they can think of to survive. Hunger changes a man, makes him do things he wouldn't normally do. Envy forces a man to look away from himself in the mirror—if he has one to look in—to shave his face in or come to terms with his place in the world. I wouldn't take this cowboy's harassment personal if I was you. You didn't do anything, ma'am, except pull into the wrong gas station at the wrong time. It's that simple. As much as I'm sorry to say it, if you were traveling with a man at your side none of this would have happened."

"There's nothing else you can do for me?" Edith said, staring at the box of cartridges before her.

"We've done everything we can. Like I said, you're free to go."

Edith sat in the Pierce for a long time, not ready to leave the security of the Wichita Falls police station. The Smith & Wesson sat in its place in the passenger seat, loaded, next to the box of ammunition. Her hands felt glued to the steering wheel.

The episode with the cowboy, from start to finish, had taken a huge chunk of her day away from the drive. She should have been closer to Wellington than she was, and closer to Sonny. Closer to finding out if he was going to welcome her, or be like the detective, and tell her that she belonged at home. She couldn't imagine the long drive back to Huntsville if Sonny rejected her, if he was angered by her nerve. What would people think? How would she get on with her life? That kind of rejection would be worse than death itself.

The sun angled toward the west, disappearing into a line of slate blue clouds that promised to bring some kind of weather. On a regular day, Edith would have longed for rain no matter the amount. Even a thunderstorm would have been welcome. Lightning, torrential rain, remnants of a hurricane pushed from the south—any kind of bad weather was a blessing these days. The way she saw it the world needed a good cleansing. But on this day, any kind of adverse elements from the heavens was the last thing she wanted to deal with. She speculated that the clouds were nothing more than wind, even though that could birth a sandstorm, leaving her stuck and buried alongside the road, easy prey for the cowboy—or anyone else of his ilk—if he was still alive. She hoped he *had* crawled off and died some-where. It was a terrible thing to hope, but a desire she embraced with open arms. The world would be better off if the cowboy was dead. He had put her through hell, and hell was where he deserved to be. Dead, face to face with the devil, on fire, suffering in the eternal flame.

With that thought, Edith started the Pierce's engine, slid the gearshift into first, and pulled away from the police station. She didn't look in the rearview mirror, didn't allow her fear to bind her to the building or its false sense of security any longer. Instead, Edith pointed the hood ornament, the silver archer, north, and started to navigate the streets of the city, aiming once more for the highway.

The buildings in Wichita Falls fell away and the open road greeted Edith once again. She was none too thrilled to be driving alone in little traffic. Now she knew how it felt to be a mouse trying to outrun the shadow of a hawk. Even if the attack wasn't imminent, the threat of it hovered overhead in every cloud—or for Edith, in every truck that appeared behind her or passed on the opposite lane. If only she could be sure that the cowboy was dead.

If she could have done it all over again, confronted the man and pulled the trigger, she would have only shot him once. That shot would have been to the heart. Then she would have dragged his body into the police station and deposited it where it belonged. But there were no do-overs when it came to life and death situations like the one she had faced. Or any situation for that matter. She had learned that lesson the hard way when Billy Bunson had walked into her house in Huntsville with nothing but killing on his mind. But Edith knew right then and there, revving the engine, pushing it harder than she had since she'd been on the road, that she wouldn't make the same mistake twice. If the cowboy ever came into her aim again, she would kill him without thinking twice. She would be the one to send him to hell for certain. There would be no more wondering, no more looking over her shoulder. That was no way to live.

The slate blue clouds turned darker, flirting with black, and the afternoon light was replaced by a false gloaming. Nighttime rushed toward her hours earlier than it was scheduled. She had to turn on her headlights to see the road before her. A strong wind from the west buffeted the Pierce, making the automobile difficult to steer, difficult to keep on her side of the road. Every mile was a fight, requiring more arm strength from Edith than she knew she possessed, especially the farther from Wichita Falls she got. Sand, dust, and anything loose pelted the steel and glass body that she was encased in. Twigs, nuts, and loose cloth from who knew what swept across the road in front of her. More times than once Edith was tempted to swerve but kept the front of the Pierce steady. She was driving right into the storm, could feel the wind intensifying, but not one drop of water had fallen from the sky to the parched ground. There was no turning back even though that made the most sense. Stopping alongside the road was out of the question. All she could do was keep on driving.

The evening grew even darker from a combination of the day ticking toward night, and the relentless cover of clouds that had deepened overhead. A glance at her watch told her that she wasn't going to make it to Wellington by true nightfall, and that concerned her even more. Being on the road alone with the fear of the cowboy still being out in the world, chasing after her if he was still alive, if that was possible with two gunshot wounds, considering the shape she had left him in, was one thing. But being alone and driving in the dark of night frightened her even more. If the cowboy had somehow managed to put himself into his truck and continued his pursuit of her there would be no way to see him coming. Still, she kept on going until she could go no more. Whether she liked it or not, she was going to have to stop for food and gas. She didn't have enough of either to make it to Wellington.

She found a small two-pump Phillips 66 gas station in Quanah and pulled into the empty lot with reservation, to fill the tank. The yellow brick building sported a red tile roof, and all of the lighting and pumps were painted the same color red as the roof. A tanker truck sat behind the building, and all of the lights burned bright inside. It was the only building along the road that looked alive, that had people in it, was open.

A short, plump man with greasy hands toddled out of the building like Fatty Arbuckle as Edith turned off the engine. She dropped the Smith & Wesson into her purse, then moved the purse from the passenger seat to her lap before she rolled down the window. The windstorm still raged, pushing the man's thin salt and pepper hair into the air. It had been a wise choice for him not to wear a hat. Anything that wasn't attached would have ended up in Oklahoma. Pings and pops continued as debris and small dirt particles pelted the side of the automobile.

"Can I hep, you?" the gas attendant said. He looked to be in his early fifties and had dull, bored eyes. Edith assumed he might have been the station owner.

"Fill the tank, please," Edith said.

He looked past Edith into the Pierce, and said, "Will that be all?"

She didn't understand what he meant. What else could there be? "Yes," she answered, then rolled the window closed as quick as she could.

The man stared at her, then walked around the automobile and got to the task of putting gas into the Pierce's tank.

Edith sat stiff in the driver's seat, watching the man in the rearview mirror, tracking him as he went like he was a threat, even though she didn't feel like he was. There was no one else in the Phillips building that she could see, and no one loitered around anywhere. The station sat off the road and every once in a while, a truck or another automobile passed by; all of them fighting the wind like she had. She clutched her purse as tight as she could, ready at any second to pull the Smith & Wesson from its hiding place. Her heartbeat was faster than normal. She could hear it inside of her ears and feel it inside of her chest. *Was she going to be this scared when she stopped every time?* she wondered.

Gas ran inside the tank while the attendant hurried to check the oil and the air pressure in her tires. He raised from the tire Edith had changed, looked to the gas pump, then hurried inside the building. The attendant was back outside in a blink, carrying a wrench, in a hurry, on a mission. Once he got back to the Pierce, he disappeared from Edith's view as he leaned down to work on the tire. The automobile lurched a bit as the attendant tightened something. From there, he hurried back to the pump and finished with the gas.

Edith rolled down her window, and said, "How much do I owe you?" when the attendant came back around to collect payment for the gas.

"It's a good thing you stopped, lady. The lug nuts were pretty loose on that tire. If you would have kept goin' that tire would have come off and you could have killed yourself. Did the front end shake as you was drivin'?"

"I thought it was the wind I was fighting."

"Whoever put that tire on didn't have a clue about what they was doin'."

Edith didn't claim responsibility for mounting the tire. She thanked the man, then repeated her question. "How much do I owe you?"

"Be two dollars and seventy-five cents."

Edith counted out the money, dropped it in the man's hand, said "thank you," and closed the window as fast as she could again. She left her purse in her lap, started the automobile, and put it in gear. She almost didn't hear the attendant say thank you as she drove away. All Edith could think about was getting back on the road, moving as fast as she could. She wasn't a target then. It would be harder for anyone to attack her if she was speeding toward Wellington at fifty miles an hour rather than sitting in a gas station being lectured to about putting a spare tire on an automobile.

Whether she liked it or not, Edith needed to stop to get something to eat. She was famished. Her head was throbbing, and her hands were shaking. It was all she could do to hold onto the steering wheel.

It wasn't long before she came to the town of Childress and knew from her map that this was the last hard turn she would have to make. Wellington was north. To get to the intersection she would have to drive through Childress and its downtown. She drove down a main street, passing an elaborate theater, the Palace, like a lot of decent-sized towns had. There weren't any places to stop to eat until she came across a place called Gay's. It was a wide single-story building, painted a creamy yellow, making it hard to miss, at the intersection of the highway she needed to turn north on.

Her headlights cut across the parking lot, catching a few automobiles; two black sedans and one older maroon coupe. After finding a parking place, Edith tried to get a glimpse of herself in the rearview mirror, but the light was too diffused. All she saw was a pale white face washed away by gray shadows. Her appearance didn't matter. Not after the day she'd had. Besides, she thought, I don't know a soul in Childress, Texas.

Edith couldn't help herself from running a comb through her hair and fluffing it a bit before exiting the Pierce. She held her purse tight, like it was sewn from golden cloth, as she walked inside the restaurant. The place smelled of grease and cigarettes like every other café she had walked into since she'd been on the road. The interior was fitted with overhead lights that reflected off of an ordered collection of white tabletops with bright yellow seats. Everything inside looked crisp and clean. A row of booths sat butted against a back wall while a low-slung bar with round pedestal seats fronted the interior of the café. The round seats were yellow like the chairs; a dozen suns that rotated when a customer moved. A cash register sat at the end of the bar. Five people were eating their dinner. Two couples and a single man, all scattered about the oversized room.

A waitress, much older than Stella in Ennis, stood wiping down a pie case, looked up when Edith walked in and said, "Sit anywhere you want, honey."

Edith made her way to a table that faced the window. She sat down so she could see the door, so her back was against a wall. The table was clean, and a menu sat open on top of it. Edith didn't want much. A hamburger and coleslaw would be fine, which was what she told the waitress when she came to ask for her order. The waitress looked to be in her late fifties, not much older than Edith, a little on the heavy side, and stuffed into a yellow dress. Her name tag said: Madge.

"Save some room for some pecan pie, honey," Madge said. "Earl makes the best pies in Texas." She spun around and headed back toward the kitchen with her order pad in hand.

Edith wondered if every waitress in Texas said that. Stella had said the same thing. She nodded, agreeing that she would, but deep inside knew she wouldn't. Dessert was for special occasions and this wasn't one of them. All she wanted to do was eat and get back on the road. Her next stop would be in Wellington. And no matter how Sonny welcomed her, she would be safer there than she was anywhere else.

Automobiles were sparse on the road outside the café. Their

headlights cut through the darkness like they were butter knives. There one minute, gone the next. Edith kept a lookout for a truck like the one the cowboy had been driving when he'd stopped the last time—when Edith had shot him. Wondering—hoping—if the man was dead, was never far from her mind.

Satisfied that she was safe, Edith relaxed as much as she could, though not enough to move her purse off her lap. She looked at the couple closest to her. Three tables away. They looked to be in their mid-thirties. Working people. He had on black boots and denim pants. The woman, a buxom blonde with a sour face that was so common that Edith would have been shocked to have seen anything else, wore similar clothes to the man she was with. There was no reason to assume they were married, and no reason not to. They both looked glum, tired from the day. No one smiled these days. Humor was a rare bird that no longer migrated to this part of the country. The other couple was older, more her age, and they talked low between each other. He wore horn-rimmed glasses, had gray hair, and a loose tie hung from his neck. His white shirt suggested that he was a businessman of some kind. The woman with him was dressed nice, too, in a pink dress, offset by silver hair coiffed by a professional. She wore glasses, too, that shone in the light like they had been polished with pride. That left the lone man, who wore businesslike attire too, tie, glasses, and shiny black wingtip shoes. Edith was about to start wondering about all of their stories when the bell on the door dinged, taking her attention away from the café patrons, returning it to the entrance. She stiffened her back against the wall and tightened her grip on her purse.

Two boys walked inside. Edith would have been surprised if either of them were twenty years old. They wore work clothes and heavy boots, similar to the man sitting with the sad woman. One of the boys wore a denim jacket and the other had on a dark long-sleeved flannel shirt.

"Find yourself a seat, fellas," Madge hollered from the pass-through window. Edith wondered where this Earl was that the waitress had spoken of. She had yet to see him. From the looks of things Madge was doing all the cooking *and* waiting tables.

The boys, one with oily black hair and the other with greasy brown, ignored Madge's welcoming, walked to the cash register, and stood there in wait. They were silent as two cats ready to pounce on an unsuspecting mouse. Neither of them said a word to the other. They stood as still as carved statues celebrating the angry youth of the day.

Madge peered out of the pass-through window, exhaled deep enough to send an echo throughout the café, then stomped to the cash register. "You two want an order to take out or what?"

The black-haired boy said, "No. I want what's in the cash register."

As soon as the first utterance of a word had come from his mouth, the brown-haired boy spun and pulled a knife out of his pocket, then pointed it toward the seats in the café. "Nobody moves and nobody gets hurt," he yelled.

Edith gasped, shocked to be in the midst of a robbery, though something deep inside of her wasn't surprised. The road trip had revealed a world desperate to survive, to express its rage, and to take whatever it wanted without consequence.

The brown-haired boy was blocking her view of the other boy now, but it looked like he was poking something from the inside of his jacket. A gun? Or a finger pretending to be a gun? It was hard to tell. But one of them had a weapon—a knife— along with everyone's attention inside the café.

"We got a gun, too," the brown-haired boy continued on, his eyes darting off the three men in the café calculating which one to be the biggest threat. His eyes landed on the single man and stayed there.

"Give me all of the money in the till, lady," the black-haired boy said, jabbing whatever was inside his jacket at her.

Madge put her hands on her wide hips, and said, "I ought to reach over the counter and box your ears. Does your momma care about where you are? I bet she'd beat your ass if she knew what you were a doin'. Good thing I don't recognize either of you or I'd be happy to tell her. Yes, sirree, I would. You can count on that."

None of the men in the café moved a muscle. They stared at the confrontation, watching the boys with a high amount of interest. If there was fear in the air, Edith couldn't smell it.

"You say one more thing about my momma and I'm going to shoot you, old woman, then help myself to the money anyways." It was the black-haired boy, who was red in the face and tense as a guitar string about to be plucked.

The brown-haired boy turned away from the men in the interior of the café and pointed his knife at Madge. He thrust it forward without warning, and said, "Do what he said, lady."

Madge darted out of the way of the blade. It didn't catch anything but air. A look of concern fell across the woman's face. The attempt on her life had got her attention, convinced her in that second to take the boys seriously.

With the focus off all of the people in the restaurant, and the lack of action by any of the men, Edith didn't hesitate any longer to reach into her purse and pull out the Smith & Wesson. She wasn't going to sit there and let Madge get hurt. Nobody was going to get hurt if she could help it.

Edith let the purse fall away, stood up, and leveled the pistol at the brown-haired boy. Neither of the boys noticed, but the rest of the customers did. They were surprised, drew back, and focused on Edith as she walked past them.

The inside of Gay's Café was silent as an empty casket. Something hummed from inside the kitchen. A light buzzed. A fan clicked as it turned. But all of the sounds were so distant, Edith couldn't hear them. She felt like she was floating until she stopped midway to the cash register. "Both of you boys better drop your weapons and get on out of here," Edith said as strong as she could. Her voice didn't crack once, and she stared at both boys with an assurance and sternness that she meant business. "Nobody has to get hurt, but if you don't do what I tell you, I can promise you that I will shoot you before you can say Jack Sprat."

Edith had surprised the boys. They both turned to her and assessed her seriousness. The barrel of the Smith & Wesson was pointed at the brown-haired boy's head. There was no waver in the barrel. Edith held the gun as steady as an executioner.

Neither of the boys said another word. Without any hesitation, they turned and ran out of the door, one trailing after the other. Both of them were gone as quick as they had come in, leaving a bewildered Madge and a relieved group of people inside the café.

A man, who Edith assumed was Earl the cook, came walking out of the kitchen carrying a stack of green serving trays, not paying any attention to anything else inside the creamy yellow building.

Edith dropped the gun to her side and looked out the windows into the darkness of night, looking for any sign of the boys. They were nowhere to be seen, and for a second, she wondered if what had happened was real or imagined. The tremor in her hand told her that the robbery had been real. A cold shiver confirmed that feeling for her.

"What's going on here?" Earl said. "Did I miss something?"

"Where were you?" Madge snapped.

"Outside smokin' a cigarette. Why?"

"You about got us all killed is why." Madge walked out from behind the counter and went right to Edith. The waitress wrapped her in a powerful hug. "Thank you, honey. Your meal's on me. That was awful brave of you," she said as she cast a disapproving look to the closest man. The rest of the customers remained silent; their eyes fixed on the two women.

After a heartbeat, Edith pulled herself from the hug and made her way back to her table. She could hardly believe what she had done. She couldn't believe it was her own face staring back at her in the reflection in the window.

CHAPTER TWENTY-SIX

Sonny stared down at Aldo lying in the bed. The Mexican's face was swollen and battered. His eyes were closed like he was sleeping, but that was not the case. Rubo had told Sonny that Aldo was unconscious, hadn't woken up since they'd found him. Aldo was shorter than Sonny, but he had never looked like a child, always an old man with thick hair spun white from years spent traveling around in the sun, and dark brown skin, wrinkled and fragile, worn like a good saddle. He lay on his side in a fetal position pulled into himself, the only movement coming from the repetition of one shallow breath after the other in his slight chest. A push of wind would shatter him like a rock thrown at glass. He looked like a baby born an old man, tortured by every day he had spent on earth.

"You hang in there, *amigo*," Sonny said, restraining to touch Aldo, to offer him comfort. That had never been their way. The distance of race and position had stood between them from the first day they had met. Instead, Sonny turned to leave the small bedroom, silent, his head hung low while his feet shuffled toward the door in a slow funeral march. The room had smelled of healing salts and urine, was bitter to the nose, and Sonny almost tripped over his own feet as he heard Aldo gasp and rattle. He didn't dare to look over his shoulder. He feared he would see the grim reaper come to take his friend away.

Rubo and Jesse were standing outside the room waiting for Sonny. He held his hat in his hand and acknowledged the three sitting Mexican women as he passed. Each of the women held a rosary in their hands, fingering the holy beads with a mumbled prayer. Sonny had no idea what the words being offered to the invisible god in the sky were, but he figured whatever they were, they couldn't hurt. If Aldo was to live, it would take a miracle.

Once he was outside the shack, Sonny turned to Rubo and said, "You're sure he didn't say anything? Give you a hint at who did this to him?"

Rubo looked down to the ground. "No. He was the way he is when he was found."

"I still think you ought to take him to the hospital."

"I fear he will not survive the trip into town."

"All right," Sonny said. "But I'd like to stop at the hospital and tell Doc what has happened. If he comes out here will you let him tend to Aldo?"

Rubo offered a slight nod. "If he makes the trip, he will be welcomed here. Aldo would not work at the hospital if the doctor was not a good man."

Jesse stood solemn at Sonny's side, keeping quiet, allowing his eyes to search the vacant horizon.

"I'll tell him," Sonny said. "I have some stops to make, some questions to ask."

"You have an idea who might have done this, Mister Sonny, don't you?" Rubo said.

"Maybe. I'm not sure why, or what he was looking for at Aldo's house, but I'm going to go talk to some people to find out if I'm right."

That got Jesse's attention. "We'll let the sheriff decide that," he said.

Rubo ignored Jesse. "You give him to understand that he is the enemy of the Hernandezes if he did this to our Aldo. He is our enemy and we will have our revenge."

Sonny put his hand on Rubo's shoulder. "There's been

enough blood spilled on this day, *amigo*. Jesse will see to it that we find out who did this to Aldo. You don't need to worry about anything else."

"You tell that to Aldo." Rubo walked back inside the shack and slammed the door behind him, rattling Sonny's teeth and soul.

Jesse, Sonny, and Blue were all settled in their places in the Plymouth, heading into Wellington. A wall of dark granite blue clouds reached out from the west, promising to catch the automobile no matter how fast Jesse drove. The wind had strengthened while they had been inside the shack. Bits of dust and dirt pinged the automobile; it sounded like someone had opened fire on them with buckshot. Neither man seemed to notice that the Plymouth was being sandblasted. The shine of the paint was lost forever.

"Looks like another storm comin'," Jesse said. "There's been a spate of 'em. I keep hoping for snow or even an ice storm. Anything but the dusters. I think the grit travels inside my veins."

"There's no escaping it."

Silence settled between the two men, but it didn't take long before Jesse had to put some extra effort into holding the Plymouth on the road. He locked both elbows and stared down the road. "Jonesy has to be aware of what has happened to Aldo, Pa."

"All I want us to do is go talk to Leo Dozier. We need to figure out how he's tangled up with that Harmeson girl. I don't see a problem with talking to him."

"Do we have to do this again?"

"No." Sonny allowed any tension in his voice to resign itself. "But I don't trust Jonesy right now. Do you?"

"No, not really."

"Then why are you heading into town?"

"Because I gave the man my word that I wouldn't overstep my boundaries. You taught me that my word is gold. It's all I have. Or did I misunderstand you?" Jesse flicked his eyes over to Sonny, then turned his attention back to the road, letting the look speak for itself.

The wall of weather had rolled closer, but Jesse was doing a fair job of outrunning it. More buckshot pebbles took a crack at the Plymouth, bouncing off the Detroit steel like it was hail dropped out of a cold sky. The roar of the wind had invaded the interior of the automobile, promising any words would go unheard—so Sonny said nothing. He eyed the storm, which was a good mile to the side of them, not disputing anything Jesse had said.

By the time they reached Wellington, the storm, void of rain, and heavy on sand, dust, and debris, had started to kiss the Plymouth's bumper. Jesse drove to the courthouse, determined to keep his word. Sonny was happy to be a passenger for once. It was hard to fight the wind in his truck. He didn't have the strength in his arm and prosthesis, or the desire to wrestle any automobile in a storm. Riding with Jesse allowed him to sit and think about what he should do next. He could get used to the shotgun seat—even if he disagreed with Jesse about talking to Leo Dozier.

"There's Jonesy's vehicle," Jesse said, pulling to a stop in front of the courthouse, craning his neck to look two automobiles down. "I'll run in and talk to him."

"Good idea. Me and Blue'll wait here for you."

Jesse reached for the door handle and stopped with a jerk. "I'm serious, Pa. Don't leave here without me."

"Why would I do that?"

"Because you're you."

"I hadn't thought about leaving you here." Which was the truth. Sonny hadn't considered ditching Jesse to go find Leo

Dozier, but he thought it was an idea worth considering now that Jesse had mentioned it.

"You swear?" Jesse demanded.

"I swear."

The promise satisfied Jesse. He pushed his way out of the Plymouth and struggled to the door of the courthouse, leaning forward into the wind, holding onto his white Stetson with his right hand, keeping his other hand stiff at his left side. His pant legs flapped like flags struggling to free themselves of a pole. Left standing there, Jesse's clothes would have been ripped to shreds by the latest sandstorm.

The dark blue clouds had turned black, sucking whatever light remained out of the day. Interior lights flickered on around the square, illuminating the café, the grocery store, and the hardware store. The street was empty of traffic, giving Sonny pause. Downtown was deserted. In the blink of an eye, it looked like midnight outside instead of late afternoon. Everyone had taken refuge, saw the storm coming, were hunkered down. Waiting out a storm was a common practice—like cleaning everything after it was.

Sonny had no intention of stepping foot outside of the automobile unless Blue signaled that it was necessary. Jesse would lose his mind if the dog peed on the seat. Sonny looked over his shoulder and made eye contact with the dog. Blue seemed comfortable to ride out the storm safe from the shooting sand and dust in the backseat. The dog had good sense about him that was for certain.

Sonny closed his eyes for a second, allowing everything around him to disappear as best he could. The wind howled a song of striking rage, shaking the Plymouth with the threat of turning it over onto its side. There was no worry about that. Sonny had never seen such a thing. The most unsettling thing was the unending spray of flying grit shooting at the windows.

Sonny had seen shattered glass after a strong storm. He felt exposed, vulnerable. Closing his eyes took him away from that feeling for a brief second. Then another more urgent feeling arose, one that was more unknown and unwelcome. That feeling was fear. Not for himself, but for Edith. He realized that she was on the road alone, facing the same irascible weather or something worse. He couldn't rush to her and save her. If he could find her, he would have betrayed his promise to Jesse right then and there and taken the Plymouth without a second thought.

Sonny reached for the door handle, but when his hook tapped against the metal instead of flesh, a heavy dose of reality came flooding back to him. There were brief periods of time when he felt whole, healthy, with all of the appendages that he'd been born with. Brief moments that ended with a child's stare, a reach for something with the expectation of fingers that had been there to grab whatever it was that he was after, or when he woke from a dream where he had both hands. The realization often triggered despair or anger. He could condemn Bonnie Parker for her deed, but she wouldn't hear him, buried in a grave in Dallas like she was, her body riddled with so many bullet holes the embalming fluid ran out of her as soon as it had been poured into her. She'd got her due. Hamer and Gault had seen to that. Sonny's rage against Bonnie Parker had subsided early on, but it had never disappeared all the way. Sonny knew he'd made the choice to go after Bonnie and Clyde on his own. That had been like climbing into a viper pit blindfolded. He blamed himself as much as he blamed Bonnie. She was a bad seed set on fire by something no man could ever understand, and Sonny had a similar urge to extinguish the mean ones before they hurt someone else. The two of them were more alike than Sonny ever cared to admit.

He tapped the hook against the door handle again, and felt

trapped, claustrophobic, unable to move. He hated confinement. But his concern about Edith had forced him to open his eyes and allowed him to see a truck passing by. A truck he knew and recognized right away. The truck was a ten-year-old black Model T Ford with a dual rear axle. The bed was outfitted with a boom and a hook, used as a wrecker when the need arose, and belonged to Leo Dozier's father, Wilmer. The Doziers owned a junkyard north of Wellington, and regardless of the oversized tires and bigger engine than most trucks were equipped with, no fool in his right mind should have been out tooling around in a sandstorm. Not even the Doziers.

Any thought of Edith disappeared from Sonny's mind. *What the hell?* he wondered as he twisted around in the seat to follow the sight of the truck as it passed by. Sure as he was sitting there, it was Leo Dozier behind the steering wheel, driving the wrecker.

Sonny looked to the door of the courthouse, thought about honking the Plymouth's horn, to alert Jesse, but he knew there wasn't going to be time. He was going to have to break his promise and take the automobile. *Jesse,* Sonny reasoned to himself, *would have done the same thing.*

Sonny slid over on the bench seat and started the Plymouth. "Hang on, Blue, this could get interesting."

The dog cocked its head at the mention of his name but didn't move.

Sonny threw the Plymouth into reverse with his left hand and reached over with the hook and pulled the lights on. It was an orchestrated move that forced him to cross his arms, concentrate on using both appendages, use his foot on the clutch all at the same time—something that would have been impossible for him to do only months before.

The harsh, unrelenting wind screamed out of the west and Sonny was heading south. Leo had turned on his lights, too, giving Sonny two red dots to aim the front of the Plymouth at. He had to focus on keeping the automobile on the road since he was being pushed so hard by the wind. It took both his hand and his hook to keep the hard steel Plymouth straight. He struggled to find the strength in his arms.

Pebbles, dirt, and anything else that was loose on the ground battered the steel and windows, trying their best to get inside and bury Sonny, destroy him before he could catch Leo—it was like they were in cahoots together. Nothing had shattered yet.

Sonny was going to do everything he could to catch up with Leo, to see where he was going, what he was doing. There was no reason for anyone to be out in this kind of weather. It made no sense. Unless Leo was running away from something. Or going to something. The jaunt may have been a wrecker call, a duty of his father's business, a hero's journey.

Sonny had been trained to think the worst of people. Leo's name had turned up from the start, when the mailman, Clifford Jones, had told Sonny about the CCC camp trouble. Then Aldo had brought Leo into the story. And Jonesy and Betty Maxwell, too. Even Ida Harmeson, the dramatic farm girl, twisted in grief over the death a Mexican man, had named Leo. Or was that it? Sonny wasn't sure because Leo had been there, had delivered the news and blamed the circus people. Leo. It was always Leo. There first. In front of Sonny, and then gone. Until now. Leo was in Sonny's sights and he wasn't letting him go. Not this time.

The pair of red taillights grew dimmer, then disappeared, turned off. Sonny could still see the outline of the wrecker as it rushed out of the grasp of the buildings in town and into the vulnerable openness of cotton fields flung into the air; he imagined mad children throwing sand in the air. Sonny had no choice but to try and catch Leo. The boy was on the run. He was trying to hide. That's why he turned the lights off.

The wrecker matched Sonny's acceleration.

Did he recognize Jesse's Plymouth? That it was a Texas Ranger on his tail?

Once Sonny had enough control of the Plymouth, he reached into his coat pocket and pulled out the Colt revolver. He tossed it on the seat next to him so it was there if he needed it.

Grit and dust infiltrated the Plymouth, and Sonny had to spit to clear his lips and mouth of the taste. It didn't work. The dust lingered. There was no way to get rid of the stuff. Some days he felt like the sand and soil had become a part of him, were trying to bury him inside out one grain at a time. Jesse had said the same thing.

Even with the high beams on, the road became difficult to see. Snakes of dirt attacked the Plymouth from all sides. Visibility had dropped to a few feet and Sonny was driving on faith and instinct, doing his best not to blink, not to close his eyes. He was driving faster than he should have been, over forty miles an hour. The Plymouth complained and all of the bolts threatened to unscrew. Leo's truck had disappeared, and Sonny feared he'd run smack-dab into it, doing even more damage to his relationship with Jesse than to the automobile.

The risk wasn't worth it.

Sonny slammed on the brakes before he killed himself and Blue.

The Plymouth came to a stop in the middle of the road, then coughed, shuddered, and died.

No one in their right mind should have been out in this kind of weather. Not even Sonny Burton chasing down Leo Dozier for a reason he didn't understand. All he knew was when the compass insisted on pointing in one direction, you followed it no matter what.

CHAPTER TWENTY-SEVEN

As quick as the sandstorm had started, it stopped. Solitary grains of dirt dribbled down from the sky as the back end of the gray wall pushed east. The leftover view of the horizon was a mosaic of blue, gray, and black splotches; clouds bruised and battered, but still breathing, too tired to catch up with the rest. Evening had not fallen all the way to the ground. A fresh light cast itself into the interior of the Plymouth. The roar of the storm still clogged Sonny's ears, but his vision was fine. He could see through the shifting sand on the windshield, down the road. His eyes landed on the object they sought; Dozier's motionless wrecker twisted sideways, propped up on a boulder twice the size of an eight-cylinder motor. The featureless, nameless boulders were a common sight in Collingsworth County—dug out of cotton fields in their infancy—marking property lines and intersections of farm-to-market roads. A head-on collision with one of the massive stones could kill a man, send him flying headfirst out of an automobile. Leo had the advantage of driving a larger, oversized truck, but it was still damaged. He had found a sudden end he hadn't counted on no matter where he was going or why.

Sonny grabbed the Colt, then looked back to check on Blue. "You stay here, boy," he said, then pushed his way out of the driver's side door, leaving it open. He stopped at the edge of the door, using it as a shield as he tried to get a better look at the wrecker. The pistol dangled from his hand, loaded and ready to use. He'd become a fair shot left-handed, but he would never be as good as he was with his right. All he needed to do was protect himself. This was no competition.

At first, he didn't see any movement in the wrecker at all, with the exception of the front left wheel, spinning, gearing down to a stop brought on by force, impact, and nothing else. Sonny wondered how fast Leo had been going when he'd hit the boulder. Then he saw a head bobble into the open window, followed by a bloody hand grabbing hold of the steering wheel, desperate, in search of a life raft in an ocean made of loose dirt and obvious pain.

"You all right in there?" Sonny called out. He wasn't about to rush over to the cab. Leo's state of mind was a mystery. Never touch an injured cat came to his mind; a voice from the past, an adult offering him serious advice. Sonny couldn't identify the voice when it had been spoken to him, but he heeded the warning from his memory. He stood still, calculating, waiting to see what Leo did next.

The only thing that answered Sonny's question was the dying wind and the receding roar of the storm. He had to lick the grit off his lips and clear his throat before he said another word. His skin tasted like ash and earth and smelled of decay; old and unspeakable. "I ain't here to hurt you," Sonny said, boosting the words from his chest, not quite a yell. His voice caught on the weak wind, but it was hard to tell if his plea had been delivered. The three of them, Sonny, Blue, and Leo, were the only source of life to be seen or heard for miles. There was nothing around to reach out to. Not even a shack. Everything was gray and soiled, buried or blown bare by the force of the wind and the angry sky. Even the sight of a crow would have been welcome.

The head and the hand disappeared from inside the cab, and Sonny stood fast. He held his focus where he first saw movement. A barrel slid out the window and before he could take cover, Leo fired off a shot in his direction.

The bullet buried itself in the earth a few feet from Sonny's boots, spraying the Plymouth with a thin shower of dust and dirt. The controlled explosion inside the handgun echoed across the fallow fields, racing to catch the fleeing storm. A ring of gun smoke lingered, then disappeared, sucked away by a vacuum left behind from the storm.

The shot had caught Sonny off-guard. He hadn't expected Leo to open fire on him. There was nowhere to run to except back inside the automobile. He dove into the front seat, head down, doing his best to hold onto the Colt in his weak hand.

"You go on and get out of here," Leo yelled from inside the wrecker. "Ain't no call for you Burtons to stick your nose where they don't belong."

"I'm here to help you," Sonny answered back. "You're hurt."

"I said *get!*"

"Why in the hell are you shooting at me?" Sonny couldn't see Leo, or inside the truck. The angle it was perched at on the boulder wouldn't allow him a good look. For a second, he wondered if Jesse had a set of binoculars stowed away in the Plymouth somewhere. He knew there wasn't time to search, to move around, and put himself at risk of being shot.

Leo didn't give a reason for his actions. He stayed silent, leaving Sonny to ponder his next move again. All he could do was assume, which he loathed to do, that Leo had something to do with Rafael's hanging. Though, if he was going to speculate, and he already had thought about what was going on plenty, he would have put Heck Kilbride and Clyde Jones at the hanging, not Leo Dozier. But it *was* Clyde Jones who had taken Leo's spot at the CCC camp, and it had been Rafael who had taken tequila to the meeting, then got into a fight with Leo. If Leo was the blaming kind, he could have taken a grudge out against

Rafael for costing him his spot. The thought made sense to Sonny as he stared at the wrecker, his Colt in hand, ready to fire back if he needed to.

The speculation might have made sense, but it didn't help him out of the predicament that he'd found himself in. If the injuries had got the best of Leo, then silence would prevail, giving Sonny a chance to make his way safely to the wrecker. If not, then time would tell what was going to happen. Sonny was a patient man. He had nowhere else to go. Sooner or later Sonny was going to have to face Jesse and explain why he broke his promise and left Jesse at the courthouse. But that could wait.

Leo was not as patient as Sonny. And he had no clue as to the damage he'd done to the wrecker. Or if he did, he was still going to try and get away. The wrecker engine roared, sending a flume of thick blue smoke out from the exhaust pipe, and a loud roar that almost matched the pinnacle of the recent storm. The engine clanked and complained as Leo put the truck in gear, vibrating against the solid rock underneath it.

Without warning, the Model T lurched forward on the boulder sending a shower of sparks to the dry ground; weak, unintended Fourth of July fireworks in January. The truck only moved a couple of feet before Leo let off the accelerator. If he kept moving, there was a good chance that the truck was going to tip over onto its side, making things worse instead of better. Leo backed up to his original position on the boulder, then revved the engine again. The air smelled of diesel fuel, soot, desperation, and failure.

From his angle, Sonny could see Leo struggling inside the cab with the steering wheel and the gearshift. All he could do was watch and grip the Colt in his hand as tight as he could.

Leo Dozier was preoccupied with the potential of escaping. If Sonny was going to make a run to the wrecker, it was now or never. He chose now. He jumped out of the Plymouth, Colt first, leading with his left hand, his aim on the open truck window. Then he scurried as fast as he could, zigzagging to avoid being shot, taking cover at the rear of the truck.

Crouched down, ready to run if the truck was put into reverse, Sonny held his bead on Leo's head through the back window. It took him a second to catch his breath. He was old and out of shape. When he was younger, the run for cover would have fueled him instead of weakening him.

Settled, and breathing, Sonny saw something else that he hadn't been able to see before: a head in the passenger seat. He had assumed that Leo was alone, that he was fleeing or heading somewhere by himself. That wasn't the case. Leo had someone with him.

It was difficult to get a clear look at the person with the fading evening light and the boom and hook obscuring his view. He couldn't make out who was in the truck. Leo's father? Heck or Clyde? Or someone else? It was hard to say.

Leo turned off the wrecker's engine, returning silence to the open fields. The solitude of failure was met with the sound of Sonny's fast-beating heart. Blood careened through his veins, spiked by the alcohol of adrenaline, mixed with the foul-tasting tonic of fear. He stiffened, did his best to blend into the shadows, and waited to see what Leo was going to do next.

Leo opened the driver's side door and tumbled out of the truck onto the ground. He rolled toward the front of the Model T, came to a stop in a crouch, and spun around to face Sonny. One more unexpected move from the Dozier boy.

Sonny edged to the corner of the wrecker, holding his Colt as steady as he could, and aimed the barrel at Leo's head.

Leo was armed, too. He held a similar gun, a six-shooter pistol, aimed at Sonny's head in return.

"Looks like we got us a Mexican standoff, Ranger Burton," Leo said.

"It's Mr. Burton to you."

"Oh, that's right. Them Rangers ain't kin to no one-armed men, are they?" Leo was a stocky, muscled, bulldog of a boy of nineteen or so. He wore a nose broken more than once, which contributed to his dense, pugilistic gaze. Blood trickled down from a gash in Leo's wide forehead, and his left hand dripped like he had stuck it in red paint. His skin was pale, topped by a head of black hair, a wavy unfurled flag in serious need of an iron.

"What's this all about, Leo?" Sonny said, standing firm. His hook was pulled tight to his side. He could feel the cold steel on his skin through the fabric of his pants. "Who do you have in the truck with you?"

"Ain't nothin' for you to be concerned with now, is it?"

"It's me," a voice hollered out from inside the wrecker.

It was a voice that Sonny knew well and wouldn't confuse anywhere. The voice belonged to Jonesy.

"You okay, Jonesy?" Sonny called back, doing his best not to show any surprise. *Why was Jonesy in the truck with Leo?* The sheriff was the last person Sonny had expected the passenger to be.

"Hell, no, I ain't all right. I'm handcuffed to the door," Jonesy said as loud as he could.

"Shut up!" Leo said, then, as quick as the flap of a fly's wing, he turned his pistol from Sonny, pointed it inside the truck, and pulled the trigger.

The unexpected boom caused Sonny to jump. Glass shattered out of the passenger window, and Jonesy screamed, "God-damn it!" Three beats, one after the other in a song that was rushing toward a sad ending.

Before Sonny could take another breath, Leo had his pistol pointed back at him.

"This ain't no game, Ranger Burton," Leo said. "Next shot kills him."

"What are you doing, Leo? You're messing with the rest of your life." Sonny had squared his shoulders and gathered himself as quick as he could. The shot had been a warning.

"I'm bleeding in here," Jonesy yelled.

Leo didn't flinch, didn't seem the least bit concerned about the sheriff's state of health. "My life's already ruined. The sheriff done saw to that."

"What's Jonesy got to do with this?" Sonny said.

"You tell me exactly what you think *this* is?" Leo wiped his bloody hand on his pants. They were already marred with plenty of blood. Denim mixed with red. His pants looked purple, dirty instead of blood-soaked.

"All I can say is Rafael Hernandez is dead. Heck Kilbride and Clyde Jones are missing. And you're sitting smack-dab in the middle of a fallow cotton field taking potshots at the sheriff inside your truck. Now, I got reason to believe you know something about Rafael's death, though I would have been happy to have pinned that on Heck Kilbride, but you wanted it that way, didn't you?"

"That Mexican had it comin' to him for what he went and did to Regan Harmeson."

"Regan? I figured this had something to do with the middle one, Ida."

"That little girl loves a drama is all. She butts in where she don't belong all the dang time. Especially when it concerns her older sister. That girl don't get no peace in that house."

"So, you told Ida that the circus folk hung Rafael to throw the scent off you. And for some reason, you knew she would believe you. Why is that, Leo? Was she sweet on Rafael and not you? Little girls like Ida get crushes on older boys their sisters like. Were you jealous, Leo?"

The end of the barrel of Leo's pistol wavered, trembled for a second. Sonny had hit a nerve. But he was still confused about the connection to Regan, the oldest Harmeson girl. "You want to clear this up for me, Jonesy?" Sonny said, stopping short of a yell. "You've been acting like a trapped badger ever since you took Rafael to jail. If Rafael is dead because of something you did, then now's the time to admit to it. We all make mistakes, Jonesy. I've made my fair share."

"I told you I was bleedin'," Jonesy said from inside the truck. Sonny still couldn't see him. "Glass went everywhere."

"You gonna live?" Sonny asked.

"You stay out of this, Ranger Burton," Leo said. "This is between me and the sheriff."

"I'll live," Jonesy offered.

"I told you, Leo," Sonny said. "I'm not a Ranger anymore. I'm a concerned citizen, nothing more."

"Yeah, and I'm a choirboy."

"Nobody would have ever said that about you, Leo, but from what I've heard, you were a decent boy. Short on temper, which was why wrestling in high school was a good thing for you. And you were at the top of your class, too. You got smarts. Otherwise you wouldn't have had a chance at going to the CCC camp. Now what have you done? Gone and wrecked your life is what. And what for? Can you tell me that? Let me help you, Leo. No matter what you think, or what's between you and the sheriff, I can help you. You have to tell me the truth about what's going on here."

Leo stood staring at Sonny. Jonesy remained quiet, not offering to join in the conversation to clear himself. Sonny found that discomforting.

"I had my way out of this town made," Leo said. "And then the sheriff screwed it all up so his nephew, Clyde, could take my place at the CCC camp. He knew I had a grudge agains' that

258

Mexican. Didn't you, Sheriff? You knew I'd pop a cork if I saw Rafael Hernandez tryin' to make a play for a spot on the CCC."

"Why's that, Leo? Because he's a Mexican?" Sonny said.

"There is that, but it's like I told you. It's what he went and did to Regan Harmeson, then the sheriff let him off for it. Why's that? Why would a white man with a badge on his chest let a Mexican go free after he violated a white girl? They lynch Negroes for less. Look at that fella in Shelbyville. Same thing happens here."

Sonny stood as motionless as he could, not wanting to stop Leo from talking, watching for an opportunity to disarm the boy and save Jonesy. "Why don't you let the sheriff tell his side of the story. Let him out of the truck. Let me see if he needs tended to."

"Ain't nobody gonna tend to him," Leo said. "I can see him. He's alive. Ain't hurt bad. I see what you're tryin' to do, Ranger Burton. You said it, I ain't no dummy. I got smarts about me. I'll figure my way out of this. You wait and see. I will."

"You can start by letting the sheriff speak for himself. I'd like to hear what Jonesy has to say."

"Nobody asked you here, Sonny," Jonesy shouted. "Why don't you leave this to the boy and me."

Sonny was tired of not being able to see Jonesy for himself. He edged out from behind the wrecker, holding the Colt steady, still aimed at Leo's head. The movement surprised Leo and he tensed a bit. Sonny figured if the boy was going to overreact it would be then. But Leo didn't do anything. His face was pale and sweaty even though the temperature had dropped a good ten degrees.

The evening light was almost gone, and darkness was winning the bet to take over the world, making it harder to see. Sonny had counted on that, counted on Leo being a little disoriented so he wouldn't shoot when he was the most vulnerable.

"Why don't you put the gun down, Leo," Sonny said. "And let me take a look at the sheriff. I really don't want to hurt you. I really don't want to shoot you. I can help you. Let me help you." The words hung in the air as well as pierced Sonny's memory. He had said the same thing to Billy Bunson, had begged Billy to put down his gun so Sonny could help him out of the situation he'd put himself in. He really didn't want to kill Leo any more than he had wanted to kill Billy Bunson.

Leo lurched forward, cocked the gun he was holding, and let out a scream that sounded like it came from the deepest part of his soul; primal, full of unrequited pain.

Sonny put a little more pressure on the trigger of the Colt. Time stopped. There was no wind. No sound. A blink of the eye between life and death.

Out of nowhere, from behind Sonny, Blue charged out of the Plymouth, growling, barking, teeth barred, running at Leo.

The dog surprised Leo, but not in the way Sonny expected. Blue had sensed that Sonny was in danger and had acted on his own. Sonny was surprised, too.

Leo turned the pistol and fired into the cab of the truck, then brought the barrel to the side of his head.

Sonny didn't hesitate. He pulled the Colt's trigger and shot the gun out of Leo's hand. The force of the shot staggered the boy as Blue jumped into his abdomen, sending Leo into a backward fall.

Sonny was on him in a swift run. "You move another inch, and I'll finish you," he said.

"No, you won't," Leo quibbled. "No, you won't."

A roar came from behind Sonny, capturing his attention. A parade of automobiles come to find him, if he was guessing.

Sonny wasn't the least bit surprised when the first one stopped and Jesse rushed out of it, angry and relieved.

Jonesy was handcuffed to the passenger door of the wrecker, gutshot, losing blood quicker than any man ought to be able to and still talk. "It wasn't Rafael who got that Harmeson girl pregnant, Sonny," he said. "It was Clyde. That girl was dancing between two boys. But I pinned it on Rafael because Clyde's my family. I started this mess. It's all my fault. I was only tryin' to keep Clyde out of trouble."

One of the deputies had a key to the handcuffs, and Hal Buckworth, the ambulance driver, stood in wait to help load Jonesy onto the gurney.

Sonny held a wad of cloth against the wound in Jonesy's stomach. "You don't need to worry about all of this now."

"You've got to find out what Leo did with Clyde and Heck," the sheriff begged.

"What did he do?"

"He said I'd never find them is what." Jonesy's words were weak. His eyelids fluttered, then he gasped like a fish taking its last breath. He went limp and his eyes closed for good before he could say another word.

Sheriff Jones was dead. Something Sonny never thought he would see, and he was sad that he had to witness another senseless death.

CHAPTER TWENTY-EIGHT

Edith followed the beam of her headlights, sighing with relief as the light swept across a hand-painted sign that said: Welcome to Wellington, Texas. Night had fallen right on schedule, covering the world in a cold January blanket of solid darkness. The wind had drawn down to a whimper that couldn't even be called a breeze, but there was evidence of the most recent sandstorm everywhere. A drift of dirt, dust, sand, and debris clung against the two posts of the welcome sign, promising to bury it if another storm came along. Edith, to her surprise, was in one piece, but as lost in her destination as she was on the long road that had got her there. She had no idea where Sonny lived other than the post address, RR #1, Box 78, that she sent his letters to. That could have been anywhere.

She stopped at the first place she came across, a homegrown service station called Suggs. The bell dinged when the Pierce rumbled over it, alerting a young boy of average height, smooth face, and tired eyes, who ran out to greet her. A glance to the fuel gauge told her that she had half a tank of gasoline and didn't need to worry about getting any more. She rolled down the window and smiled at the boy. His name tag said he was Bob.

"Can I help you, ma'am?" He looked up and down the side of the Pierce, his eyes coming awake as if for the first time, then whistled. "This sure is a fancy ride. We don't see too many of these kinds of automobiles around here."

Edith hated it that the Pierce stood out, made her an object of curiosity, but was not surprised. The yellow automobile was like a miniature sun driving down the road; she could never outrun the brightness and glare it brought to her. The Pierce had caused her a slew of problems on the trip. She felt a little better now that she was in Wellington, though she was more nervous than a rabbit being chased by a dog. She hated looking over her shoulder every five seconds for the cowboy, too. "Thank you," she managed to say as politely as she could. "I was wondering if you could tell me where Sonny Burton lives?"

"Sonny Burton, you say? The Texas Ranger?" Bob Suggs said.

"He used to be a Texas Ranger," Edith answered. "I believe his son, Jesse, has that position now." She turned off the Pierce's engine, glad to be able to hear Bob without the agitation of a running motor.

"Why, yes, you're right. That's the Sonny Burton here in Wellington. I saw him a day ago. It was the queerest thing. A bearded lady and the tallest man on earth drove in with a stolen cow in the back of their truck, and Mr. Burton, well, he talked to those folks like they was real people and not guilty of a crime of any kind. The circus passed through town. That's why the lady had a beard."

"That sounds like my Sonny Burton." A smile formed on Edith's face when she said his name. She was so happy to be in Wellington she could almost squeal with delight. But that wasn't her way. There was too much trouble behind her and too much uncertainty ahead of her.

"You need directions to his house, you say? You must not be close to Mr. Burton that well if you don't have directions to where he lives." Bob leaned down so he could get a look inside the Pierce. It was lit in shadows, radiated by the dim service station lights that hung overhead. Astonishment hung on his young face like frozen peach fuzz; stunted, excited, in wonder at its own existence.

"I've never been to Wellington before," Edith said. She didn't want to explain herself any further to the boy. Her reason to visit Sonny was not any of Bob's business.

"Oh, well," Bob said, "I ain't allowed to give out personal information about no one in town. I get in enough trouble sayin' one thing or the other about things that happen around here. Like that cow I told you about. My pop, he owns this place. He don't take kindly to gossip or that kind of thing. But you seem like a nice lady, so I could tell you."

"If it troubles you," Edith said, looking around Bob for anything that moved, a coyote, a hawk, or a cowboy, "you could call his neighbors, the Harmesons, and have them deliver a message asking if it is okay if you give me directions."

Bob pulled himself from the window and whistled low again. "Boy, this automobile is as purty on the inside as it is on the outside. I ain't gonna bother them Harmesons. They got problems enough without me rattling the bell on their phone in the dark of night. No, if you know so much about Sonny Burton, I figure you deserve to get what you're askin' for." Bob stood and pointed the opposite direction that Edith had come in from. "You'll have to head north, go through town, and turn left at the second farm-to-market road you come across. There's nothin' there except a gigantic old boulder the size of a tractor tire. You follow that road for a good stretch, go around a bend, and you'll come to another intersection of country roads. You turn right there and go on for a bit, down a deep dip, then when you top it, that there's the Harmeson place. You're almost there. Keep a goin' and the next house you come to, that one is Sonny Burton's house. There's a #78 painted on the mailbox. You got that?" Bob had been twisting his arms around in a mapped expression, showing her the way with his hands, body, and memory. When he was done talking, Bob stood rigid, waiting for confirmation that Edith had understood everything that he had told her.

"I think so," Edith said. "Head north, turn left, turn right, go down a dip, and then I'll be there."

"Uh-huh, that sounds right. You can get lost out there this time of night, and you'll have to be careful of debris on the road. That was a mighty fierce storm that blew through here earlier this evening. Powerful enough to knock down trees and litter the road with knee-deep piles of sand. Don't try to drive through 'em. You could mess this beauty of an automobile up so bad it couldn't be driven. That'd be a darned shame. It sure would."

"Thank you for your concern, Bob," Edith said. "I appreciate that."

"Can I get you some gasoline?"

"No, I think I have enough to get where I'm going." Edith smiled and restarted the Pierce's engine. "Thank you, Bob. You've been helpful."

"You be careful out there." Bob stepped back from the Pierce, admiring the sight of the yellow automobile all over again. He looked at it like it was a dame with the finest set of legs he'd ever seen.

Edith hesitated, wondered what Bob knew or saw, then realized he was only being decent and nice. She smiled again and drove out of the service station slower than normal, recounting the directions in her head that she had been given. The last thing she wanted to do was get lost in the middle of nowhere.

Edith drove through Wellington proper, catching nothing but a glimpse of the town in darkness. Like Huntsville, and every other town in Texas, Wellington rolled up its sidewalks and tucked them away for future use at the first sight of the evening star. There were few lights on in any of the businesses. Even the sparkle of the movie palace, the Ritz, was dimmed, turned off, asleep. No Shirley Temple stories to cheer the Depression-afflicted Wellingtonians. *Bright Eyes* would have to wait for another day.

It wasn't long before Edith found the second farm-to-market road Bob Suggs had told her about. She turned left at the sight of a tractor-sized boulder sitting alone at the intersection. How many boulders could there be here in this county? she wondered, taking the turn on faith, hope, and uncertainty. Her vision darted back and forth in front of and behind her without thought. She still feared that she was being followed, tailed, hunted down like a wounded animal. The back of her neck twitched like it did when she was being stared at by someone from afar. Even if that feeling was her imagination, she didn't like it. Not one bit. *I'm almost sixty years old, and for the first time in my life, I'm afraid of the dark.*

The narrow hardpan road held straight for a few miles, maybe three but it could have been four. Then out of nowhere, the road curved into a bend and Edith relaxed. Her headlights thrust two long spikes of manufactured light in the blackest night she could ever recall seeing. There were no stars overhead and no light of any kind on the horizon. There was nothing but the road ahead of the Pierce, dotted with piles of sand, dust, and the occasional tree limb. She kept her speed slow, wary of doing any damage to the automobile this close to her destination. Long stretches of the road gave Edith the feeling that she was lost in a desert; the land was flat and unforgiving, but void of heat of any kind. The night had turned cold. Her toes felt like they were made of ice instead of flesh and bone.

Like Bob Suggs said, there was another intersection of roads after the bend. Edith slowed and made her final turn toward Sonny's house. Her stomach dropped along with her confidence and any hope she held tumbled right along with it. But she couldn't let her mind linger in the barren land of fear and doubt. She'd come too far and been through too much to be afraid, to turn around now. Edith Grantley was no quitter. There hadn't been time for that kind of thinking, that kind of reaction. Not from the time she'd been a little girl until now. There had been a battle to fight, a reason to keep going. This was no different— even though facing Sonny on his own land, in his own house, made her tremble like a frightened bird, trapped with nowhere to go.

Once the silver archer was pointed in the right direction, Edith had no choice but to keep driving at a moderated rate of speed. The road was still an obstacle course made from the thrust and fury of the sandstorm. Her eyes fell on a sudden surprise of light, and the ground underneath the tires quavered like an earthquake had found its way to the Panhandle of Texas. Her attention was drawn down the road to a sight so unusual Edith thought she might have been hallucinating.

She slowed the automobile to a crawl, edging the berm, if it could have been called that, avoiding what looked like some kind of oncoming parade.

A farm truck with a fenced bed led the way, sporting a bright spotlight anchored on the driver's-side door. The beam stretched down the road and flooded the interior of the Pierce like a beacon on a treacherous sea, searching for a lost ship. Edith shielded her eyes with her left hand and kept her right hand steady on the steering wheel, driving into the light. The aim of the Pierce was direct and safe as long as there was nothing in the road that she couldn't see. The operator of the beam of light turned the spotlight from Edith's automobile, lighting the empty road beyond her. There was nothing behind her that she could see with a glance over her shoulders.

The ground continued to rumble at steady and predictable

intervals. There was no sign of what could be causing such a disturbance until Edith was able to look past the stake truck. She gasped at the sight of an elephant. It was the last thing she expected to see. A second look at the truck as it passed by her allowed her to see ripped and shredded banners dangling from the boards on the bed of the truck; it was full of people, sitting, standing, looking down at her as she drove by. Two men walked behind the truck, both carrying torches, lighting the way for the biggest animal she had ever seen in her life. The elephant wore a purple satin bib the size of a bedsheet and kept a respectable distance from the torch bearers. Edith was tempted to pull off of the side of the road and watch the parade go by. She had never seen a circus parade or an elephant before. But she kept driving, unsure of the land she was on, and bothered by the existence of the parade in the first place. *Why would they be traveling at night?*

Once she got past the elephant, she looked in the side mirror to make sure the giant beast wasn't a figment of her imagination. When she turned her attention back to the road, her eyes fell on a camel and two white stallions, being led like the elephant, by two more men carrying torches. Behind the horses came another jalopy pulling a long pole that rolled along on a pair of small wheels. Another truck followed, packed with items that Edith couldn't make out, but she assumed was the canvas that made the big top. Beyond that was another group of people, including a man so tall he looked like he could grab the moon and take a bite out of the yellow orb like it was a piece of fruit. Two more men with torches brought up the rear of the parade. As Edith drove on, they all disappeared as she headed down a deep dip in the road.

When she came up the other side of the road all Edith could see was dancing flames diminished in the distance, smaller, but no less surreal. Seeing the parade at night, in the middle of flat, almost vacant, country, was something she wouldn't soon forget. The sight had distracted her from the worry and fret she carried forward. The elephant had provided a short respite for what was to come at the end of her journey. Edith's mouth went dry at the thought.

A white farmhouse sat on the left side of the road as she continued driving at a slow pace. And then she was almost there. The next house she saw would be Sonny Burton's house. Her stomach flip-flopped at the thought, at the realization. Her shoulders fell with relief, but her heart seized in fear that it would be rejected soon. Then what would she do?

If Edith had slowed to a crawl as she had passed the circus parade, then she was now moving along at a snail's pace, her eyes searching for a mailbox that said #78. It only took another long minute before she spied the number she had been searching for in the darkness for so long.

Edith brought the Pierce to a stop in the empty road and left the engine running. Blackness covered the fields all around her as tight as the clouds covered the sky, keeping the stars and moon hidden from her. She had passed the only house to be seen for miles, and it was behind her.

A single light shone in the window of Sonny's house, and his truck, a Model A pickup, sat next to the front door. From where she sat, it looked like Sonny was home. All she had to do was drive to the house, get out, knock on that door, and present herself. But all of the muscles in her body had frozen, atrophied like they had not been used in years, unable to move. Every "what if" she could think of played out in her mind. Every reason she could think of to keep driving, to turn around and go back home, made sudden sense to her. Her feet were cold now that she was within yards of her goal, of her desire, of her final destination, the place she wanted to be more than anywhere else in the world.

"What are you waiting for?" Edith said aloud in the darkness. "The worst thing he can do is tell you to leave, that he never wants to see you again." And that, she decided as fast as she had said the words, wouldn't be the worst thing at all. Not knowing would be the worst thing. If she drove off now, she would always have to wonder what kind of life she might have had if she had parked the automobile in Sonny Burton's front yard and followed her heart to the door.

Still, she sat motionless, looking out into the darkness, hoping for something to urge her on, to spur her to move one way or the other. In the end, it was nothing more than the tick of the clock and the turn of the earth. She was running out of time. So was Sonny. The chance for love of any kind was lessening by the second. Old age and death were waiting for them around the bend, which seemed closer now than it ever had. This might be her last chance to love and be loved, and Edith Grantley knew that was the deepest truth that she had discovered on the journey to Wellington, Texas. There were forces in the world waiting to take what was yours, what belonged to you, no matter your age or station in life. Death stood with outstretched arms waiting for you to walk into its embrace. There was no escaping the coming of darkness, the end of life. Years rolled by like a fast-moving river. Even if you could outrun a maniac cowboy, there was something else waiting to take his place. Time and regret forced Edith to make a decision, to move, to grab the door handle with a sweaty palm and fingers.

Ready, willing, or not, Sonny Burton was about to have a visitor in his life. Edith hoped he was ready. She hoped she was ready, too, because there was no turning back now.

CHAPTER TWENTY-NINE

"What is it, Blue?" Sonny said.

The dog sat up, ears erect, roused from a deep sleep. It had been a long, tiring day for Sonny and his four-footed friend. Blue had come in handy by distracting Leo Dozier, making a contribution, ending the standoff, unbidden, untrained, with limp and all, overcoming his infirmaries with an unrealized dash of courage. An extra helping of mashed potatoes fell to Blue after Sonny had settled in at home and eaten his own dinner.

Sonny was still amazed by the dog's action, his show of protection. Nothing like that had ever happened in Sonny's life before. Leo sat in the jail now, helped there by Blue. Sadness, however, weighed Sonny down. He was bereft about the senseless loss of Jonesy but was distracted by Blue's wakefulness. The dog had already shown he knew more than Sonny thought possible. He wouldn't underestimate his companion again so soon.

Blue scurried out of the front room, favoring his good hind leg. He stopped at the kitchen door and sniffed the jamb, whimpering as his long nose flared like a bellow.

Sonny followed and stopped to stare at the door and the dog. This was more unusual behavior from Blue. This wasn't how he signaled to be let out, or alerted a threat of some kind, real or imagined, lurking beyond the door. This was something different.

Blue barked, stood back, looked at Sonny, then barked again.

Sonny grabbed the .22 caliber varmint gun that sat next to

the door in case he needed it, and made his way past Blue. When he opened the door, his eyes met Edith Grantley's and locked. Blue rushed outside, barking, yipping, and dancing around Edith's ankles. She ignored the dog for as long as she could, holding eye contact with Sonny as if she couldn't believe that he was real. Sonny felt the same way. He knew that Edith had been traveling his way, but his shock and grief about Jonesy had pushed the thought of her on the road by herself to the back corners of his mind.

"Edith," Sonny said. "You made it."

She leaned down to pet Blue, trying to sate his enthusiasm, but that was not possible, at least in the short term. Blue danced like a circus dog after giving the performance of his life.

The dog was of no interest to Sonny. He was focused on Edith. She was a welcome sight, wearing nothing but a simple dress. There was no coat in sight. A purse dangled from the tentative grip of her left hand. The dim light from the house covered Edith in shadows, and there was a stiffness to her movements and a grayness about her that was unfamiliar to Sonny, even as she made over Blue in her subtle way. Still, she was the most beautiful sight he had seen all day.

Edith broke away from the dog, stood up, and faced Sonny.

"I've been worried about you," Sonny said. His words were low, soft, as they spun around on the slight breeze that blew across the empty fields. "I called your house and spoke to Marcel. He told me that you were on your way." He sat the .22 against the house. There was no need for it. "I couldn't imagine you on the road alone."

Edith's blinked her eyes in quick succession. They were covered in a glaze of tears preparing to fall. "You're not angry, are you?" She shivered, not taking her attention off of Sonny. It was almost as if she couldn't believe that she was standing before him.

Sonny didn't say another word. He couldn't say what he felt, not after the day he'd had, or how empty the time away from Edith had been. He had never shared intimate words and thoughts with a woman before. Not once in his life. If he had ever expressed soft and gentle feelings to Martha, she would have suspected him of doing something untold, like stepping out on her, or betraying her in some way or another. Acknowledging feelings with his dead wife had never been their way. Matrimony was a duty, honoring a vow, and avoiding each other as the long years of dissatisfaction and resentment accumulated into a distance that could not be traveled. Sonny Burton didn't have the vocabulary—in his mind or his heart—to answer Edith's question. She deserved more than his usual solitary no.

Whatever he wanted to say, what he had to say, came in the form of movement instead of words. Sonny stepped down so he was face to face with Edith, and pulled her into him with his left hand, his left arm, then wrapped his right arm and hook around her waist as gentle as he could. She melded into him like two pieces of broken glass being glued back together. She welcomed his embrace, fell into Sonny with a sigh. He couldn't help himself, didn't try to regulate his manners or decide what was right or wrong. Instead, he kissed her as deep and with as much passion as he had the first night they had slept in the same bed together.

Blue had vanished. The sky and the earth had disappeared right along with the dog. The only thing that existed was longing, regret, relief, and something else Sonny felt that he couldn't name. It could have been love. He only knew what he felt. For the first time since he had left Huntsville, he could relax and allow the world around him to go away. All that mattered was the embrace, holding onto something he thought had been lost, and didn't ever want to lose again.

"I missed you," Sonny said, after pulling away from Edith.

His face was flushed red, and his heart raced like a horse crossing the finishing line after running a long endurance race.

It looked like Edith was having the same trouble as Sonny at finding the right words to say. A tear dripped off her cheek and splattered onto the dry, hard ground beneath her. A second tear hit the thirsty earth as Edith shook her head, unable to say what was inside of her. She looked happy and sad, twisted and torn, relieved and in grief all at the same time—if that were possible.

Sonny took Edith by the shoulder, guided her toward the door, then grabbed the .22 with his good hand. "Come on, let's get you inside where it's warm."

She walked inside the house. Blue danced, barked, and circled around the two of them, shuddering from nose to tail, happier than Sonny had ever seen the dog. It almost looked like Blue had four good legs instead of three.

Sonny closed the door and deposited the rifle in its place, then faced Edith again, who was standing in the middle of the kitchen, patting Blue's head. The dog looked like he was attached to her calf. He was panting, and if it were possible for a dog to smile, then he was.

"I think he missed me," Edith said with effort, catching her breath, and forcing her own smile. Her face looked like porcelain, white and shiny, ready to crack at the first suggestion of stress. She stood, pulling herself away from the dog once more.

"He did. We both did," Sonny said.

"I wasn't sure. You didn't answer my letters."

Five feet separated Sonny and Edith, and he longed to be next to her like the dog. "I'm sorry. Writing with my left hand is nothing but chicken scratch. You wouldn't have been able to read a word. I found a typewriter and taught myself how to write a letter on it, but I guess I mailed it too late. You were already gone before it had a chance to get there."

Another tear trailed down Edith's cheek. She broke eye contact with him and let her eyes trail down to his prosthesis. "I'm such a fool," she whispered. "It never entered my mind that you would have trouble writing anything. You're the most normal man in the world to me. I'm sorry." Her faced twisted in pain, the porcelain cracked, and she trembled again. "Can you forgive me?"

"Forgive you? For what?" Sonny said. "I'm happy that you're standing in my kitchen. I can't tell you the day I've had and seeing your face and finding you safe and sound makes everything so much better."

"I may not be sound. I have a story to tell you, too," Edith said. "It was a difficult journey to get here."

"Can it wait?" Sonny stepped forward, then stopped in front of her, waiting for her answer, waiting for her to give him a sign that he had overstepped a boundary, that he was too close to her.

She didn't show any sign of opposing the nearness of him. Edith didn't say a word. She stepped into his space as close as she could, leaned into him, and kissed him with a hunger that Sonny recognized and matched right away. He had to be careful of the hook as he pulled her into him, but every other part of his body was easy to forget. They were ageless, lost in a youthful whirlwind of falling clothes and desire.

The bedroom was dark, but it wasn't lonely. Moonlight shone through the window, falling across the tangled bed, touching their flesh with a soft glow. Edith laid against Sonny's chest as he stared off into the distance, half asleep, half awake, not sure if he was dreaming. A line of clouds threatened to overtake the moon and steal away the light of the night. The front of the weather, if that's what it was, must have crawled over the house, because in the blink of an eye, large flakes of snow started to fall from the sky.

"Look," Sonny said, "you brought a drink of water with you."

Edith propped herself up, doing her best to not leave Sonny's touch, smiled, then grabbed a blanket and covered them with it. "It's beautiful." The flakes sparkled like silver diamonds as they spiraled to the ground. "I saw the oddest thing on the way here," she said.

"What was that?" Sonny adjusted the blanket with his left hand so his stump was uncovered, atop the blanket. It got too warm sometimes.

"A circus parade in the night."

"They've left then," Sonny said. He looked away from Edith and stared at the ceiling. The memory of eating dinner with the circus people, and Frances Avalon demanding that he use his hook to shake hands, washed over him.

"You sound sad about that," Edith said.

"They showed me a kindness. I took shelter in a storm with them. They treated me like I belonged there, is all."

Edith flicked her head in understanding. "Isn't it dangerous for them to travel at night?"

"They didn't want to draw any attention to themselves." Sonny went stiff as he remembered his conversation with Bob Suggs when Frances Avalon had pulled into the station to get gasoline for her truck. Bob had speculated that the circus would leave in the middle of the night after they had stolen enough food to feed their animals. He hoped Bob was wrong about that. He hoped he was right, that they didn't want any more undue attention, and that was all.

"There's all kinds of things in the darkness that could bother them."

"Like what?"

It was then that Edith went on to tell Sonny about her encounters with the cowboy on the road. First at the Magnolia station, then at the café in Ennis, and along the road where she found that she had no choice but to shoot him and leave him behind. "When the police went out to the sight there was no one there. His truck was gone. He was gone. And I haven't seen him since. Detective Spurling has my phone number and address if he needs to contact me," Edith said. "But I don't know if that cowboy is still alive or not. I've looked over my shoulder the rest of the way here. I think I always will."

"You're safe here with me," Sonny said.

"I can't stay here forever."

"Why not?"

Edith didn't answer Sonny, so he let silence fall between them. Her face was washed in the soft white glimmer of moonlight that peaked inside the window.

Sonny reached up and stroked the side of her face, could see that the question had troubled her. What shine of happiness and satisfaction that had hung on her face only seconds before had followed the moonlight into grayness. "We don't have to talk about that now. There's time for that later."

She sat up and looked at Sonny. "It's like now. I'm embarrassed to tell you that I need to visit the privy, but I don't want to go out there by myself. I feel like a little girl afraid of some imaginary monster."

Sonny sat so they were shoulder to shoulder. "That monster was real. Come on, I'll go with you. Me, Blue, and my father's Colt." He stood then, grabbed a robe out of his wardrobe, and offered it to Edith.

She left the bed and took the robe while Sonny put on his pants and pulled an undershirt over his head. There was no need to bother with buttoning a shirt or putting on the prosthesis. He could grab his coat on the way out the door.

Blue didn't need instructions. He was awake and ready to go. Once they were dressed and armed, Sonny let the dog out the door. If there was anybody lurking around, Blue would alert him to the presence.

Nothing got Blue's attention, allowing Edith to hurry to the outhouse. Sonny stood watching with the Colt in his left hand, cocked and loaded. He hoped this cowboy, whoever he was, had crawled off and died, but if that was not the case and the fool had the audacity to follow Edith to Wellington, then Sonny was more than willing to finish the job.

The moon disappeared behind the clouds, taking the last bit of glow with it. Snowflakes the size of nickels continued to fall, drenching the dry ground with droplets of frozen moisture that thawed as quick as they hit the ground. There would be no accumulation, but there would be a drink for the parched earth. He opened his mouth, tasting the snow, letting it splatter on his face like he had as a little boy.

Sonny wondered what the grass would look like when it was green and vibrant. It would take more than a flurry of snowflakes for that to happen, but at the least, Sonny could hold onto to a glimmer of hope, see a world in the future that was alive and growing. Maybe it was being with Edith, or the snow itself, a rare sight of recent. Either way, it was a lighter feeling, and one he welcomed.

Edith made her way back to him, apologizing as soon as she was within earshot for dragging him and Blue outside. "It's been a long time since I felt snow on the tip of my tongue," he said. "If you weren't here, I would have missed that."

Edith cooked breakfast the next morning and found that the larder was low. Sonny had been surviving on Spam, Van Camp beans, biscuits, and coffee. "We should go into town, then," Sonny said.

"What will everyone think when they see you with me?"

"Nobody knows who you are."

"They know you."

"I'll tell them you're my friend. That's the truth of it, and anything else is none of their damned business."

"They'll figure out I'm staying here with you. A single man and a widowed woman alone in a house in the country. You'll be a scandal, Sonny Burton," Edith said. "What do you think about that?"

"I think it's about time."

Sonny saw Jesse's Plymouth parked alongside the road as soon as they came to the dip in the road. "That's Jesse's automobile. I better stop and see what this is about," he said.

Edith sat next to Sonny on the truck's bench seat. Her eyes followed his, and she shrugged. "It'd be good to see Jesse again."

"He knew you were coming." Sonny pulled behind the Plymouth and parked.

"What did he have to say about that?"

"Doesn't matter to me if it doesn't matter to you."

"I hope he warms to me over time."

"We *are* talking about Jesse."

Edith smiled, and waited in the truck until Sonny got out, walked around to the other side, and opened the passenger door for her to slide out. The winter day had turned out to be a nice one; clear blue skies, warm sunshine, no sign of snow or the flakes it left behind. They had left Blue at the house. With the threat of the circus gone, the dog was free to wander outside like he did when Sonny was away. All things considered, Sonny wanted the dog to keep an eye on things and trusted him to do so.

Jesse and Peter Harmeson were standing in a barren field, face to face, having a conversation. It was a good fifty-yard walk to them. Sonny and Edith walked in step over the ground that was packed down, trampled on, compressed by the days the circus tent had spent pitched there.

When he got closer, Sonny could see that Peter was leaning on a shovel, which struck him odd, in the middle of an empty field in January.

"Pa, Mrs. Grantley," Jesse said once the two of them came to a stop.

Peter Harmeson looked at Edith like the stranger she was, then to Sonny, a little surprised.

"This is my friend, Edith Grantley," Sonny said. "Edith, this is Peter Harmeson. He owns this piece of land and has been a good neighbor to me ever since I moved to Wellington."

Edith extended her hand. "A pleasure to meet you, Mr. Harmeson." As soon as they finished shaking hands, Edith turned to Jesse. "And it's good to see you again, Jesse."

"Peter," Sonny said, as he shook the man's hand with his hook. It had been an action without thinking, only Jesse and Peter noticed, but said nothing about the strength of the handshake.

Jesse said, "Ma'am," then grabbed the top of his hat as a push of wind whistled across the field. The temperature was in the low forties, so it wasn't bitter cold. All of them were dressed for the weather in coats, gloves, and warm hats. Edith had carried her purse with her instead of leaving it in the truck.

"What's this all about?" Sonny said.

"Mr. Harmeson called me out," Jesse said.

"Didn't know who else to call since Jonesy is, well, not the sheriff no more. Now I hear tell we're gonna be without a Texas Ranger in the county." Peter's voice was low and fell to the ground as soon as the words came out of his mouth.

"Come Friday, that's right," Jesse said. "Though they might change their minds now that the county is without a sheriff."

"I told Jesse if they let him go, he ought to run for sheriff hisself," Peter said. He was wearing a brown field coat patched at the elbows, and knee-high mud boots that didn't look they had been cleaned since the last century.

"It's a little too early for that kind of talk," Jesse said. "We still have to honor Jonesy."

"It's not a bad idea," Sonny offered. Edith stood still by his side, and Sonny looked past Peter to a shallow hole that had been dug. "So, why'd you call Jesse, Peter? Edith saw the circus leaving last night. I hope this doesn't have anything to do with those folks."

"I think it might," Jesse said. "We'll have to see. It's all right to show Pa what you're thinkin', Mr. Harmeson."

Peter dug into his pants pocket and pulled out a sliver of bone. "Looks a bit like a finger to me," he said, holding it away from himself like it was poison. "Sorry, ma'am," he added, nodding at Edith.

"A finger?" Sonny said.

"Yes, sir," Peter said. "That bearded lady promised me that I could help feed the lion and tiger if I let them stay here. And she kept her word. Gave me a pail of slop to feed to them is what she did. All kinds of meat and such. I didn't think much about it once I was convinced they'd bought Tom Young's milk cow instead of stealin' it. But that pail, it didn't smell like any cow I ever smelt. I didn't say anything. I stood there and watched that lion and tiger eat their meals. I ain't never seen anything like it. Not even a tabby shreddin' a mouse. Anyways, once I knew they was gone, I started pokin' around, and I found this bone and some others. I went back to the house to get the shovel and figured I should give somebody a call—in case I was right about what I was thinkin'."

Sonny nodded and understood what Peter was suggesting. "You think that might be what's left of Clyde Jones and Heck Kilbride, don't you?"

"I heard tell they was still missin'," Peter said.

Sonny stiffened a bit as he put a few things together in his head and focused in on Peter. "Jonesy told me there was some trouble with your oldest daughter, Peter. Bad trouble where one boy took the blame for something the other one did. Rafael paid for that mistake with his life. Jonesy, too. He tried to cover up what Clyde did to your daughter. Heck? Who knows why Heck is dead, if that's the case, other than he was with Clyde, and well, Heck was Heck? He was a bully. Maybe even to you, Peter. Or your girls. You'd do anything to protect your girls, wouldn't you?"

Peter Harmeson's face drained of color. The bridge of his nose and his forehead was white as snow. "What are you sayin', Sonny? You think I had somethin' to do with this? Why in the hell would I call the law if that was the case? Why would I bring Jesse out here if I went and done somethin' to Clyde and Heck like that?"

"Maybe so everybody would think that Leo Dozier killed all three of them boys," Sonny said. "All he ever said was that 'nobody would ever find them.' He didn't say he killed Heck and Clyde. And I spent a little time with those circus people. They were honorable folks, Peter. Never once did I get the sense that they were killers or of questionable morals. Now, it's my guess if we go talk to them, they'd tell us that you were the one that brought the meal for the lion and tiger, not them. You can count on it that Jesse will ask them. And if that's the case, then you'll have some explaining to do, if we find more bones in that hole over there. Bones that belonged to Clyde and Heck."

Peter Harmeson gripped the shovel tighter, then shimmied the handle up his hand as quickly as he could, spinning the shovel in an attempt to swing it like a weapon. But Peter had only been paying any attention to Edith and Sonny. Before Peter could force a swing of the shovel, Jesse had pulled his .45 out of his holster. "Drop it, Mr. Harmeson. Drop the shovel right now," he said, aiming the pistol's barrel right at Peter Harmeson's head.

Peter Harmeson did as he was told, then said, "I didn't have nothin' to do with all of this." The shovel dropped to the ground with a useless thud.

"You best tell me what all this is about, Mr. Harmeson." Jesse was rigid as a cat about to leap on a mouse. Sonny reached over with his left hand and pulled Edith back a step out of the way so Jesse could handle the situation that had just arose.

"It was Leo Dozier that done all of this," Peter said, his voice shaky and weak. "Why else would he shoot Jonesy for what he had done, lettin' Clyde off for what he went and did to my girl."

"That doesn't explain this pile of leftover bones you're burying, Mr. Harmeson."

"I swear to you that Leo killed 'em all."

"But you helped? Or did you make a deal with him that you get rid of the evidence? But you got worried you'd get caught, or that Leo would start talking, so you figured you better do something to throw the scent off yourself and onto the circus folk who were here. That's what this is about, isn't it? You got scared," Jesse said.

Sonny had to fight the muscles in his face to keep from smiling as he watched Jesse back Peter Harmeson into a corner he wasn't going to get out of. No matter what happened, Jesse was going to be all right. One way or another there would be a badge on Jesse Burton's chest. A phone call to Frank Hamer would make sure of that.

For the second time in a week, the road along the Harmeson place was lined with police automobiles and an ambulance. Sonny and Edith sat in his Model A pickup truck watching as a parade of men wandered from the field to the Harmeson farmhouse and back.

"Never in my life would I have thought a man like Peter Harmeson would have done something like that," Sonny said.

"I'm not sure I understand what just happened with that man," Edith said.

"Well, it seems that everyone had thought Peter Harmeson's girl got caught up in a triangle of sorts between Rafael and Clyde Jones. But there was something going on between her and Leo Dozier all of the time, too. Jesse needs to go talk to them Harmeson girls, especially the middle one, Ida, to make sure. I'm gonna stay out of that. Anyway, the girl got herself in the family way, but nature took care of that, it seems. Rafael got pegged with the trouble when Peter went to the sheriff. But Jonesy knew, or thought he knew, that Clyde was really the guilty one who'd been with Regan Harmeson. So, Jonesy used his position to get information from Rafael and turned him into a snitch. This is where Jonesy made his mistake, protecting Clyde. Other than sending Rafael into the CCC camp training. Jonesy knew there'd be a fight with Heck Kilbride there, and his intention was to get Clyde to take Leo's spot, so he could get his nephew out of town and as far away from trouble as possible. But he had no idea that Leo had feelings or a relationship with the Harmeson girl. He lit that boy's fuse is what he did. I'm not sure who Leo killed first, but I'm guessing he went after Clyde Jones, because Clyde not only took his place at the CCC camp, but he had been with Regan, too. I thought the triangle included Rafael, but it was really Leo. Rafael was the fall guy, in the wrong place at the wrong time, and a Mexican, to boot. Rafael was easy to blame and took the attention off of Clyde. I think Rafael was already dead when he was hung in that tree down from the circus. I can't say if Peter helped then or not, but I imagine Leo went to Peter, who had a grudge against Clyde, and probably Heck, too, and convinced him to help get rid of the bodies. Well, the circus was right there, and what better way to get rid of something than let them big cats eat the evidence. Nobody would ever know."

"Except there are bones left over," Edith said.

"And Leo is still alive, able to talk," Sonny answered. "Leo killed all three of them boys, and my guess is he beat Aldo to a pulp, too, when he went looking for Rafael and found him. If Aldo lives, can talk, he'll be able to confirm that. Peter Harmeson helped hide the evidence, which is a crime in itself."

"So, Leo got his heart broke, then somebody came along and took what was rightfully his and he snapped. It was all too much for him."

"That sounds about right," Sonny said.

"Revenge is a bitter pill that can't often be refused," Edith said. "Getting back at somebody for what they take from you is stronger than we think. That story rings true to me right now. I'll always wonder what that cowboy was after, and if he's dead or alive."

"I'm sorry you had to experience that, Edith."

"It seems there's no escaping the madness of some men. You should be proud of Jesse."

"I am. He turned out better than I thought he would. Are you all right?"

"I am now that I'm sitting here next to you."

Sonny leaned over and pecked Edith on the lips, then looked out into the field to see Jesse talking to Hal Buckworth. It looked like Jesse had everything under control. There was no doubt that the circus people would be interviewed, and Leo Dozier still had some explaining to do, along with his own crimes to answer for. But none of that was Sonny's problem. Not now. Not anymore. Peter Harmeson and Leo Dozier's foul deeds were the law's problem, not his.

"Let's go to the grocers another day," Sonny said. "I think it's time to go home."

"And where would that be?" Edith asked.

"Wherever you are," Sonny answered. "My home is wherever you are."

ABOUT THE AUTHOR

Larry D. Sweazy is a multiple-award-winning author of sixteen western and mystery novels, and over eighty nonfiction articles and short stories. He is also a freelance indexer and has written back-of-the-book indexes for over nine hundred and seventy-five books in twenty years. Larry lives in Indiana with his wife, Rose, where he is hard at work on his next novel. More information can be found at www.larrydsweazy.com.

The employees of Five Star Publishing hope you have enjoyed this book.

Our Five Star novels explore little-known chapters from America's history, stories told from unique perspectives that will entertain a broad range of readers.

Other Five Star books are available at your local library, bookstore, all major book distributors, and directly from Five Star/Gale.

Connect with Five Star Publishing

Visit us on Facebook:
https://www.facebook.com/FiveStarCengage

Email:
FiveStar@cengage.com

For information about titles and placing orders:
(800) 223-1244
gale.orders@cengage.com

To share your comments, write to us:
Five Star Publishing
Attn: Publisher
10 Water St., Suite 310
Waterville, ME 04901